I0548216

E.F.T.

A Noir Thriller

Matt Hughes

Trigger Warning

E.F.T. is a novel that deals with aberrant psychology and sexual assault.   If those subjects are likely to trigger a traumatic response in you, you should stop reading now.

E.F.T.

© 2019 Matt Hughes
ISBN 978-1-927880-19-7

FOREWORD

The story dates from far back in my writing career – circa 1984 – when I was a freelance script reader for Telefilm Canada, the Canadian government agency that underwrites film and television properties in development. I wrote a number of screenplays, none of which survived to actual production, though I did get paid for a couple.

My main source of income in those days was freelance speechwriting, and one of my clients was the British Columbia head office of The Royal Bank of Canada. I was still working on IBM Selectrics when I was tasked to write a speech about data security and was trying to get my head around mainframes and remote terminals and computers that could be lugged around – albeit clumsily – in a suitcase.

One day, while standing in line at my bank, the idea for *E.F.T.* popped into my head. Having recently read a biography of Alfred Hitchcock, whose story-making genius I admired while deploring his sexual weirdness, I did what he used to do: I wrote an extended treatment of the story, got it printed, and tried circulating that to anyone who might take an interest.

Nobody did. I came to understand that nobody but Hitchcock ever did extended treatments, or if they did, they were ignored. The thing to do was write a screenplay. So I did that. It didn't sell, either.

Years went by. In 1996, I had an opportunity to take some time off from speechwriting and write some crime fiction. I wrote two novels based on my unsold screenplays: *Paroxysm* and *E.F.T.* They were good enough to land me a New York literary agent who started sending them out.

Then I was struck by one of the freakish events that have made my fiction-writing career so unusual. My agent suffered a family crisis that took her away from the business for months. I let her go to deal with what she had to deal with, and went looking for another agent.

But here's the rub: if a book has been sent out by an agent and has failed to sell, no other agent will be interested. My two crime novels instantly became "trunk books," author-speak for manuscripts that didn't make it. And never will.

Later on, after I had sold a few novels and made a faint murmur in the publishing business, I updated both books and tried selling them on my own. That didn't work, either. A couple of years back, I self-published *Paroxysm*, selling it on my web page and through Amazon, Kobo, and Smashwords. Lately, I have licensed the UK and Commonwealth ebook rights to SF *Gateway*, an online marketing arm of Gollancz/Orion.

E.F.T. was a different kettle of fish, however. It dates from 1984, when electronic funds transfer – the meaning of the title – was a practice largely confined to big businesses and financial institutions. ATMs and debit cards were just on the horizon, on-line banking didn't exist because the internet was used only by the military-industrial-academic complex, and laptops and smart phones were no more than a gleam in Bill Gates's eye.

So today it would qualify as a historical novel – a return to those thrilling days of yesteryear, when nobody had heard of a computer virus except heads of data security at companies and institutions large enough to own a mainframe. And me, a guy who had to write a speech about it.

But I think the idea behind the story still holds up, even if the technology has passed it by. And I like the character, Harry Lukovitch, that I created to be the sleuth at the center of the mystery. I would have liked to write a series of stories about Harry, another one of my oddball-outlier protagonists, but what happened to *E.F.T.* meant that he came into the world stillborn.

Finally, as I stated in the trigger warning, this is a tale that involves sexual assault. My views on the appropriateness of such material have evolved in the thirty-five years since I wrote that treatment.   I probably wouldn't write a book like *E.F.T.* today.

But I did write it.   So here it is.

Chapter 1

It was the old something at first sight again. Detective Sergeant Harry Lukovitch never knew what to call it -- love, infatuation, fascination, obsession. But, whatever it was, he knew it when he felt it, and he felt it the moment he saw Dory Novello. And he knew that once he felt it he would have to do something about it.

She hadn't been there when he met the other women seated on either side of him at the head table. She came in late, after everybody else was sitting down. She took a place at the far end of the long table, beyond a row of female hands lifting forks to female faces under well coiffed heads that nodded and bobbed in counterpoint to bright conversation.

So Harry didn't know she was there as he worked his way through the entree -- some kind of fish, with naked little potatoes and still-born carrots under a sprig of parsley -- then progressed to the soggy cake.

Between bites, he politely fielded the questions people like to ask police detectives who come to speak at club luncheons. Most of them were asked by the woman who would be introducing him. Katherine Tower was a compact forty-five-year-old with champagne-colored hair and a no-nonsense face that went with the information on her business card. It said she was a vice president and chief financial officer of Hamilton Lynch Inc., a billion-dollar forest products company.

"It's not like the stuff you see on tv," Harry said. "Maybe ninety per cent of cases that are cleared, it's because of information received."

Katherine paused a forkful on its way to her mouth. "Information received?"

"Somebody tells us who did it."

"Stool pigeons, squealers, is that what you mean?"

"Snitches, we call them."

"And the other ten per cent?" she asked.

"Occam's Razor takes care of most of it," said Harry.

Her eyebrows went up.

Harry chewed and swallowed, then launched into the explanation. "I learned it from my original partner, Zip Metcalfe. He was an old timer, would read anything he got his hands on. He said there was this guy way back in the middle ages, name of Occam -- or maybe that was his home town -- came up with a method for cutting through the fog to get to the reliable facts. That's why they called it his razor."

"And this has something to do with police work?"

"No, it has to do with figuring out any complicated situation. Occam's Razor says that the simpler the answer, the more likely it's the right one. Like for example, there's a murder, odds are the murderer is somebody close to the victim. Because they're the people most likely to have a motive. Money, sex, jealousy, or maybe it's just thirty years you've been hearing him say the same damn thing every time he comes in the door."

"I'm not married," she said.

"Still, what I'm saying," Harry continued, "the more complicated you make the explanation, the more pieces that have to fall into place before it will stand up. Or the way my partner used to put it, if ten different things have to happen just so or your theory doesn't make sense, that's a lot less likely than if only two things have to happen."

"Let me see if I get this," Katherine said. "We can forget Sherlock Holmes and deductive reasoning. Ninety per cent, somebody tells you, 'Joe Blow did it,' so you pick him up. Most of the rest of it is pretty much fill in the blanks, so you arrest the wife or the business partner."

"Or the neighbor."

"Okay, the neighbor. My question is: what are we paying you guys for?"

Harry smiled. He had a sad smile that some women warmed to. It went well with the quiet eyes and the rumpled face. "Mostly, you're paying for the paperwork," he said.

"I'm going to introduce you now," she said.

He didn't listen to the introduction. He straightened his little pile of blue index cards, the kind Letterman used for his top ten lists. He realized his mouth had suddenly gone fossil dry, and fumbled for a glass of water.

He gulped the liquid, looking out over the tumbler's rim at a room full of cloth-covered round tables, each of them with its circle of well dressed women. They were all looking at him. He badly wanted to reach under the table and check his fly, but he was sure everyone would know what he was doing.

He put the glass down, breathed in deeply through his mouth and expelled the air slowly through his nose. The department's public relations officer had recommended controlled breathing as a preparation for public speaking. It wasn't helping today.

Katherine Tower came to the end of her introduction. He heard "please welcome Detective Sergeant Harry Lukovitch," and a ripple of applause. He got to his feet and moved to the lectern at the center of the head table. He and Katherine worked their way around each other in the confined space between the head table and the wall.

He put the index cards on the lectern and gripped its sides with both hands. A microphone snaked out of one corner and he pulled it closer to his mouth, bending its segmented steel neck, and blew into it.

Don't blow into the mike, the PR officer had said.

"Ladies and..." he began, then stopped. The only men in the room were the waiters handing out carrot cake with cream cheese topping. Somebody snorted delicately.

Harry looked out across the room. *Find one friendly face and talk directly to that person,* was another of the PR guy's handy-dandy public speaking tips.

He looked for the woman who had snorted, and found her with her chair tipped back to lean against the wall behind the farthest table. She was short and wiry, with cropped mousy brown hair and green eyes set a few millimeters too close together. Her cheeks were high and her chin had a point. She wore a green blazer and slacks, and looked like Tinkerbell gone a little bad.

Both the face and the snort were familiar as well as friendly. She was Mack Sinclair, his partner on the sex crimes squad for more than two years. She bared her teeth at him and winked. She was enjoying this.

Harry knew a German word -- *schadenfreude* -- that roughly translated as the enjoyment of other people's discomfort. He knew a few other words that summed up his opinion of people who liked schadenfreude; he wouldn't be using any of them in today's speech to the West Coast Businesswomen's Alliance.

But he knew that Mack was entitled to a certain amount of enjoyment at his expense. In their two years together, she had done more for him than a partner was required to do -- like helping him to break up a continuing relationship with bourbon whiskey that had almost made Harry a naturalized citizen of the Nation of Alcoholism. He also had a pretty good suspicion she'd like to do a lot more with and for him, if he ever gave her the sign.

But, for all the time Mack had known him, the only signs Harry had given off said, *Closed; Out of Order; Next Wicket Please; No Emotions Available for Public Use.*

He hadn't always been a dry hole in the desert. A psychiatrist had once told him that -- perhaps because of his peculiar upbringing -- Harry was liable to great sweeps of emotion. Where other people got an easy ebb and flow of the tides of feeling, Harry would always be potentially in the path of a tsunami.

"You're essentially a nineteenth-century romantic. It's like they found Mary Shelley's Frankenstein frozen in the polar ice, thawed him out and dumped him into the 1990s," the man had said. "To use a nineteenth-century term, you are *passionate.* You ought to be writing tragic poems in heroic couplets or painting pictures of shipwrecks. All this irony and sarcasm you indulge in is the thinnest of veneers. One day, it will crack and out will pop Childe Harold, the melancholy romantic, ready for another romp through the landscape of sentiment."

Harry had stopped seeing the psychiatrist. He had denied any risk of emotional tidal waves, and worked instead on thickening the veneer into a pretty solid carapace. He and Mack had become good partners and almost good friends. Whatever more they might have been, they weren't.

But he liked her, liked the edgy tension that was always somewhere in the quips and banter that peppered their working-day conversations. Now he fixed his gaze on his partner's wry face and began again, reading from the cards, "Ladies, I am very pleased to have an opportunity to speak to you today."

The text was standard department issue, put together by the same PR officer who'd been so free and easy with tips on speaking technique, after Inspector Mason volunteered Harry for this assignment.

From time to time, look around the room, the flack had advised. So Harry did. Later, Mack would tell him it had put her in mind of a lighthouse, the way he started with the head table on his left side, then swept his eyes across the assembled members of the Alliance, panning continuously until he was looking down the head table to his right.

At Dory Novello -- and that's where it started.

The way she chewed, that was what he first noticed about her. That and the fact that, unlike every other woman in the room, she was not looking at him. She stared straight ahead, methodically chewing the anonymous seafood.

Later on, he would recall the scene and be reminded of a rough attempt at trick photography -- one of those gag photos where somebody's image is clipped and pasted into a crowd shot, somebody who wasn't anywhere near the scene when the original picture was snapped. Everyone who's legit is looking in this direction and being lit from that angle, while the interloper squints the wrong way from under the wrong set of shadows.

That was his later impression, when he knew the whole story. His first take on Dory was that she stood out from the rest of them. The way the muscles in her jaw bunched and rolled as she chewed. The way she stared straight ahead, as if she could see something much more compelling through the back wall of the room. He knew she would do everything with just such a focused intensity.

There was something there, something that broke right through Harry's outer shell and stirred up the soft, warm vulnerable quick he kept hidden. Even though he had seen no more of her than her profile, he was hooked.

She was tall, even sitting down, with a round head under a rough-cut thatch of blond hair, a sculpted jaw and a long, straight nose. He couldn't see her eyes, but he wanted to. He wanted them on him. But she did not turn his way.

Through the rest of his speech, she drew his gaze away from Mack, away from the audience. He worked his way through the blue cards, doling out the department's reassuringly good counsel, but he was constantly aware of the movements of her hand and head at the edge of his vision.

He turned over the last of the cards. "So the best advice the police department can offer is this: prudence and prevention. The rapist counts on you to give him the opportunity he's looking for. Don't oblige him. Thank you."

He looked to his right again. The other women at the head

table were all looking up at him, politely applauding. The blonde still stared straight before her.

Katherine Tower was beside him at the lectern, saying something about taking questions. Harry pulled himself back together and said questions would be fine.

A woman at one of the front tables got up. "Mr. Lukovitch, prevention is great, and any one of us could give you chapter and verse. But what do you do when prevention fails?   How do you deal with a rapist?"

Harry put the blue cards back on the table beside the lectern. "Ma'am, I wish I had an easy answer for you. Look, I've specialized in sexual assault cases for almost five years, ever since... well, anyway, I've known victims who beat the crap out of their attackers, and I've known women who offered no resistance and still got slashed or..."

He shrugged. "I'm sorry, there just isn't a simple answer. If it happens to you, you've got to handle it the best you can. But the main thing is prevention. Don't let yourself be a victim."

There were a few more questions. What about personal alarms?   What about pepper spray?   What about self-defense classes?   Harry gave them the straight department line, while sneaking looks at the blonde woman on his far right. She paid no attention.

Finally, Katherine Tower called time. She thanked Harry, touching off another ripple of applause, then the room began to empty. Mack Sinclair pushed her way through the welter of chairs and tables toward her partner.

Harry gathered up the blue cards and shoved them into the inside pocket of his sports jacket. He'd worn the green one without the ripped cuff; it was his best. He watched the blonde woman move toward the door.

Katherine took his arm. "You didn't get to meet everybody, Sergeant."

She called to the blonde. "Dory!   Don't go just yet!   I want you to meet our guest speaker."

Dory Novello was almost at the door. She turned and came back into the room, threading among the flow of women headed for the exit.

It was Harry's first sight of her, full on. She wore a well

tailored skirt and jacket over a high-necked silk blouse, with something made of gold wire and enamel where a soldier would have worn his medals, and a necklace of big creamy beads. Her eyes were gray under precisely plucked brows, but what struck Harry was the curious, iconic stillness of her face, as if she wore a mask made of her own flesh.

As she came toward him, he could actually hear the sound his blood made pulsing past his eardrums. He felt a breathless tightness in the center of his body, as if something was squeezing his diaphragm. A small part of him was cataloging these sensations with alarm; all the rest of him was locked onto the woman who was moving into touching distance.

She barely glanced at him as Katherine Tower made the introductions.

"Harry Lukovitch, Dory Novello. Dory's only been with the Alliance a couple of months, but she gets things done."

Dory held out her hand. Harry took it. It was cool and firm, with no hint of welcoming warmth. He felt a slight tremor, but didn't know whether it was his or hers.

"Nice to meet you," she said. Her voice was soft and low. "I'm sorry, but I have to go."

Harry held onto her hand. "You seem upset. I hope you weren't bothered by anything I said."

She looked directly at him then, a brief, cool brush of her eyes across his face. "Why would I be bothered?   It had nothing to do with me. Excuse me."

She turned and walked away.

Katherine's arm was still locked in Harry's. She looked from Dory's departing back to the detective's face. and said, "I don't know what I'd call it, Harry, but something just happened."

Harry said nothing. He watched the blonde woman disappear through the ballroom doors.

Katherine cocked her head and regarded him. "I don't know Dory too well. I don't know you at all. I'll probably never see you again, so let me be blunt. Is there a Mrs. Lukovitch?"

"Ex," Harry said. "I'm divorced."

"Well, far as I can tell, Dory Novello's as manless as Mother Teresa."   She squeezed his arm. "I think she needs somebody."

Now that she was out of his sight, Harry found he could

gather together most of his usual composure. He gently removed his arm from Katherine's grip. "Ms. Tower," he began.

"Katherine."

"Katherine, I only came to give a speech."   He looked to Mack for support, but his partner was inspecting the ceiling tiles.

Katherine tilted toward him. "Listen, Harry, I've had two husbands and two divorces, and I've learned two things. When you want something, you don't wait for it to come to you. You go and get it."

"Okay. What's the second thing?"

She smiled. "It's fun to meddle in other people's lives."

Harry offered her his hand. She shook it.

"We've got to go," he said. "There's bad guys need catching. Thanks for the lunch."

"Thanks for the speech."

The hallway was empty. Harry set a brisk pace toward the escalators that went down to the lobby. Mack had to move fast to keep up with him.

Emotion always made Harry move. It didn't matter whether he was running toward something, or away from it. He just had to be in motion. Right now, if he stood still, he was going to have to think about what was going on inside him, and he wasn't ready for that. Not yet. Maybe not ever.

He stepped onto the moving stairs and started down, Mack right behind him. He crossed the lobby, gave the parking elevator a pass and took the service stairs two at a time. He pushed aside the door with *P2* painted on it, and strode to the blue sedan that had "unmarked police car" written all over it in letters that were invisible only to straight citizens.

Mack stretched her legs to match him step for step, until he came up against the locked driver's door, where he fumbled in his pockets for the keys. The car had an electronic lock activated by remote control.

"I drove, remember?" said Mack, holding up the remote and shaking it like a hostess summoning the maid to clear away the dishes.

"Let's go," Harry said.

Mack made no move. "So what was that?" she asked.

"What?"

"Don't give me what," she said. "You're so busy staring at the blonde you read the same card twice. Then you gawp at her like Teddy Teenager and forget to let go of her hand."

"Open the car."

"So this is, like, love at first sight?"

"Open the car."

"I mean, I want to know. If somebody has got through to wake up the sleeping prince, the least he can do is tell the neighbors."

Harry drew his lips into a flat line and said nothing. Mack nudged him away from the driver's door and unlocked it. He still said nothing while she drove them back to police headquarters on Main Street off East Hastings.

She watched him from the corner of her eye. She had seen a number of different Harrys in the past two years. She hadn't seen this one before. Something had finally slipped under his hard surface and now it was bubbling in there. She didn't know whether to make a joke about it -- or pull over and put an arm around him.

"You okay?" she asked.

"I'm okay," he said.

They parked in a multistory garage down Main Street from the ugly old building that housed most of the VPD's investigative divisions, although the brass had recently relocated to the new headquarters on Cambie Street. They went up to the squad room and caught up on paperwork until end of shift.

#

Katherine Tower lived alone. She had bought her one-bedroom condo in a new high-rise overlooking English Bay just before a tidal wave of Hong Kong money swept the price of Vancouver waterfront real estate out of reach. It was a good place to be. When the setting sun filled the small space with gold, she could look out past the bulk freighters and container ships, dark against the metallic sheen of English Bay, and see the lights of West Vancouver climbing the North Shore mountains. It was quiet up here, well above the street noise.

She ate a boil-in-the-bag dinner and put the single plate and cup in the dishwasher. She closed the living room and bedroom drapes, then went into the ensuite bathroom, started the bath water running and tossed in a handful of sweet-smelling salts. Her cotton robe was hanging on its hook behind the door; she removed her office clothes and put them into the dry cleaner's pick-up bag, then slipped into the robe's comfortable warmth.

She wiped away what was left of the day's make-up and regarded her face in the mirror over the sink. The mist from the hot bath soon clouded the glass and hid the crow's feet. Just as well, she thought.

She liked to drink a glass of chilled aperitif wine while she soaked. When the water had foamed up and filled the tub, she turned off the tap and went back to the kitchen for the wine.

The masked man was in the living room. She saw him as she stepped through the bedroom door. He was coming silently toward her across the deep red of the carpet. His shoes were highly polished. He wore a dark three-piece suit with a white carnation in one lapel, and he moved with the speed and strength of youth.

His head and face were completely covered by a rubber mask. It gave him the features of a young girl, burlesqued into a cartoon rendering -- gap-toothed grin, freckles, button nose, straw-colored hair in pigtails -- that was contradicted by wraparound skier's sunglasses taped to the rubber.

Katherine froze in the doorway. If he had made any noise, she might have reacted more quickly. But the silence made the man's presence seem dreamlike, and she delayed a second before she moved.

Then she slammed the bedroom door closed and reached for the lock. She was too late.

The knob turned in her hand, and his shoulder struck the wood. The impact pushed her off-balance and she stumbled back a half step.

It was all he needed. He put his foot between the door and the jamb, and pushed.

She threw herself against the panel. But he had weight and strength. He forced her back.

"No, you don't," she said. On top of a dresser was a fist-sized globe of clear plastic on a black marble base, an award from the Institute of Certified General Accountants. Still pushing against the door, she reached, closed her hand on it and swung it toward his head.

He was too fast. His right fist came up, a short pistoning

blow to the left side of her jaw. It rocked her. She dropped the paperweight. Before it touched the floor, he hit her again, this time a calculated uppercut that lifted her onto her heels and sent her backpedaling across the small room to sprawl across the bed. She heard a rushing sound in her ears, then everything fell away.

When she regained consciousness, she knew she had only been out for a brief time. But it had been long enough for the man to tape her wrists and ankles to the short legs that supported her bed. She lifted her head and saw that she was naked.

The man sat on a kitchen chair at the foot of the bed. He had turned off the bathroom and bedroom lights. He was back-lit only by the spill of light through the open bedroom door. She could see only the outline of his head and shoulders; he still wore the mask.

Katherine pulled against her bonds. They did not yield. "You son-of-a-bitch, limp-dick bastard!" she growled. "I'll make you wish you'd..."

He got up, and she saw the knife. It was long and thin-bladed, and it caught the light from the doorway.

He walked along the side of the bed, drawing the flat of the blade along her inner thigh, across her belly and up between her breasts. The metal was cold against her skin.

He held it a handsbreadth from her face, angling the blade so that it reflected a bar of light across her eyes. She concentrated on it, on memorizing the details: it was a dagger, military, she thought, with curlicues engraved on the steel, maybe an ivory handle, with a silvery pommel that looked like an eagle's head poking out of the other end of the man's fist.

The knife went away. The mask bent over her, came closer. A gloved hand cupped her left breast.

"You bastard," she said.

The hand left her flesh and went to the little girl's lopsided grin, a finger to the rubber lips mimed <u>shush</u>. The knife came back, and this time its needle point rested on Katherine's cheek, just below her eye.

Katherine swallowed and nodded, then turned her head to the other side of the bed. "Goddamn you," she whispered.

He closed the bedroom door. Now the room was almost completely lightless. She heard the sound of a zipper, then felt the bed settle as he knelt between her legs. He lowered himself onto her.

#

Harry twisted the cap off a second bottle of Shaftebury Cream. It was an English-style dark mild beer made by a micro brewer in Victoria, and it cost him three-and-a-half bucks for a bottle that comfortably filled a pint glass he'd lifted one night from a designer beer joint near Kits Beach. He refilled the glass now, letting the head form naturally, leaned back on his couch and took a good mouthful. The beer was his last luxury. It was his last connection to the old Harry, the one with the big appetites, the one with so much curiosity about the world that he sucked in knowledge like a vacuum cleaner, the one that Mack had sometimes heard about but had never known.

Since his marriage broke up, three years back, he had rented a bare-bones studio apartment in a concrete high-rise whose plans might have originated in Stalinist Russia. The furniture was bought used from a rental place. The couch still gave off a hint of garlic when anyone sat on it; not that anyone but Harry -- and, once or twice, Mack -- ever had. His mismatched pots, pans and dishes were from Goodwill Enterprises's going-out-of-business sale. There were no pictures on the walls.

The orange drapes were closed, cutting off the view of parking lots and Brentwood Mall, a low-rise shopping center on this side of the Lougheed Highway, and the car dealerships and light industrial zone across the divided four-lane arterial. He kept the windows closed in an successful attempt to mute the unending growl of traffic. When he was home, the tv was always on -- the constant ebb and flow of sound and image sometimes kept him from thinking.

Right now, Nigel Kennedy was doing an amazing job of reinterpreting a Bach partita that Harry's mother used to play as a warm-up piece. He listened to the precise clarity of the successive notes, each individual element of Bach's invisible architecture appearing exactly where and when it had to. The bowing was amazing -- perfect -- no difference between the forestroke and the backstroke.

The segment was a filler on one of the new cable channels, a few minutes between longer programs. But while those few minutes lasted, Harry was up and away, moving through a simpler, clearer place. It was a place where there was no need for feelings, where all that was expected of him was an intellectual delight in the flawless ordering of the notes and phrases -- an expectation he could deliver on.

Kennedy finished and an art movie came on. Harry lay back on the couch and took another mouthful of the good beer while he tried to concentrate on the story. But his mind kept wandering back to the luncheon. To the blonde woman with the odd air of dissociation from her surroundings.

He didn't want to think about her, about the strange something that she had called up in him. His thoughts kept nibbling at the edges of it, but he pushed it down and away. He sensed that there was danger there, profound danger to the sparse and orderly universe he had established around himself and in himself.

If he kept nibbling, he would next take a bite. And if he took a bite, he would swallow it whole, and then he would be swallowed by it. He was sure of that. He had walked around a corner of his own being, and found something sleeping there. He dared not wake it up. If he did, it would take him in its jaws and run him pell-mell through the world.

There was a rustling sound from the discarded fast food wrappings and empty containers on the floor beside him. A dark shape was nosing after scraps in a cardboard french fry sleeve.

On the coffee table were the remains of a clubhouse sandwich. Harry dug through the drying bread and pulled out a fair sized hunk of lettuce. He held it gingerly by one corner and offered it to the scaly head that lifted out of the paper debris at his feet. A moment later, the leaf was tugged from his hand, and he heard the slow methodical crunching of reptilian jaws.

His partner had named it The Mystery Turtle. It had appeared in the apartment one morning, about six months after the divorce, when Harry was in what Mack called his Jack Daniel's period. He had probably bought the animal off some other drunk in a bar, or maybe he'd won it in a bet. For all he knew, he might have held up some pet store owner at gunpoint -- there were a lot of blanks in his calendar then -- except nobody ever came forward to complain.

He had been intending to take it to a zoo or somewhere appropriate, but he kept forgetting. It seemed to get along on a diet of potato chips, french fries and beer; the same was substantially true for Harry at the time. About once a week, it left a small pool of urine wherever it happened to be; otherwise, Mack said, it was a ideal companion for him.

After a week, Mack took him to the library, where they found a book that positively identified the animal as a Sulcata tortoise. It was supposed to live on high-fiber vegetables -- "beans and greens," Mack said -- and most of the time that's what it got, but it was always interested in any combination of potatoes and grease.

Harry found another piece of lettuce and handed it over. The phone on the coffee table rang.

"You wanna get that?" Harry asked, but the tortoise was busy chewing. He reached for the phone. It was Mack.

He listened for a few seconds, then said, "The words, 'off-duty,' they don't mean that much to you, do they?" He was wrapping himself in his practiced persona -- cool and ironic -- like a naked man belting a raincoat over his exposed flesh. He knew he was going out again into one of life's cold places.

She told him she'd be there in ten minutes.

He waited inside, looking out through the glass doors of the apartment block at the beginnings of a Vancouver April rain, working on not thinking about the job ahead. Mack came right on time, pulling up in her efficient little red Geo. He squeezed into the passenger seat and snugged the seat belt over his incipient paunch.

"You got a mint?" he asked.

She looked him over.

"One pint of beer and two sips of a second," he said. "Not an inappropriate amount for an off-duty detective. But the breath needs help."

She reached back and fished around in her purse that was on the back floor of the car, came up with a roll of something minty and gave it to him. He popped one in his mouth. "Okay," he said, "tell me about it."

"Sexual assault, single perp. Had a knife, didn't use it."

"And this has what to do with me?"

"The ineffable Inspector Mason," Mack said. "He admires your work."

Harry sighed and sucked on the mint. "I don't think I would apply the word 'ineffable' to Inspector Mason. I think I would call him the most effable police inspector ever to fall to earth from the hands of God."

He rubbed his neck. "I take it the good inspector views this as no garden variety violation."

"He does not. It appears to have trimmings. That's why he wants you to catch the case."

A few drops of rain spattered on the windshield and she switched on the wipers. Every few seconds, the black blades brought clarity and order, but after each pass the droplets came randomly back, inexorably turning Harry's view into a distorted muddle of shapes and lights.

He was not comfortable in the Geo's artfully designed seat. He scrunched down and watched the landscape flow past, saw cars nosing down driveways onto wet asphalt, like crocodiles sliding into a dark jungle river.

Chapter 2

At Katherine Tower's apartment, the uniformed crime-scene specialists were putting away their bags and powders and tweezers, preparing to move on to the next show. Harry and Mack collared the senior member of the team, a sergeant named Fitzgard, in the hallway.

"No way you make this one on physical evidence, Harry," said the NCO. He was a big blond man who liked chewing gum.

"What are you telling me?"

"We got dick all from the scene. Guy wore gloves, no prints. Mask over his head, so no hair samples. No semen stains on the bed cause he used a condom."

Harry held up a hand. "It's depressing I got to stand here and listen to you tell me what you don't have. So what *have* you got?"

Fitzgard shrugged. "Few clothing fibers. A carnation petal."

"A what?"

The cop held up a plastic baggy that contained a small white object. "Guy wore a carnation in his lapel. We found one petal on a kitchen chair he brought into the bedroom. Smack dead in the middle of the seat."

Fitzgard's tongue rolled the wad of gum over. "You ask me, he wanted us to find the petal."

Harry blew out his cheeks and looked at Mack. "Trimmings," he said. "How I hate trimmings."

"How'd he gain entry?" Mack asked.

"Had to have a key," Fitzgard said. "Victim says doors were locked, one regular, one deadbolt. No signs of tampering. He even locked up after himself."

"How considerate," said Harry. He let Mack get the rest of the information from the crime-scene crew, and went into the apartment.

Katherine Tower sat on the edge of her leather couch in her bathrobe, her eyes looking everywhere except the open bedroom door. A uniformed policewoman sat with her.

Harry came in and the uniform got up and moved away. He sat down on the couch, not too close. "Katherine," he said, "I'm sorry we have to meet again under these circumstances."

Her eyes rested on him only a second before continuing their constant circumspection of the room. "Uh huh," she said.

"I have to ask you some questions," Harry said.

"Sure."

"Did you know the man who attacked you?"

"No."

"Are you sure?"

"Absolutely."

"Who else has a key to this apartment?"

"Nobody. The building manager, I guess."

"Has anyone been in here lately?   Carpet cleaners, plumbers, that sort of thing."

"No."   She snorted. "I always tell people I'm lucky. Got a condo that doesn't fall apart day by day."

"What about unexpected visitors -- door-to-door sales, people canvassing for the Heart Fund?"

Katherine shook her head. "It's a no-soliciting building. The only people I've had in are from the Alliance -- you had lunch with them today."

"Can you give me a list of their names?"

She named them, and Harry wrote the information down, fitting his recollection of each woman to the name. Ellen Wiens, he remembered as a brisk, sharp-edged woman in her mid-twenties; she was executive assistant to the president of MacroFiber Industries. Maria Chen, diminutive and in her early thirties, was a partner in the local office of a Japanese merchant bank; Carla Gonsalvez was plump and thirtyish, and a senior market analyst for Fat Choy Developments, a Hong Kong-funded property firm. Dory Novello, he remembered very well; Katherine described her as a consultant.

"All right," Harry said. "Now, I got to ask you to help us catch this son of a bitch, Katherine. I know you can't give us a detailed description, and I know he's the last thing you want to think about. But right now you're the only one who knows the things we need to know."

Her eyes came round to him and narrowed. "Like what?"

"I just want your impressions of him. What kind of guy are we looking for?"

"You're looking for a piece of shit!" she hissed.

"Yes, we are," said Harry. "But shit comes in all different

kinds. What kind is this one?"

Katherine took a deep breath and let it shiver out. "He's... cold-blooded, that's what he is. Bastard never said a word, like a goddamn robot." She stopped, remembering, then her hand slapped the leather couch, the impact loud as a pistol shot. "No, wait a minute! He *acted* cold, like it was some kind of performance and he'd rehearsed all the moves, but underneath, that sorry bastard was having the time of his life!"

A tear ran down the side of her nose. "I'll tell you this much," she said, "you're not looking for some schmuck who can't help himself. This asshole loves putting other people through hell!"

Harry got up. He wanted to put a hand on her shoulder, but he knew better. "Thank you, Katherine," he said. "I'm going to leave you my card. If you think of anything else, give me a call. Now, this officer will take you to the hospital."

He beckoned to the policewoman.

Katherine stood up. She angrily wiped away the tear, and took his card. It crumpled in her fist. "You just catch him!" she said. "Catch him and put him away! And then you let me know the name of the jail and the day he gets out!"

She turned away and let the policewoman move her toward the door. But in the doorway she stopped, and her eyes locked onto Harry like a pissed-off lioness. "And get my goddamn award back!"

She stalked out. Harry looked at Mack, "Award?"

Mack consulted her notes. "Big plastic paperweight on a marble base. She tried to brain him with it. Appears to be the only thing missing."

"Trophy hunter," said Harry. "I hate them."

Mack sighed. "She's observant. Gave us a pretty detailed description."

"Of what? We got no face, no prints, no voice. Asshole even polished his shoes so he wouldn't leave any red river clay for Inspector Poirot to identify. Leaving us with what? A banker's suit, a carnation in the buttonhole and a dime-store Halloween mask."

He went out into the hallway, locking the door behind him. Mack followed him toward the fire stairs as he examined the carpet.

"There's the knife," she said. "Unusual piece, might be able to trace it."

He opened the door to the fire stairs. "Yeah, right. Way the bastard waved it around, you know he wanted us to get all excited about it. Probably been in the family since World War Two."

Harry descended a few steps. The stairwell was enclosed in gray concrete, lit by bare fluorescent tubes fixed lengthwise on the low ceiling.

"The knife's a blind, a decoy. Like the bank robber who wears a red rubber ball on his nose, like a clown. The teller can't take her eyes off the clown's nose, and it's the only thing she can remember when we ask her for a description."

He looked up at Mack. "Come on," he said. "We'll go down the stairs. Maybe this is the kind of asshole likes to leave clues to tease us."

She followed. "Are you going to get worked up about this one, Harry?   Cause I need to know whether this is a normal case where I'm working with my normal partner, or if it's gonna be one of those times you turn into some kind of crime-fighting Jekyll and Hyde. I mean, I just need to know."

It didn't happen often. Maybe one or two cases a year. There'd be something in the circumstances that would throw a hook into Harry's depths and drag all kinds of deep stuff out into the open. Then the case would consume him; he'd live it, eat it, sleep with it, rub his face in it twenty-four hours a day.

When he was like that, Mack couldn't ask him about the weather or his weekend or what he might be reading. There was nothing of Harry but the case, and there would be nothing until he charged a suspect and handed the file over to the Crown prosecutor's office.

Mack had seen it three times so far, and had heard about previous episodes from Harry's old partner, Zip Metcalfe. She wasn't sure how she felt about it. To see the man who shared her working life become suddenly obsessed was scary; but it was also exhilarating to bump along in his slipstream.

Besides, it made her think about how much fire was contained somewhere in Harry's core, and what it might be like to draw that power out of him for herself.

Harry didn't answer her question. They trudged in silence down the sterile stairway, all the way to the exit door. Then he said, "I don't like rape artists. I don't like them dumb, and I really don't like them smart."

He pulled open the outside door, examined the lock plate and the jamb. "No scratches. He didn't leave it taped."

"So he had a key," said Mack.

"Where'd he get a key?" said Harry.

"Maybe he used to live here. Or had a friend lived here."

"That gets him into the stairwell and up onto Katherine Tower's floor. But how'd he get a key to her apartment?"

"When we know how, we'll know who," said Mack.

#

The rain was coming down steadily as Mack drove them back to Hastings and Main. "I like the way you handle victims," she said.

Harry was slumped in the passenger seat, his head tilted to rest against the side window. "Well, I took that course."

"I know, after your wife was attacked."

Harry straightened. "Whatta you know about that?"

"What you told me. Your wife was raped in a parking lot. You had some trouble dealing with it."

"I got weird," Harry said.

"Okay, you got weird, your marriage fell apart, and you stayed weird."

"I told you all this?"

"Uh huh."

"I guess I was drunk."

"There was a time, just about when we started working together, that you were drunk a lot, Harry."

"I never touched it when I was on the job."

"That's true. We wouldn't have worked together otherwise."

"And I told you about Jeannie?"

"You told everybody. The other guys said, I'd be working with Harry the Confessor. That's what they called you. They said, 'on the job, there's nobody better, but you get a couple of shots of Black Jack in him, the gates open, and it's mea culpa all the way."

"I don't remember telling you, that's all."

"It was only the one time. I didn't like you drunk. And then you sorta pulled yourself out of the bottle, leveled out. Now, its like..."   She shook herself. "Hey, what am I saying?   It's your business."

He kept his eyes fixed on the road in front of them. "No, it's okay. You say what's in your head."

"Well, the other guys, they tell me what you were like before, you know, it happened. The things you used to say. The way you used to be. And I spend the day with you now, it's like I've got the shareware version, not the full-tilt, registered user edition."

"I don't know what that means, that computer stuff."

She stopped at a red light and looked at him. "It means I'm only getting a part of you, the cop part."

"That's the only part there is."

"I don't think so."

"The light's green," Harry said. When they were moving again, he rubbed his eyes with thumb and forefinger. "Listen, Mack, you're a good cop and a good partner. But I'm just here to do my job."

"Come on, Harry. What's it been, two years?   I think maybe you've beat yourself up enough. Maybe it's time to get back in the race."

She wheeled the Geo into the rear parking lot and nosed it up against the bland brick wall of the police building. Harry opened his door, then looked at her. "I'm not in any race, Mack," he said.

"Yeah, you are," she said. There were so many things she wanted to say to him, but she knew she ought to keep it flip and witty. Talk raw to Harry and he closed up. "It's the human race, and we don't accept resignations," she said.

"I got a report to write," he said, and got out into the rain.

She followed him to the lighted doorway. "Harry," she said, "if I'm outta line on this, just say so."

He pulled open the heavy wired-glass door. "It's okay, partner. You want to give me a pep talk sometimes, that's fine. But talking about maybes and might-have-beens doesn't change what is."

He went up the stairs, two at a time and she matched him. "Yeah, and what is this 'what-is'?"

He stopped at the squad room door on the third floor landing, only a little out of breath. He turned to her and it all came out fast.

"Jeannie's car wouldn't start that night. She called me, said 'come and pick me up,' and I said I would, but I was involved in some case, and I sat there at my desk going through interview notes, while the time passed and she got tired of waiting, so she went back to the garage and tried to start the car again, and two punks robbed her and beat her and made her suck them off, and all the time she's waiting for me to drive up and help her, and *I wasn't there.*"

She put a hand on his arm, lightly, no pressure. She wished it were a poultice that could draw the pain out of him. "So you made a mistake," she said. "It happens."

"Not to me. Not again."   He went into the squad room.

#

Michael worked out for two hours at the Nautilus center, then came home to his side-by-side duplex on the south side of a quiet, tree-lined street in the Marpole district of Vancouver, near the Fraser River. He parked his Honda Accord in the carport behind the house, took a canvas suitcase out of the trunk and unlocked the back door.

He was a nondescript man of twenty-nine, the kind that the eye slides over in crowd scenes, because there is nothing about the person behind the face that holds an observer's attention. He wore a lightweight beige windbreaker over a tee-shirt and jeans, with inexpensive sneakers, and he moved with an economy of motion.

His half of the house was the west side. The back door led into the utilitarian kitchen, its surfaces clean and uncluttered. Closing the door muted the distant noise of traffic from the Oak Street Bridge, and the only sounds from either side of the duplex were the whirring of his refrigerator's fan and a barely audible hum from the stove's fluorescent light.

Michael walked through the shoe-box shaped dwelling to the closet with the folding louvered doors in the front hall. He put down the canvas suitcase, opened the closet and took off the windbreaker. He arranged the jacket on a plastic hanger and hung it from the rod that ran the length of the closet. The only other garment sharing the closet space was the belted trench coat he had bought to keep the rain off when he first moved to the west coast.

A telephone rang in the other half of the duplex. Michael pushed aside the windbreaker and the trench coat. The rear wall of the closet was a thin sheet of plywood, painted white. He knelt and inserted a finger into a small hole in the lower left corner of the panel. It slid aside, revealing the interior of the front closet in the other half of the duplex. Several coats and jackets hung there, all of them conforming to the taste of a successful, conservative businesswoman.

The phone rang twice more, then Michael heard the

answering machine in the living room come on. The taped message said, "This is Dorcas Novello. I can't take your call right now, but please leave a message, and I'll get back to you."

The machine beeped, and a woman's voice said she was Sonya from Fine Line Carpet Cleaners with a great special on area rugs. She left a number and hung up.

Before the telephone solicitor was finished reciting her canned spiel, Michael had slid the panel back into position and closed the closet doors. He carried the suitcase down the hall to the bare-walled bedroom and laid it on the narrow single bed with its precisely neat covers.

He unsnapped the suitcase and lifted the top. Inside was a three-piece business suit on a plastic and steel hanger, the buttons of its jacket done up. He lifted out the suit, shook it gently, then took it to the bedroom's small closet and hung it up, turning it on its hook so that the front of the suit faced outward.

Then, item by item, he removed from the suitcase a pair of crepe-soled shoes wrapped in a plastic bag, a pair of latex gloves, an ivory-handled dagger in a steel scabbard, and a rubber mask with sunglasses. He placed the shoes below the hanging suit, tucked the mask between the shoulders of the hanger and the bar that supported the suit's folded pants, and put the gloves and the weapon into the pockets.

When he was finished, the suit hung in the closet like a facsimile of a human being. The sunglasses taped to the little girl mask made the effigy appear like a hybrid of a human and insect.

Michael regarded it for a moment. His face was still, his mouth slightly open, his features unanimated by any expression. Then he lifted the white blossom from its lapel and closed the door. He went into the ensuite bathroom and flushed the flower down the toilet.

When he came back into the bedroom he noticed that the answering machine connected to the phone on the bedside table was flashing its "message received" light. Michael sat on the bed and pressed rewind. While the minicassette whirred its way back to the starting position, he looked at the framed photograph that stood beside the machine. It was the room's only decoration. It showed a delicately featured woman in her twenties, her straight dark hair cut chin-length, her head slightly bowed to make her dark eyes look hopefully up into the camera.

Her name was Monica, and it was her voice that now issued from the answering machine.

"Hi, lover. I know you don't like surprises, but I guess I've got one for you. They're shutting down the plant for renovations, and I get a week with pay. So I booked a seat on one of those cheap flights, and I'll be there soon. Hope your energy level's up, 'cause I need my ever-lovin' man. See you."

The machine paused, then a computer-generated voice announced the day and time the message was received. Michael stared blankly at the phone for a moment, then suddenly reached for the handset and began punching numbers. He heard the buzz of a phone ringing in the Toronto suburb of Markham almost three thousand miles away, then a hiss as the call was answered by Monica's machine.

Her tone was breezy. "Hi. I'm probably not here right now, so leave a message."

The machine beeped. Michael licked his lips and spoke into the phone, the words tumbling over themselves. "It's me. Got your message. Listen, I'm really involved in a big project right now. It's better if you hold off coming out for a couple of weeks. When it's done, I'll be pretty well finished here, so what do you say I come see you?   Get back to me, please."

He hung up the phone and placed his hands palms down on his thin, hard thighs. For several seconds, he sat motionless as a mannequin, the only movement a slight bulging of his jaw muscles as he ground his teeth. Then he rose swiftly and went into the hallway, reaching into a pocket for his keys.

The door to the basement stairs was secured by a deadbolt lock. Michael opened it, switched on the naked bulb that illuminated the stairwell and descended.

The basement was unfinished, its walls and floor of smooth gray concrete, roofed by the joists that held up the floor above. Plastic pipes and sheet-metal heating conduits connected to the natural gas water heater and furnace at the dark end of the long, rectangular space where an overhead light bulb had burned out and not been replaced.

At the other end, where the floor was partially covered by a carpet remnant, stood an angled drafting table, a small desk and a swivel chair. An adjustable light fixture was clamped to the side of the table, and a notebook computer lay on the desk.

Michael sat in the swivel chair and switched on the lamp. The basement was unheated and the cold raised goosebumps on his flesh. He rubbed his arms as he scooted the chair closer to the drafting table, and inspected the large flow chart pinned to its surface.

The chart consisted of several parallel lines that connected series of boxes precisely drawn with a t-square and black ink on white paper. Each box contained a few words or a date neatly lettered in the restrained penmanship taught in technical schools to those who must prepare plans and documents for others to see -- though Michael did not intend for anyone ever to see what he had created in this bare room.

The chart read from left to right. The first box, on the top rank at the left margin, contained the words *FEB 15, OPEN OFFICE*. A flow line connected it to the square on the right, which read *FEB 16, K. TOWER, HAM-LYNCH*. From that box, two lines emerged, thin as spider's silk in black ink. One went sideways to a box that read *FEB 18, PROPOSAL*; the second line went downward to a space that contained the words *FEB 19, JOIN ALLIANCE*. From that box sprang a half a dozen connections.

The chart was three feet wide and densely covered with rectangles. Most of them were bisected by neat lines drawn through them. Michael picked up a pen from the gutter at the base of the table and drew a diagonal slash through a square that read *APR 04, TOWER, AWARD*. His hand trembled slightly as the pen moved downward across the paper; the resulting line was the only one on the chart that was not rigidly precise.

He tapped the end of the pen against his lower lip. The next box read *APR 07, WIENS*. After a moment, he crossed out the seven and drew a five above it. Then for the next several minutes, he worked at the chart, changing dates, creating new connecting pathways between boxes on the right side of the chart, crossing out some of them altogether.

When he was finished, he regarded what he had done with a sour expression. The elegance and balance of the plan had been compromised. But he shrugged and turned his attention to the last square on the chart. It rested against the far right margin of the paper. All the connecting lines that flowed across the scheme ended here, at a box that contained the words *APR 27, E.F.T.*

Michael stared at the printing. Then he crosshatched over the number in the date and inked another number above it. He inhaled a deep breath through his nose and expelled it slowly through his mouth. It was not neat: that bothered him, but it would do. He supposed it would have to do.

He put down the pen and slid the chair over to the desk. He opened the notebook computer and powered it up. While he waited for the operating system to lay out its array of tools, he tapped his index finger on the dog-eared paperback that was the only other object on the desk. It was by an eminent forensic psychiatrist, a man who had testified at trials that made the evening news. Its title was *PROFILES IN SEXUAL DEVIANCY*.

The notebook was ready. Michael spun the track ball to move the cursor to a program and pressed *enter*. The internal hard drive whirred and data came up on the screen. He scrolled down, frowned in thought for a moment, then began to tap keys.

#

MacroFiber Industries occupied the top seven floors in a tower of golden glass that stood on the former site of Vancouver's world's fair, Expo 86. The smooth denizens of MacroFiber's senior executive suite could look out over the reclaimed industrial slum called False Creek and watch the muscular young women of the home-town dragon boat team dig their paddles into the salt water, practicing to retake the championship laurels at the world finals in Hong Kong.

The boardroom, as well as the offices of the company's chairman, president and executive vice presidents, were done in glass and aluminum, the furniture made of chrome, glass and pastel shades of butter-soft leather. The carpets were thick and the art hanging on the walls reflected the enterprise's aggressive posture as a developer and supplier of crucial components for a select list of high-technology manufacturers on both sides of the Pacific Ocean.

Ellen Wiens had the smallest office in the penthouse, positioned next to the expansive corner suite of Rhys Maitland, with a view that was not quite half as good as her boss's. An aluminum plaque on her door read *Executive Assistant to the President*.

As the digital clock on her perfectly organized desk flicked past noon, Ellen was one of the few MacroFiber employees on the top floor. The corporation's senior officers and board of directors were meeting for lunch in the executive dining room, one floor below. Their secretaries had gone down to the coffee shop in the lobby or taken their bag lunches to eat on the sea wall overlooking False Creek.

Ellen expected to skip lunch today. Rhys Maitland was making a presentation to the board at one o'clock, and he expected his assistant to ensure that the briefing books that supported his pitch were waiting on the boardroom table when the directors took their seats. Naturally, there had been some last minute changes, and Maitland had left it to Ellen to add new data to several pages and interpolate them into the three-ring binders the board would review.

She hunched over the keyboard of her work station, completing the last alteration to the draft marketing plan, then instructed the spell-checker to scan for errors. Pages scrolled down the monitor screen, but there were no mistakes -- Ellen could spell and type. Most days, she could also outthink her boss, or at least get to the same conclusion before he did.

But she lacked the drive that propelled second-rate minds like Rhys Maitland's into the land where seven-figure salaries and plump perks ranged free for the roping. She knew herself well enough: she was bright but brittle; she could plan a battle, even help fight and win one, but she didn't enjoy the taste of other people's blood on her teeth. And without that blood lust, she could never be a chief executive officer, even if she hadn't been born without a penis.

The spell check complete, she told the computer to print out the new pages on the LaserJets she shared with the support staff. When she heard the printer kick into life in the photocopying room on the other side of the empty executive suite, she went to collect the finished material.

Her secretary, a plump and thick-legged long-time employee named Joan Foster, came out of the washroom as Ellen was passing. She took a motherly interest in her boss's welfare. The girl was too skinny, too pale and too wound up in her work.

"Will you be going out for lunch?" she asked.

Ellen kept moving, tossing her reply back over her shoulder. "No time. Have to prepare the boardroom for Rhys's one o'clock."

Joan did not approve of skipping lunch. "Want me to get you

something downstairs?"

"Sure, whatever looks good. Thanks." Ellen's voice faded as she disappeared into the photocopy room.

Joan said something under her breath, went into the lobby and pushed the elevator button. She would bring back something with meat in it.

Ellen lifted the sheaf of pages from the printer's out tray and took them back to her office. The printer had already collated them. She quickly punched holes in the left margins and distributed the pages among the binders. When the last folder was snapped shut, she assembled the books into a stack and carried them to the boardroom.

The gold-tinted floor-to-ceiling windows that made up one wall of the MacroFiber Industries boardroom gave an odd polarity to the light that streamed in from the south, so that the air contained in the room seemed heavier and more substantial than that breathed by the tiny people thirty stories below. Ellen felt an air of power in the room, even when she was its only occupant.

She distributed the three-ring binders around the long glass and steel table, placing one precisely in front of each plush chair. From the credenza near the door she brought out a stack of note pads and a clutch of pencils, and put one of each beside the binders. Finally, she took a tray loaded with small bottles of juice and mineral water from a refrigerator that masqueraded as a cabinet, and placed it on top of the credenza. Joan would brew fresh coffee and bring it in just before the meeting began.

She stood at the boardroom door and methodically checked each item in the room. All was ready. She turned to leave, but stopped at the sound of an elevator's discreet chime.

It was a private elevator, set in the wall of the boardroom opposite the door through which Ellen had been about to leave. It rose directly from a rank of reserved parking spaces in the upper level of the underground garage, and would not operate unless its passenger inserted a plastic card that had a black stripe imprinted with the right electronic code. Ellen had such a card in her desk drawer. She had never had occasion to use it.

The elevator door opened. It was a small compartment, the kind with a single narrow door only half the width of the car. It appeared to be empty, and its overhead light was not working.

The door closed, then immediately opened again. The door

began to vibrate and make the chuttering sound that marks an unhappy elevator. Ellen's face took on a *what now?* expression. She could well imagine Rhys Maitland's reaction, if any directors got stranded in a balky elevator the day he made his big move. Her boss was neither an understanding nor a forgiving man.

She walked the length of the boardroom, put her palm on the vinyl bar that worked the door release, and gave it a shove inward. The door continued to shudder. Gingerly, not wanting to be stuck, she stepped into the dark interior.

The masked man was inside, waiting for her. As she reached for the *door close* button, his gloved hand seized her by the arm and swung her around into the far corner. He hit her once, hard, a short driving blow to the solar plexus that whooshed the air from her lungs and left her gasping.

The door closed. The elevator was lit only by a dim glow from the control panel. The man pushed the *down* button and the car began to descend. Seconds later, he pushed *emergency stop*. A bell sounded briefly, and the elevator jerked to a halt.

The man seized Ellen by the shoulders and spun her so that she faced into the corner. The hollow aching in her middle, the shock of the sudden impact, the desperate need to concentrate on drawing air into her starving lungs, all combined to rob her of her will to resist. Besides, this couldn't be happening. Not really. Not to her.

She heard a rip of tape being pulled from a roll, then felt her wrists yanked together. He bound them tightly together then, swung her around to face him. The sight of the mask's idiotic smile broke through her paralysis. A wordless, panicky noise came up from some part of her. She leaned her shoulders into the corner and tried to put a knee into his groin.

He made no sound, just turned his thigh to receive the blow. She opened her mouth to scream <u>NO!</u> like the women in a tv documentary she had seen. But he silenced her with one gloved hand, while the other brought up the dagger.

She saw the red light of the emergency stop button reflected in its thin blade, then felt the prick of its needle point beneath her jawbone.

Ellen stopped struggling. Her legs filled with cold jelly. Her panic cleared, to be replaced by a chilling, helpless fear. He took his hand away from her mouth.

"Please don't," she said. The soft rubber of the mask moved around the gap-toothed grin. *He's smiling*, she thought. That frightened her even more.

He put a hand on top of her head and pushed down, a steady pressure that forced her to her knees. She shut her eyes. There was the sound of a zipper, then she smelled the sharp odor of latex rubber close to her nose.

She opened her mouth and concentrated on living through the next few minutes.

Chapter 3

Fitzgard was watching one of his crime-scene crew vacuum the elevator when Harry and Mack came into the boardroom. The uniformed NCO caught the detective's inquiring glance from across the room and shook his head.

"Go see what little joy Fitz can offer," Harry said to Mack, and went to where Ellen Wiens stood, trembling, fists clenched, staring through the ceiling-high windows at a clouded sky. A Pacific system was moving in from the southwest, burying the horizon under a wet, gray pall.

A policewoman stood beside her, notebook open, the top page blank. She looked at Harry and shrugged.

"Ms. Wiens," Harry said. She didn't turn. "Sgt. Lukovitch. We met yesterday."

Ellen gave no response.

"It would help if you could tell us about it," he said.

She ground her teeth. The sight of her jaw muscles working triggered a sudden image of the blonde woman from the luncheon, and a strange bubble of emotion burst through the surface tension of his mind and floated free across his awareness.

He watched it go by then brought himself back into focus. "Ms Wiens," he said. "Ellen. I want to catch this evil man for you, catch him and put him away with other evil men who will do to him what he did to you. You have the power to help me. Please."

She turned and looked at him then. Her face was pale and her eyes were red and swollen. She shook her head and looked back to the gray world outside.

"All right," he said. "Maybe later."

He detailed the policewoman to drive her to the hospital. A matronly woman had been anxiously hovering by the door, prevented from entering by the uniformed cop Fitzgard had placed there. She put her arm around Ellen's shoulders as she left the boardroom and spoke softly to her. Harry saw the young woman's shoulders shake, and she began to cry.

Mack came up to him. "Same guy," she said. She showed him her notes. "Left us another carnation petal, and some used duct tape."

"Anything special about the tape?"

She shook her head. "Find it in a million hardware stores."

A movement from the doorway caught Harry's eye. A beefy man in a discreetly expensive suit was signaling to him. The motion spilled flecks of light from the diamonds set in gold on his ring finger.

Harry leaned his head toward Mack and spoke quietly. "My old partner used to use the expression 'to beckon imperiously' from time to time. Would you say that's what it refers to?"

"I think I would," she said.

"Well, who the hell is it who's beckoning so imperiously in our direction?"

"I believe that's Rhys Maitland, the chief executive officer of the company. Fitzgard says he was the one found the victim trussed up in the elevator after lunch."

"Tell me more," said Harry. He gave the company president a bland smile and raised a finger in a gesture that said, *Be with you in a moment.*

Mack looked at her notes. "Private elevator, runs between here and the parking garage. Attack took place between floors. Then the perp tapes the victim's hands, feet and mouth, rides the elevator down to the basement, sends it back up to the penthouse with her in it. All over in two minutes."

Harry sucked the inside of his cheek until it caught between two teeth. "Private elevator needs a key, right?"

Mack nodded.

Harry said, "Find out who's got keys and if any are missing. Then check building security, see if they've got cameras in the parkade. Maybe we'll get lucky."

"Okay. You going to talk to Mr. Corporate there?"

"I have the special training such duty requires."

Mack squeezed past the uniform and Maitland in the doorway, deflecting the executive's impatient queries by gesturing over her shoulder to Harry.

Harry waited until the man's eyes were on him before beckoning him into the room. The gesture was not quite so imperious as Maitland's, but it was close.

He held out his hand, but the CEO ignored it and went first to the boardroom table. He counted the binders Ellen had distributed, making sure that none was missing. Then he swung around to face Harry.

Harry extended his hand again. "Sgt. Lukovitch, sir."

Maitland gracelessly took it and said his own name. "We need to get this wrapped up, Sergeant," he said. "I have an important meeting."

"We'll try not to delay you unduly. I understand you found the victim?"

"That's right, but I can't tell you anything more than that. I came in to check the arrangements for the meeting and found her trying to get out of the elevator. She'd pushed the *door open* button with her nose."

"Uh huh," Harry said. "To your knowledge, does anyone have a reason to hurt Ms. Wiens?"

"No."

"What about her private life?   Has she got a husband, boyfriend?"

"She's not married. I don't know anything about her private life."

Harry looked down at Maitland's shoes. They were Italian. He bet they cost more than his own off-the-rack suit. He couldn't think of anything more to ask this completely self-centered man, but he enjoyed making him wait. He reminded Harry of Inspector Mason, only a little more up-market.

"Is there anything else, Sergeant?"

Harry turned toward the big table. He reached out and touched a corner of one of the binders, moving it slightly out of alignment. "I think not."

"Then when can we make use of our boardroom?   I've got several very important people sitting in my office, waiting to make a decision on a thirty million dollar project."

"And they are unable to make a decision there?" Harry used his most innocent voice.

A spot of color appeared in each of Maitland's smoothly shaved cheeks. Harry forestalled the explosion. "Well, I think we're all wrapped up here," he said. "I'll ask Sgt. Fitzgard to move his people out."

The CEO subsided slightly. Harry shepherded the crime-scene team to the door. Maitland had already forgotten them. He was straightening the binder Harry had touched.

Harry paused at the door. "Oh, one more thing, sir," he said. "Where would I find your head of personnel?

Maitland snapped a name and a floor number at him.

"Thank you, sir," Harry said.

#

The twenty-fifth floor was only fifty feet below the senior executive suite, but the comfort level dropped even further. No chrome and leather chairs waited for the personnel department's staff to return to their screened cubicles from their forty-five minute lunch break. No avant garde art encouraged them from the bland beige walls.

Harry found the place cramped even with the staff gone. It would be an anthill once the workers got back to their phones and work stations, and started generating the noise and bustle of a busy office.

He reasoned that the vice president in charge of personnel would have a corner to himself. Across the tops of the cloth-covered screens he could see a fairly spacious glassed-in office, one of a number that lined the outer wall, with one of the ubiquitous aluminum name plates beside its door. Rather than walk the long way around the outer rim of the huddle of cubicles that filled the intervening space, he entered a passageway that snaked among the screens and began to work his way across the room.

He was soon wandering at an angle away from the place he wanted to get to. The passageway wormed among the cubicles as if it had been intended to lead him astray. He came to a point where the path diverged in two directions, took the left hand because the vice president's office was now somewhere off to that side, and ultimately found himself in a cul de sac among the screens. Taped to one of the barriers was an ancient poster of a kitten dangling by its front paws from a bar, with a tag line underneath that read *Hang in there, baby!*

Harry began to think he should have brought a ball of string to unravel behind him, like the old Greek hero who went down into the labyrinth to kill the Minotaur. He retraced his steps to the intersection and eventually broke free of the maze by moving a screen aside and stepping into the clear only twenty feet away from the big corner office. A moment later, he looked through its glass wall and saw that it was empty.

He looked around. The place was silent except for the buzz of fluorescent lights, and the occasional shush of air as cars went up and down the central elevator shaft. Then Harry heard the muted clatter of a computer keyboard from somewhere nearby. He went toward the sound.

It came from a small office two doors down from the vice president's. The bracket that should have held the occupant's name plate was empty. Harry tapped on the wood and opened the door.

Dory Novello looked up from the monitor. Harry saw surprise flash across her face, then fade under an expression he could not name. *There's conflict there*, he thought. *She's glad to see me but at the same time... she's not.*

His own reaction was unsettling. What he had felt at the luncheon came back full bore. When she looked back to the computer screen, fingers skittering on the keyboard, right then he wanted nothing more in the world than for her to look at him again.

Something in her face spoke to a part of him he couldn't quite identify. It was as if his mind had constructed a woman just like her in some forgotten dream, and created a roil of powerful emotion between his dream self and a fantasy pastiched together from bits and pieces of real women he had known, or seen passing in the street, or watched in a movie. Then, without warning, he was faced with the living reality -- and while the workaday Harry scratched his head and wondered what was bubbling up inside of him, the dream Harry was dredged from the well at the bottom of his mind, to gape at Dory Novello and yell, *That's her!   That's the one!*

He didn't like having other Harrys surfacing inside him. He wanted his inner landscape bare and uncluttered. He knew he should step away, right now. The way she drew him bordered on terrifying. He could feel thick-skinned bubbles of strong emotion rising in him. *Move away!* he thought, *this woman can make you crazy* -- but instead, he watched himself push the door open wider. "Hello," he said.

She glanced toward him. "Hi," she said, very low, then her eyes went right back to the monitor.

It's all right, he reassured himself. *I can handle this. I'll just be businesslike, a cop asking cop questions.* "You remember we met at lunch the other day?" he said.

She didn't look up. "Yes. What are you doing here?"

"I'm looking for the head of personnel."

"That's Mitch Lucas," she said. "He's out to lunch."

"Well, maybe you can help me. I need a list of employees."

"What for?"

"A woman was attacked on the thirtieth floor."

Her hands rested on the keys. "That's awful. What happened?"

He was doing all right now. If he focused on being Harry the cop, he could stand this close to her, and still ignore the yammering under the floorboards of his mind. "I can't talk about a case under investigation," he said. "You'll have to wait for the office gossip."

"Did anyone see the attacker?"

"What makes you think we didn't catch him?"

"You wouldn't be looking for a list of employees if you had."

Harry smiled. "Good one. You could be a cop."

She looked at him now. *She likes being told she's smart*, he thought. *And I like making her smile*. He pulled himself back into cop mode. "So how about the list?   Can I get one?"

She returned to the computer, cleared the screen and typed a string of digits. When she hit the enter key, a stream of words and numbers flowed upwards for five seconds, then stopped.

"As of noon yesterday," she said. "this company employed 4,368 people in fourteen business units spread over five countries."

"Including you?"

She shook her head. "Not including me. I'm a consultant."

"Oh yes?   And what would I consult you about?"

"Data system security."

"You're one of those computer geniuses who keep the bad guys from -- what do they call it? -- hacking into the filing system?"

She nodded. "Or stealing market information competitors could use. Or a just a list of employees' names and addresses they could sell to a mail-order house."

"Or stealing money?"

She looked back at the screen and typed something that cleared it again. "Or stealing money. Now I have to get back to work."

"Defending the four thousand against junk mail."

"I'm very busy," she said.

He felt her pulling away from him again. They had made a

little contact; he'd handled it without going weird, but she seemed to be as skittish as he was. "I'm not making fun of you," he said. "You obviously have a lot of brains and talent. I respect that."

She called up another screen of data, made an entry. "How progressive of you," she said.

Harry chewed his lip. "Just one more thing."

"Yes?"

Suddenly, there it was, as powerful as the first time -- the inexorable pull. He knew he was about to step off the edge of the cliff into free fall. He hadn't meant to, but now some part of him was grabbing for the controls, taking over. His mouth was dry. He fought down an impulse to cough. He said, "Could I, maybe, see you sometime?"

She didn't look at him, but her hands froze above the keys. Her voice was tight in the back of her throat. "I'm very busy," she said. "I don't have time to socialize. Perhaps you could wait in Mr. Lucas's office."

But Harry had no way back now. He was launched into space, flapping his arms and grasping for any little twig that might be sticking out of the cliff face. "How'd you get into this kind of work?"

"Is that police business?"

"It's a police habit. We ask questions. So, were you always crazy about computers, or what?"

She looked at him, setting her upper teeth gently into her lower lip. There was a wistfulness about the way she angled her head and spoke. "I wanted to get into the movies. They said I had a talent for acting."

Making the personal admission seemed to frighten her. Her face closed again. "I'm very busy. I can't talk," she said.

But Harry sensed the vulnerability under the ice. He had the impression there were things inside her she wanted to tell somebody about. Maybe she went through the days half hoping, half dreading that somebody would ask the right questions. Or maybe he was mixing her up with himself. Still, he pressed gently. "Why give up acting?   You got the looks."

It was a very small sigh, but he heard it. "It's a long story."

"People say I give exceptionally good ear," he said.

She looked at him for a third time. "What do you do, collect life stories?"

"Only the good ones."

"Well, you can have mine if you promise to leave me alone."

"I will if it's dull."

"It's dull," she said. She looked out through the glass at the warren of cubicles. People were returning from lunch and going back to work.

"When I was still in high school," she began, "I worked part-time for my dad. We had this little manufacturing firm. One day somebody got into our computer, copied some crucial data and sold it to a competitor, who clobbered us on a big contract bid. We were over-extended at the bank, it was just when interest rates went crazy, and we got wiped out. Dad couldn't take it. He died. Insurance had lapsed, there was no money to spare, so I took a quickie course in data security. I'm good at it. Now I run a branch office for a national consulting firm. End of story."

"Maybe," Harry said. "Or maybe the beginning of something else?

She stared at him, the wistful look again. Then it went away and she shook her head. "No," she said, and this time the doors slammed tight, leaving no crack into which Harry could insinuate himself. "Please," she said, "let me get on with this."

The impulse that had broken through the shell Harry kept around himself had weakened. He knew enough about himself to recognize that he was affected by vulnerability in women. Those who were in need of protection tugged at him. Those who didn't scarcely registered. So when she drew herself together and stared him down, the strange pull she exerted on him faded in its intensity. "Okay," he said. "Another time."

She said nothing. He backed away and closed the door.

"Can I help you?" said a male voice beside him. A smooth man in a brown suit was standing in the door of the corner office.

Moments later, Harry was sitting in Mitch Lucas's visitor's chair -- blond wood and woven fabric was good enough at his level -- and explaining to the vice president of personnel why he wanted a list of the company's work force. Or at least of those who worked in or regularly visited the head office.

Lucas booted his own computer and began tapping keys. "There'll be a print-out in the copy room," he said.

Harry got up. "How well do you know Ellen Wiens?" he asked.

The personnel chief gave him the answer he expected. They didn't have a great deal of contact, it was all business and not much of that. While Harry listened, he watched the twenty-fifth floor staff come back from their lunch break. A slim man with a mustache went by Lucas's office. He was dressed in a blue coverall and carried a six-foot fluorescent tube. He glanced down at Harry sitting in the visitor's chair, then slid his eyes away.

Across the maze of screens, Mack appeared from the bank of elevators. Her eyes cast around for him. Harry waved through the glass and, when she saw him, he signaled he'd be with her directly.

He thanked Lucas and asked for the location of the copy room. The man went to the door of the office with him, and pointed to a metal and glass door beyond the cubicles. Harry waved Mack in that direction, and set off around the perimeter of the maze.

He glanced in passing into the office where Dory Novello had been working. She was gone.

\#

The squad room of the sex crimes section of the Vancouver Police Department was a drab and uninviting place even when sunlight leaked through the venetian blinds and lit up the dust particles floating in the air. On a wet and drizzly spring afternoon, it was worse.

Mitch Lucas had narrowed down the MacroFiber personnel list to males under fifty who worked at the company's headquarters or at the R&D shop in Richmond, a thirty-minute drive from downtown Vancouver. The printout of the names, dates of birth, addresses and social insurance numbers of more than three hundred men made a stack of paper an inch thick.

Harry was flipping through the pages when Mack came back from the lunch room, carrying two styrofoam cups of the department's acrid coffee.

"I ran Mr. Three-piece through the system," she said. "He didn't ring any bells. He's either a new boy, or a repeater with a new M.O."

"Or his particulars are sitting on some Mountie's desk in Chilliwack, waiting for an idle afternoon," Harry said.

A mass of useful data on serial killers, rapists and other

violent repeaters was supposed to be available to police forces in British Columbia at the touch of a computer key. The provincial government had shelled out major amounts of money for a province-wide system that should have allowed Harry to enter the relevant details of suspects' descriptions and *modus operandi*, and receive a list of candidates.

The system worked well, if there were enough police officers to work the system -- which there weren't. It took two hours to fill in the form that would enter each suspect's particulars into the data base. Since most police forces around the province were chronically undermanned detachments of the Royal Canadian Mounted Police hired out to parsimonious municipal governments by the federal authorities, the thinly stretched horsemen usually had more pressing things to do than extra paperwork.

Harry sipped the coffee and made a face. "Whatta you think about these kind of women?"

Mack sat on the corner of the desk and began leafing through the MacroFiber printout. "What kind?"

"You know. Career women, businesswomen, consultants."

"What do I think of career women?"

"Yeah."

"I think we put our pants on one leg at a time. What's going on, Harry?"

"Nothing. Well, you remember that woman at the lunch thing?"

"The one who made your face go all funny."

"I saw her again today when I was getting this."   He flicked the list. "Whatta you think about a woman like that, you know, career, success -- what kind of guy would she be interested in?"

"Oh, I think she'd be dying to meet a worn-out policeman with a pet turtle. It's every career gal's dream."

"Get off the desk," he said.

She looked at him. "Christ, Harry," she said, "you're not at long last swimming back to shore, are you?"

"Forget I said anything."

"Seriously, Harry. I'm not just your partner. I like to think we're friends. You want to talk about stuff like that, I'm here."

She could see she was making him uncomfortable. Anytime she moved in a little, went beyond the sarcasm and banter that confined their relationship, he always yanked up the gangplank and drifted away from the dock.

She knew she shouldn't push it. "No pressure," she said.

He cleared his throat and said, "Let's just catch this asshole with the carnation." He handed her the top portion of the MacroFiber list. "Here, you take this half, and I'll take the other one."

She riffled through the pages. "Why can't we just get their computer to talk to our computer?"

"I asked. They said not without a court order. Those guys got more security than the Pentagon. Start taking names."

She dropped hers onto her own battered steel desk, then looked at her watch. "It'll have to be later," she said. "I forgot to tell you Inspector Mason booked us to see that consulting shrink, whatsisname, Treleaven, at six o'clock. This traffic, we'd better move."

She saw Harry's face close in on itself, and wondered what that was all about.

#

Mack usually drove; she was less likely to be distracted. They wove through the rush hour traffic, skirting the worst of the downtown gridlock, and took the Cambie Street Bridge over False Creek to West Broadway. Treleaven's office was in one of the big new buildings between Cambie and Oak, with a coffee shop and a computer store on the ground floor.

The sign Mack parked under made it clear that there was no parking on Broadway between 3:30 and 6 p.m., and if they hadn't been able to read it would have been clear from the expression on the woman in the gray uniform with the big book of tickets.

Harry showed her his badge as they got out of the unmarked car. "Police business," he said.

She nodded, waited for the two detectives to go into the building, then wrote them a summons and slapped it under the windshield.

#

A little more than a mile away, in the downtown core, Maria Chen left her office in Cathedral Place and took the elevator down. Five people rode with her, but three got off in the lobby, leaving two women to accompany her to the basement parking garage.

They all left the glass enclosure that surrounded the elevator waiting area as a group, but once out into the almost empty garage, they went separate ways. Maria set off toward her parking space at the far end of the row of empty spaces.

She was always careful, but she was going to be even more watchful now. Dory had phoned to tell her about Katherine and Ellen. She put her keys in the palm of her hand then opened them out through the spaces between her fingers. When she closed her fist, the brass and steel points protruded like a set of claws.

There were only one or two cars parked between her minivan and the elevators. She stayed well clear of them. She remembered what the policeman had said yesterday. *Be aware of your body language. Look confident and alert, head up and eyes moving. Don't let yourself look like a victim.*

Her heels clicked rhythmically on the concrete floor. The minivan was provided by her employers, so that she could take groups of investors around Greater Vancouver to inspect projects in which the Taguchi Kawamura Merchant Bank had an interest. Its lock was not opened by one of the metal spikes separating her fingers, but by the small black box to which they were attached. At fifteen feet, she squeezed the box, heard the on-board security system's friendly *beep* and the *pop* as it released the door locks.

The minivan's dome light came on. She glanced into the passenger area, just as the detective had recommended. It was empty. She opened the driver's door.

#

Dr. Owen Treleaven's waiting room was deliberately bland, all its corners rounded, its surfaces smooth. A pair of inoffensive abstracts hung on the walls, offering nothing to antagonize an overtaxed psyche. It was a carefully neutral space between two doors, one leading to the pain outside, the other to the possibility of inner solace.

Harry and Mack did not have long to wait. Treleaven's inner door was open when they entered from the tenth floor hallway, and he waved them into the sanctum. He was a small, tidy man in his late forties, who purposefully looked as innocuous as his antechamber, and as mild as a camp counselor.

Mack led the way into the office. "Dr. Treleaven? I'm Detective Mackenzie Sinclair. This is Sgt. Lukovitch."

The psychiatrist smiled at both of them in turn. "How are you, Harry?" he said.

Mack looked to her partner, but her unspoken inquiry was not answered.

"I'm coping," Harry said.

"Good," said Treleaven. "Take a seat. Got yourself an interesting one here."

#

As Maria opened the driver's door, the man came out of a crouch behind the rear bumper, moving fast. She turned toward him and opened her mouth to scream. He hit her with a gloved fist, hard on the side of the jaw, jolting her back against the door. Her head smacked hard against the metal frame above the window.

She staggered from the combined impacts, then recovered and brought up the fist with the keys in it. But he had already moved in to deliver a second blow to her belly. It doubled her up and she retched.

He hammered his fist down hard on the back of her neck, just beneath the skull. A shockwave of blue light flashed through her brain, followed by a rapid flood of darkness. The man caught her as she sagged, dragged her around to the minivan's side door, opened it and pushed her inside.

#

"I hate the interesting ones," Harry said. "I only like the ones where we catch the asshole with his dick still wet, he cops a plea, and we put him away. The interesting ones are usually the ones we don't get."

Treleaven interlaced his fingers and rested them on his desk. "It's still personal, Harry?"

"No, it's not personal, goddammit!   It's the facts. A lot of these guys, we don't catch. Remember the bus-stop rapist?   Never got him. The guy with the paper bag over his head?   Took us five years, for Chrissake!   The "gentleman" that used to sodomize old ladies and then fucking apologize to them for half an hour!   We never got him. If this guy's interesting, it's three to one we don't nail him."

"You got the guys who attacked your wife, Harry," the psychiatrist said.

"Yeah, and you know where they are now?   Out on parole!"

He was embarrassed to find himself shouting. He looked at his hands for five seconds, took a slow breath and said, "Forget it. What can you tell us about this one?"

Treleaven leaned back in his chair. "Unfortunately, I think you've got yourselves a classic."

#

Maria Chen came to. Her hands were bound behind her and she was kneeling with her face against the cushion of one of the rear passenger seats. There was a taste of blood in her mouth. She heard nothing, and for a moment came the hope that her attacker had fled.

But the moment she tried to lift her head, a hand pressed down on the crown of her head, pushing her nose into the seat's velour fabric. She turned her face to the side, struggling to breath, and saw the long blade dimly shining on the seat beside her.

She froze. The knife moved, the point tracing from her temple, down past her ear to her neck. Then she felt a hand probing between her legs, and realized she was naked from the waist down.

He was kneeling behind her. He entered her slowly, taking his time.

#

"This is no pea-brain acting on impulse," Treleaven said. Mack took notes, while Harry looked out the window at the wet black night.

"He's smart. He plans. He gets access. And, like most rapists, his goal is not sex. It's dominance. He has to dominate his victim totally. He's self-controlled, self-contained. What else?"   The psychiatrist riffled through notes on his desk. "He's got his fixations. The knife, the flower, the suit, every one of them a symbol. He's a textbook case. When you catch him, I'd like to examine him in depth."

"Textbook, shit!" Harry exploded. "This guy belongs in a bad movie!   Waves a knife, but doesn't use it. Wears a suit and a carnation. Leaves us a petal. Always cool, never gets excited. Like he's acting, playing a role."

"Maybe he's method acting," said Mack.

"What?" said Harry.

"Method acting. You don't play the character, you *become* the character."

Harry looked at her. "I don't see how it helps."

"What is it that bothers you about this guy, Harry?" Treleaven asked. "I mean, more than the usual."

"I don't know. Just seems like somehow he's too much of something. I don't know how to say it yet."

"Could be you're looking too deeply into it. You might feel a need to make it seem less real. A way of distancing yourself."

Harry's gaze was flat. "Concentrate on the wacko, doc. Stay out of my head."   He stood up. "You got anything else we can use?"

Treleaven shook his head. "Too early."

"Then we got stuff to do."   Mack was between him and the exit. He motioned her to go first, then followed.

"Harry," Treleaven said.

Harry stopped in the doorway, but didn't turn. "What?"

"Anytime you want to come back. We were making progress."

This time, the detective looked back over his shoulder. "What, you giving away new lives?"

Treleaven shrugged. "You know better than that, Harry."

Harry turned away. Mack was waiting at the outer door. He followed her out.

Chapter 4

The department's coffee was no better at nine o'clock, just older. Harry called it squid piss, but he poured two more cups as he and Mack systematically entered names, dates of birth and Social Insurance Numbers from the MacroFiber personnel print-out into the CPIC data base.

Working two terminals, they had run through about half of the list. Mack took the styrofoam cup and sipped the sharp-edged black brew. She watched Harry cross to his own desk, slump into his chair, and begin to hunt-and-peck another entry into the system.

She'd been thinking about the way he'd acted at the psychiatrist's. Something was fermenting in her partner's sediments; maybe it was time she made a move.

"Harry?" she said.

"Uh huh?"

"You doing anything the weekend?"

Harry watched the inquiry come up blank. He drew a line through the name and went on to the next one on the list. "Uh uh," he said.

"I was wondering..." Mack began.

Harry suddenly sat up straight. "Bingo!   Fucking bingo!" he said.

"What?"   Mack got up, came over to his desk.

Harry jabbed a finger at a name on the list. "Shaeffer, Morris J.!" he said. "Jeez, you know I think I saw him!"

"Who's Morris A. Shaeffer?"

"Morris J. Me and Zip, we busted him, maybe four, five years back. A weenie-wagger, hung around schoolyards. And now he's a janitor at MacroFiber Industries."

Mack looked over his shoulder. "What's the address?"

Harry ran his finger along the line. "On Bidwell in the west end," he said. "About six blocks from Katherine Tower's place."

"I'll get the car," Mack said.

#

Shaeffer had a ground-floor one-bedroom in a jerry-built, low-rise walk-up. Dozens of such places had mushroomed during the West End's development boom thirty years back. By the end of the century all of them would be scraps of wood and stucco in a suburban landfill, and the high-priced lots they had temporarily squatted on would be sprouting up-market condos for the small percentage of Vancouverites who could pay the kind of money it took to be close to the downtown beaches.

The building manager buzzed Harry and Mack through the door and met them in the lobby. He was a small man with liquid eyes and a pot belly. He led them to Shaeffer's apartment.

Harry knocked on the door. "Shaeffer! Police! open up!"

There was no answer. "I don't think he's in there," said the manager. "He's not here much."

"I not only think he's in there," said Harry. "I think he's had an accident and now he can't make it to the door or call for help."

The manager produced a key.

"Good idea," said Harry. "We'll help you rescue him."

When the door was open, Harry pushed past the manager and flicked on the lights. Shaeffer had few possessions, but those he had were neat and well kept. The detectives rapidly checked closets and drawers, looked under the furniture and in the light fixtures, the freezer and the toilet tank, and in all the other places people think are so good for hiding things.

"Nothing," said Mack.

Harry called in the manager. "You ever see this guy with any flowers?"

The manager shook his head. "He's not here much."

"Lock it up. And you don't tell him we were here."

The little man shrugged.

Mack and Harry sat in the unmarked car across from Shaeffer's place. "There's nothing to link him to the assaults," Mack said, "no mask, no knife, no carnations."

Harry grunted. "Maybe he's out using them."

"You want to wait, see if he comes home?"

Harry rubbed his face. "Nah. I'm thinking he made me this afternoon. He's probably holed up in some steam bath for the night. We'll pick him up tomorrow."

"You know where?"

"His mother's. He always runs home to momma. Let's wrap it up."

Mack started the car. The radio crackled and said,

"Detectives one-baker-four. Suspected sexual assault, parking garage at 975 West Georgia. See the security guard."

"Go!" said Harry. He dug out his notebook and flipped through the pages. "That's the building where Maria Chen works. Hit your lights."

Mack punched the control. A rotating blue dome light mounted on the dashboard came to life, the unmarked's left and right headlights began to flash alternately and the siren cycled between its two ear-piercing tones.

Harry spoke into the microphone. "One-baker-four responding. I want a pick-up on Shaeffer, Morris J. Tell 'em to check all the steam baths. Suspect may be armed."

The big steel security doors leading down to the underground parking lot were raised. Mack cut the siren as she brought the car down the ramp and past the attendant's booth. The lights of an ambulance were flashing at the end of the long concrete gallery of empty parking spaces. The paramedics had strapped Maria Chen to a stretcher and were loading her into their sterile sanctuary.

It was Fitzgard's day off, but a couple of his team were questioning a green-uniformed security guard while two more inspected and photographed the minivan. Mack pulled up beside them. As she got out of the car, Harry moved over into the driver's seat.

"You handle this. I gotta check something out."

"What?" Mack said. Then she realized what the setting and the circumstances must mean to her partner. "Oh, Christ. Jeannie. Was it this building?"

"That's not it," Harry said.

"Then where you going?"

"Tell you later. It's important." He put the car into gear and u-turned in the confined space. Mack watched him accelerate toward the exit ramp, then went over to where the paramedics were packing up their kit.

"How is she?"

The lead paramedic was a lean woman with micro-short hair and a well scrubbed face. "Shock and bruises. But he really taped her hands tight. If the security guard hadn't looked in and found her, there could've been nerve damage." She closed her plastic suitcase. "Bastards," she said.

Mack assumed the paramedic meant men in general. She looked at Maria's face above the thermal blanket. Her left cheek and jaw line were swollen and purple. The gash in her lower lip had been cut by her own teeth. Her eyes were closed, but tears leaked through the lashes.

One of the crime-scene cops tapped Mack's shoulder. She turned and took the plastic bag that held a single white petal.

#

Even with the lights and siren on, it took Harry ten minutes to get from downtown to the Marpole address he had for Dory Novello. It was in the 800 block of West Sixty-Third, which he knew would put it just east of Oak Park. When he reached Oak and Fifty-Ninth, he cut the siren and lights. He turned at Oak and Park, and drove past the tennis courts and horse chestnut trees to the intersection where Park angles into Sixty-Third.

He stopped the car at the corner and got out. He figured that the house ought to be no more than three or four doors from the park. It turned out to be the east side of a duplex on the south side of the block. The lights were on in Dory's half; the other part was in darkness.

There was a whining sound in his ears, and his breath was coming in hot puffs as he climbed the front steps. He listened at the door but heard nothing. The curtains were drawn over the lighted window to his left. He listened again, then pressed the doorbell.

He waited, his ear against the door. He pushed the bell again, letting it ring continuously. He heard it faintly through the wood, but caught none of the muffled noises that would have meant someone was coming to answer.

He tried the doorknob. It was locked. A Yale deadbolt sat above the standard sliplock in the handle. He could tell it was in place. He rang the bell again and pounded on the door with his fist.

He couldn't wait any more. His heart was thumping all the way up to his ears. In a distant part of his mind, he knew he was out of line, totally unprofessional. But the thought of Dory in danger seemed to dissolve all his inner structures.

Rules and procedures meant nothing. If he didn't do something -- *right now!* -- he thought he might start screaming. He pounded on the door again, listened for a response. Nothing. There was a four-foot prybar in the trunk of the car. He went down the steps.

A voice spoke from behind the front door. "Who's there?" it said.

Harry went back up the steps fast. "Dory?   Is that you?   It's Harry Lukovitch."

There was a silence. Now the voice sounded like Dory. "Look, Sergeant, I'm flattered, but I just want to be left alone."

"I think you are in danger," Harry said. There was no response. "Dory?"

"I'm here, Sergeant. And I'm fine."

"Three of your colleagues have been attacked. I have to make sure you're okay."

There was a stretched silence. "Just a minute," she said. "I'm not dressed. I was in the bath."

Harry waited on the steps. It seemed a long time before the door opened, but it gave him time to get his breathing under control. Dory Novello was dressed in a bathrobe and slippers, her hair in a towel and her face coated in some kind of cream.

"You can see I'm all right," she said, standing in the doorway. But she didn't look all right to Harry. Without the shield of make-up and well cut clothes, she seemed as nervous and gauche as a teenage girl. The look of her pulled Harry closer, into her personal space. She reflexively moved back. He stepped around her and into the house.

"Hey!" she said.

He opened the hall closet and glanced inside, closed the door and put his head into the living room. Then he went down the hall and checked each room, before returning to where Dory stood by the open front door. Under the face cream, her expression was unreadable.

"This is an invasion of privacy!" she said.

"Yes, it is," said Harry. "But I have reason to believe you are in danger from the same man who has now attacked Katherine Tower, Ellen Wiens and Maria Chen."

"That's nonsense," she said. "I can look after myself."

He heard something wrong in the way she said it, something defensive, like an adolescent's false bravado. There was fear underneath -- fear and vulnerability -- and it was pushing Harry's buttons.

He went into the living room and looked around. The place was spartan: the furniture looked rented, there were no knickknacks, no pictures. The brick fireplace had no ashes in it, but there was plenty of dust.

"Have you lived here long?" he asked.

"I'd like you to leave," she said. The front door was still open.

Harry came up close to her. He could smell the sweet rose scent of the face cream. "There's a dangerous man out there. He's attacked people you know. I think he's got a list, and there's a good chance you're on it. Please, be reasonable."

Somehow, it was the wrong thing to say. She stiffened, and her jaw clenched. "I'm being perfectly reasonable." She took a deep, slow breath. "Why do you think there's a list?"

Harry walked around the room. There was dust on the mantelpiece, and on the phone answering machine on a small table beside the couch. "He's hit three women who all know each other. That's no coincidence. I have to ask you, what is your connection with the victims?"

She closed the front door and came as far into the living room as the doorway. She stood there, one hand holding the elbow of the other arm, shifting her weight from foot to foot.

"We're on the program committee of the Businesswomen's Alliance. We line up speakers for the monthly luncheon," she said.

Harry got out his notebook. "You all work for different companies?"

"Yes. Major corporations, except Maria -- she's with a merchant bank."

"And you're a consultant?"

"I told you that."

"Do you do work for the companies they work for?"

"Yes." She rubbed her hand up and down her arm. "Look, what is this? Why are you questioning me?"

"I told you before, it's a habit. Are there other members on this committee?"

"No, we're it."

"Where do you usually meet?"

"At restaurants, or at each other's homes and offices."

"Are any men involved?"

"It's a *women's* network. I don't see what this is all about."

Harry looked at his notes. "Neither do I. Not yet."

"Look, Sergeant..." she began.

"Harry."

"All right, Harry!"   She pulled the belt of her robe tighter. "I keep myself to myself. I don't like men barging in. I don't like questions. A group of businesswomen getting together to talk shop has got nothing to do with some animal in a mask."

Harry looked up from his notes. "Where did you hear about the mask?   We've released no description."

She was very nervous now. She wouldn't look at him. "Will you leave me alone!   I don't want to get involved in this!"

The more she denied it, the more he could see that she was afraid of something. Her fear was stirring things in him again. The urge to put his arms around her, to enclose her in a shelter of his own flesh was almost overpowering.

"You may be in danger," he said. "I'm worried about you." His mouth was dry; it made his voice sound funny. "Not just officially. Personally."

She kept her back turned, spoke to the closet across the hallway. "I don't need this."

"I think you do."

"I don't care what you think!"   She put her hand to her forehead and it came away smeared with cream. "Damn it!" she said, and rubbed her fingers on her robe.

"I'm sorry," Harry said. "I don't usually act like this, doing the big domineering daddy-knows-best. But I care about you. I know we've only just met, we don't really know each other, but something's *there*, and it's making me do and say things I wouldn't normally do."

She turned toward him. He could see, even through the stuff on her face, that she was confused, didn't know how to respond to him. He put out a hand to her, but she stepped back.

"I can't take any complications right now," she said.

"I don't want to be a complication."

"But you are."

"Okay," he said. He walked to the fireplace, ran his finger through the dust on the mantelpiece. If he didn't look at her, it was easier. "Okay. Whatever I feel, whatever you feel -- if you feel anything -- we'll just lay that aside for now. But I'm still a cop, and there's still a maniac out there somewhere, and I want to know how come you know about the mask."

She turned away again. "I don't want to talk about this."

"You've got to talk about it."

"No." She opened the hall closet. For a moment, he thought she was actually going to get into it and close the door on him.

"How do you know about the mask?"

She spoke into the closet. Her voice seemed different, flatter. "He already tried to attack me."

Harry was across the room and right beside her. "What? When?"

She turned her shoulder to him, would not meet his eyes. "I don't know, last week sometime."

"Tell me."

She went into the living room and sat on the couch with her legs tucked up under the robe. Harry sat in the armchair and waited.

"Harry," she began, still in that other voice. *She's distancing herself from the experience*, he thought; he knew what that was like. "I know you're just doing your job," she continued.

"I'm not just doing my job." There was dust on the end table too. His finger drew a line through it.

She noticed. "I work a lot. I'm not here much."

"Same with me," he said. He knew she was reluctant to deal with the man in the mask, knew that he needed to get her talking so he could ease into the bad stuff. "You're not originally from the coast," he said.

Her eyes flicked to him, then away. "How do you know that?"

"Accent mostly. Also, you don't move your upper lip or open your teeth too wide. That says southern Ontario."

"I didn't think I had an accent," she said.

"Most people think accents are something other people have, but they're just normal."

"I'm not too normal." Her hands twisted the belt of the robe. "Did you run some kind of check on me? I don't like people checking up on me."

Harry shook his head. "I have no reason to run a check on you. But I've been watching you. I like you. I get the feeling you've got a lot going on under the surface."

She looked at her hands. "You like me."   She sounded girlish again.

"I do. Okay, I don't know you, but I like what I see. And there's something about you that I can't put my finger on. You're the first woman who's made me feel... anything, in a long time."

She stared at him. He saw some kind of yearning in her eyes, and it pulled at him. He wanted to tell her it would be okay.

"Dory," he said.

The tone of his voice, the look on his face, made her snap her head away. "What are we doing here?" she said.

He didn't press it. "Tell me about the man who attacked you. Can you give me a description?"

She twisted the belt again. Then she cocked her head, as if she were listening to someone he couldn't hear. Under the face cream, her features were very still. Her voice was flat again.

"Not too tall," she said. "Kind of slim. Young, but not a kid. He wore a dark suit, a flower in his lapel, and a little girl's mask. With sunglasses."

"Did you see a knife?"

She thought about it. "No, no knife. He just jumped out, tried to grab me. I fought him off and he ran away."

"Where was this?   And when?"

"I'm not sure. Thursday?   No, Friday. At my office. In the hall. I came out, and he jumped out of the elevator. It was all over in a few seconds."

"Did he say anything?"

She shook her head.

"Did you see his face?"

"He was wearing a mask and sunglasses. I can describe the mask."

"I was hoping it might have slipped during the struggle."

She twisted the belt some more. "It might have, a little."

"One thing, did he have a mustache?"

"A mustache?"

"Yeah."

"He might have. Is it important?"

"It could be."

She thought about it. "I think he did."

"Good one." He made a note. "Anything else? Scars, moles, that kind of thing?

"Not that I saw."

"That's okay. That's good." He was feeling better now, more energized. It was all pointing toward Shaeffer. The threat to this woman had a name and a face, just an ordinary loser that Harry could get his hands on and deal with. He'd bust the goddam pervert, and that would put to rest the turmoil that was ripping him up inside.

"Listen," he said, "we may have a suspect in custody by tomorrow. If we do, I'll want you to identify him."

She looked at him, at her hands, at the floor. He heard her sigh. "Look, I only saw him for a second. I really don't want to get involved. I have real trouble dealing with this."

He heard denial. He'd heard it before in sexual assault cases. Sometimes all they wnted to do was look the other way. He also heard helplessness. Though she was a grown woman, he kept seeing her as a kid who had to deal with problems that were too old for her, too harsh.

He closed the notebook. "You already are involved, Dory. Look, I can see that this is very hard for you, and I want to protect you all I can. I'm here to help."

He took out his pocket phone and dialed Mack's cell. She was in the back of a patrol car, getting a ride back to the department from the hospital. She told him there had been nothing new from Maria Chen, except that the attacker had claimed another trophy: her minivan's security remote control.

Harry asked her to call Inspector Mason and have him arrange for extra swing-bys in the victims' neighborhoods, especially around Dory's. And he wanted a car in front of Carla Gonsalvez's place

He took out a card and wrote on its back. "This is my card. Office number and cell phone on the front, home number on the back. Call me anytime." He left it on the dusty end table.

He stood up. He was feeling better now. It was always better when there was a suspect and a good chance of nailing him. "Guess I'd better go."

She got up. Something invisible hung in the air between them. "Yes, thanks for coming."

"Somebody will be around to talk to your neighbors, see if

they've noticed anything unusual."   He looked toward the duplex's common wall. "What about next door?"

Dory moved toward the front door, put her hand on the knob. "He's my landlord. He's not here very much these days."

She opened the door, but Harry stayed in the living room archway. "What's he like?"

The question seemed to fluster her a little. He wondered if there was anything going on there. But what she said argued for the opposite. "He's kind of a wimp. He just rents me space. We don't relate."

"Do you know where he works?"

"No. I don't even think about him."

"Well, the uniformed boys will find him."   She opened the door wider and he stepped out onto the porch but didn't go down the steps. He looked at her. Her eyes seemed larger, softer.

"You feel it, don't you?" he said.

She looked at her feet. "Don't."

"Jeez," he said, "I feel like a high-school kid."

She half closed the door. "Don't," she said again.

"Just let me say something."   He took a breath. "I've been alone a long time. It's been years since anyone has gotten through to me. But you do."

"Please stop."

"I can't. I've been avoiding a lot of stuff since... since something happened that I didn't deal with, not properly. Then I meet you and suddenly there's this urge to come back in out of the cold. I feel that I want you to be part of my life."

She leaned on the door. She looked very tired. "You might not like it as much as you think."

"I'm ready to take that chance."

Her voice was weak, but strong enough to cut him off. "No. This can't be. And I've got to get up in the morning. I'm bagged. Please, good night."

He backed away. "I'll call you."

"Oh God," she said, then, "sure, I guess."   She closed the door and he heard it lock. But there was no sound of footsteps moving away. He imagined her still standing there, listening to him leave.

#

The park was a treeless rectangle, its expanse of green unbroken except by four softball diamonds in the corners. Mack eased the unmarked car to the curb on the opposite side of the street, while Harry stared at the situation that was developing on the grass.

"The hell is this?" he said.

"Some kind of rally," Mack said.

A block away, on the north side of the park, the grass rolled up a gently terraced slope. Someone up there was unfurling a green banner whose three-foot-high orange letters gradually spelled out the slogan *Free Khalistan*. Toward the banner, mostly from the south where the golden dome of the temple reared above Marine Drive, streamed endless numbers of Sikhs. Most of the men wore beards and turbans, and more than a few of the headcoverings were orange, signifying their wearers' willingness to die for the faith. The women were in bright silk saris and filmy head scarves that trailed behind them as they walked.

Two police cars were parked on the far side of the park. As Harry and Mack watched, two more came down the street they were on, slowing for the crowd still flowing across the pavement into the park. The second of the marked vehicles stopped. The uniformed inspector in the back gave the detectives a once-over.

The recognition was mutual. Inspector Fleck was head of community relations. A punctilious old-schooler, he had never found his acquaintanceship with Harry Lukovitch to be rewarding. Harry felt the same way.

Fleck told the driver to stop and rolled down his window. "What are you two doing here?"

"Stake-out on a serial rapist," Mack said. She nodded toward the growing crowd. "What's that all about?"

"It's Vaisakhi Day," the inspector said. "It's a very special day honoring Gobind Singh, last of the major Sikh gurus. All the pro-Khalistan groups are going to march up Fraser Street. You two will stay clear. Community relations is running this operation."

"Nothing to do with us," said Harry. He knew that many Canadian Sikhs, along with their relatives back home, wanted the Punjab to cease being an Indian state and become the independent nation of Khalistan. If anyone had asked, he would have said that nationalism, especially when it was supercharged by religion, was the most common mental disorder of the twentieth century -- and by far the most destructive.

But nobody was asking.

"Sir," said the inspector.

Harry put his thumb and forefinger behind his ear and moved it in the uniform's direction. "Sorry?" he said.

"Apology accepted, Sergeant," said the inspector, with a wintry smile. He tapped the driver's shoulder and the marked car moved on.

"You shouldn't get them mad," said Mack. "They can make life miserable for you."

"They're too late," said Harry. He slumped down in his seat and closed his eyes.

"Think he'll show, with all these cops?" Mack said. When she got no answer, she reached over and lightly knocked on her partner's forehead. "Hey. Bring out your dead."

Harry opened his eyes. "I was thinking."

Mack put her tongue in her cheek, pressed the flesh there. "About the ineffable Ms. Novello?"

"Time to learn a new word?"

"Sorry."

"You saw her at that lunch. What'd you think?"

"You shouldn't ask me," Mack said.

"I am asking you."

Mack shrugged and stared out the side window. She didn't want to have this kind of talk about a woman with Harry. "I dunno," she said. "Women don't see women the way men do. We see clothes, hair, that kind of thing. I dunno. You ask me, though, she's sorta mannish."

Harry sat up. "What do you mean, mannish?   You saying you think she's a lesbian?   I can tell you, she's no lesbian."

Her partner's sudden defensiveness bothered Mack. She turned to him. "You didn't... do anything with her, did you, Harry? She's involved in this case, for chrissake!"

Harry pulled his head in a little. It reminded her of The Mystery Turtle. "I didn't do anything," he said. "But why are you so down on Dory?"

Mack sighed. "I'm not down on her," she said, "but let's be professional about this, okay?   I'm actually glad to see you take an interest, even if it's... well, never mind. But you can't go getting into anything with a witness in a major investigation."

"I know," he said. "I just feel this thing."

"It's good you feel something, I guess," Mack said. "Look, we get this case wrapped, you want to give her a call, that's okay. Just, right now, you don't want your judgment affected."

"Yeah," he said. "You're right."   He yawned. "You're a good partner. Gimme some of that coffee."

He poured himself a cup of black richness from the thermos Mack had brought from home. She made good coffee. He sipped it, and watched the swelling mass of people in the park. Two more cop cars had arrived, and a news crew from BCTV.

"Hell, Shaeffer's not coming this way, all these cops. Let's slide around."

Mack started the car and they went down the street. They were on East Sixty-First Avenue, two blocks east of Fraser Street, a working-class neighborhood close to the sawmills down on the river. In the past twenty-five years, it had been the area of choice for newcomers from the Indian subcontinent.

The older houses were square little butter boxes covered in stucco embedded with bits of colored glass, mass-built for returning Second World War veterans. The newer places dwarfed the old. Outside, they had lots of brick and glass, and most of them had painted pillars out front. Inside was plenty of room for the assembly of grandparents, cousins, siblings and in-laws that made up the immigrant extended families.

They drove past the house where Morris Shaeffer's mother lived. It was one of the older ones, in the middle of the block, with pink stucco and green trim. The curtains were drawn.

"She's not up yet," Harry said. "If her little boy was home, she'd be bustling around making him breakfast and listening to his sad catalog of woes."

At the corner, Mack turned right, then right again to bring them into the service lane that ran the length of the block behind the houses. A slim young man in jeans and a windbreaker was part way down the lane ahead of them. When he heard the car behind him, he turned. And then he leaped over a wood-and-wire fence into a back yard, and ran between two houses.

"Hit it!" said Harry. He unbuckled his seat belt and half-opened his door.

Mack accelerated to the place where Shaeffer had jumped the fence, slowed enough for Harry to bail out, then sped the car down the lane, lights flashing.

Harry came out from between two houses on Sixty-First. He saw his quarry whipping it across the park in the direction of the crowd of Sikhs. Shaeffer ran with a helter skelter urgency, legs and arms well off the vertical, like a puppet whose strings were too loose.

But he had speed and a lead. And the dozen cops on the grass were standing with their backs to him, watching the men around the banner trying to organize the people -- now numbering at least five hundred -- into a column of march.

Harry scrambled over a wall of ornamental concrete blocks and stumbled across the street into the park. Shaeffer was almost all the way across the grass by now. The uniformed cops from community relations were gathered around Inspector Fleck, getting their detailed instructions.

Shaeffer was already past the huddle of cops, heading for the rear of the crowd.

"Stop him!" Harry yelled.

Some of the cops looked around, saw Harry, saw the man he was chasing, and put it together. Four of them pulled away from the group around the inspector and pounded heavily after Shaeffer.

Shaeffer insinuated himself into the crowd, weaving and sideslipping between its small clusters of people. The uniformed cops plowed straight in after him, pushing the demonstrators aside. A woman stumbled and fell. A man in an orange turban was shouldered roughly out of the way.

Turbaned heads swung around. Somebody shouted in Punjabi and a growl went up from the mass. A wall of bodies suddenly coalesced in front of the pursuing cops. Young men pushed them back. A large man cursed and swung a fist. The cops drew their pepper spray. More cops came in to rescue the surrounded four.

Out in the clear, Inspector Fleck blew his whistle in long, futile blasts, but it was too late. The main body of his men had already formed a flying wedge and flung themselves into the mob. The trapped four were reached and rescued. They backed out of the mass of angry Sikhs, their uniforms torn. One had a bloody nose.

The cops formed a line and retreated a few feet. The

demonstrators jeered and shouted at them, while the march leaders up on the terrace tried to find out what was happening down in the field. More of the crowd was moving away from them, drawn downslope toward the confrontation with the uniforms.

Fleck raised his whistle to his lips once more, thought better of it, and backed away with his men. "Where's Lukovitch?" he wanted to know. The cop with the bloody nose shrugged and sniffed.

Harry had tried to skirt the crowd, running around its edge like a sheep dog looking for a renegade ram. But when the mob turned and began to move toward the cops, he was briefly caught up in an eddy of teenagers racing around from the front.

When he broke free, Shaeffer was nowhere to be seen in the surging mass of color that was the mob. Harry ran up the slope onto the terrace of grass and swung his eye over the crowd below. The only bare heads were the few westernized Sikhs who had disregarded the dictum of Guru Gobind Singh that they should wear a turban and never cut their hair. None had the nondescript brown hair of Morris Shaeffer.

Between Harry and the street that formed the northern boundary of the park was a squat building made of cinder blocks, with washrooms and storage space for park equipment. Now the women's washroom door opened and Shaeffer came out, his hands pinioned behind him. He was followed by Mack.

"If you're finished helping Inspector Fleck," she said, "we could go downtown and spend some quality time with this guy."

Mack pushed the suspect toward where she had run the unmarked car up onto the grass. Harry helped her stow him in the back, then got in beside him.

"I didn't do anything," Shaeffer said.

Chapter 5

They sat in one of the interrogation rooms on the third floor. It had three chairs, a table bolted to the wall and a tape recorder. The walls were beige and there were no windows.

"How long you had the mustache?" Harry asked. He sat beside Shaeffer, leaned in close. Mack stood behind them, shoulders against the wall.

Shaeffer stared straight ahead. "I didn't do it."

Harry sighed, and counted on his fingers. "I got you in the building at MacroFiber. I got you for access to the victim's desk and elevator key. I got you for general description. I got a witness saw a mustache. You want to talk motive?   Shaeffer, I remember you of old."

"It wasn't me."

"Why'd you run?"

The suspect put his hands flat on the table. "I was scared. I heard about what happened on the top floor. I saw you in Mr. Lucas's office. I figured as soon as you found out I was working there, you'd come looking for me."

"You own a knife?   Maybe something Dad brought back from the war?"

Shaeffer turned toward Harry. "Sergeant," he said, "you know I was never into hurting anybody. Okay, I had some problems. Unresolved personality conflicts and low self-esteem that manifested as exhibitionism. I used to be self-degrading, but I've grown beyond that now. I would never violate another person's dignity and inflict my problems on that person."

Harry leaned back. "Where the hell'd you learn to talk like that?"

"I'm in a program. They got me the job. I'm straight now, Sergeant. I come a long way. You gotta believe that."

A uniformed cop entered. "We're ready downstairs," he said.

Harry pushed his chair away from the table and stood up. "Okay, take him down."

To Shaeffer, he said, "You won't mind helping us with a line-up, will you, Shaeffer?   If you didn't, it might just shoot my self-esteem all to hell."

"I didn't do it."

"Make sure the other guys have mustaches," Harry told the uniform. "We want to be fair."

Mack watched the uniform take Shaeffer away. When the door was closed, she said, "I don't know."

"He's the one," Harry said. "I feel it."

"Maybe you just want to feel it."

He looked up at her. "You're questioning my judgment."

"Yeah, I am," Mack said. "You get manic like this, turn into the rompin-stompin crime fighter, it can make you want to get to the end of it too fast."

"You've seen me get worked up about cases before. Was I wrong those times?   Did I get the wrong guy?"

Mack shrugged. "No. You were a pain in the ass, but you came through."

"So why not trust my instincts now?"

"Cause this time it's different. This time, you've got a thing for one of the victims. And I think it may be blunting old Occam's edge."

Harry stood up, and opened the door. "I know what I'm doing," he said. "See what happens with the line-up."

"I don't feel good about this one, Harry," Mack said.

"I do."

#

When Zip Metcalfe had joined the force, they'd still been using the old British style line-up procedures. Victims had to pick out their assailants face to face, and touch them on the shoulder to make the formal identification. Nowadays, things were done in the American way -- through a two-way mirror that allowed the witness to see without being seen.

The four women were waiting outside the door to the line-up room, seated on a bench against the wall. Katherine Tower and Ellen Wiens had their heads together. Katherine's hands punctuated whatever she was saying with short, choppy blows of her right fist into her left palm. Ellen was nodding in agreement.

"It's the goddamn glass ceiling," Katherine said. "Doesn't matter how good we are, we're still women. We only get so far up the ladder and then that's it. The big toys are for the big boys."

"But what are you going to do?" Ellen said. "It's not like you organize a petition or anything, and they have to change."

"I can't wait for a new generation of CEOs who weren't raised by Donna Reed, the stay-at-home mom," Katherine said. "I want to *do* something before I'm too old."

"What?"

"We should start our own company."

Ellen blinked. "Doing what?"

"Whatever we can do that we can be the best at," Katherine said. "I don't care. Import-export. Investment services. Property development."

"It's not that easy," Ellen said.

Katherine snorted. "This town is full of first-class women getting second-class treatment. If we brought some of them together, we'd have a company that would blow the fat-assed boys down at the Vancouver Club off the field."

"It's true," Ellen said. She thought of Rhys Maitland's ass, and how he had his tailor cut his jackets extra long to cover it. "But it takes more than talent. It takes money."

Katherine's face changed. "Yeah," she said. "And the bankers don't want to see a bunch of women coming in to ask for that money. Right Maria?"

Maria Chen responded vaguely to the sound of her name. She had not been listening. Her face was swollen, the bruises the color of spoiled fruit. Her mother had insisted on coming with her to the police station. Mrs. Chen was a tiny woman in a voluminous coat, who now brought Maria water in a paper cup and said something at length in Mandarin that did not sound comforting. Maria took the water but did not drink it until her mother urged her.

Dory Novello sat a little apart from the others. She wore a severe suit of charcoal gray that contrasted with the heavy make-up she had applied to her eyes and cheeks. She fingered the trackball of a notebook computer balanced on her lap, moving its cursor around and studying the data displayed on its screen.

When Harry came down the corridor, followed by Mack, she looked up at him with an expression he could not read, then quickly returned to the computer.

Harry was surprised by the strength of the impulse to go sit beside her, talk to her, touch her. It took an effort to fight it down, to say "Good morning," to all of them and be the model policeman.

Mack opened the door to the line-up room. Harry asked the women to come in. The place was dark and narrow, small enough that the six of them filled the space. Maria's mother had to wait outside.

Harry explained the procedure. The curtain that covered the top half of one wall would be pulled back and they would see a lighted room with several men in it. The men would not be able to see them. They would be asked if they recognized any of the men there. They had to be positive about the identification, without qualification of any kind.

He asked them if they were ready. Three of the women said they were. Maria only nodded. Harry pulled the cord that drew back the curtain.

Five men stood under the bright lights on the other side of the glass. All had mustaches, all were roughly the right size. Two had been pulled from the cells: a small time cocaine dealer and a guy who had been brought in by a patrol that responded to a complaint that he had been beating his wife with a belt. Another two were off-duty cops. Shaeffer was fourth from the left.

"Do any of you recognize any of these men?" Harry asked.

The four women stared. Ellen Wiens looked at them, one after the other, and shook her head. "Number four is familiar, but I can't say he's the one," she said.

Maria searched each man's face, as if somewhere beyond the glass was the answer to her pain, then turned away.

Katherine said, "Can you ask them to do this?"   She mimed the shushing gesture of a finger to the lips.

Harry spoke into the handset of a wall phone. The men all brought a finger to their lips. Katherine peered through the glass.

"Again, please," she said.

They repeated the motion. She shook her head. "Dammit," she said, "I don't know."

Harry looked to Dory. He had seen her studying the five men intently, concentrating particularly on Shaeffer. He was the one who seemed the most nervous.

She said, "I think," -- her voice was a husky whisper, and she cleared her throat -- "I think it's number four. I've seen him somewhere."

"Ms. Tower?" Harry said.

"Ask him to do the finger again," Katherine said. "Just him."

Harry spoke into the phone. Shaeffer put his finger to his lips. He was sweating. His eyes moved, as if he could see them through the glass.

"It could be," Katherine said.

"I think it is," Dory said. She looked at Harry. He was working on maintaining a poker face.

"You have to be certain," he said. "A maybe is a no. Are you identifying number four as the man who attacked you?"

Katherine made up her mind. "I'm going to say yes."

"Me too," said Dory.

Harry looked to the other two women. "Ms. Wiens? Ms. Chen?"

Maria shook her head and looked down.

"It could be, but I can't say," said Ellen.

Harry drew the curtains on the five men. "I want to thank you ladies for assisting us," he said. "I know this was not easy for you. We'll contact you later for formal statements."

"Did we get the right one?" Dory asked.

"The man you indicated is a suspect," Mack said.

Dory let out a sigh.

"Do me a favor," Katherine said. "Put him in a cell with a big biker."

Harry opened the door, and they filed out. Maria's mother took her daughter by the arm and started to lead her away. Katherine Tower went after them.

Dory was right behind them, heading for the door to the street. Harry hurried to catch her.

"Dory," he said, "if there's anything I can do."

"No, thank you, Sergeant," she said.

Mack was giving him a look. He hunched his shoulders and put his hands up, then followed her back upstairs.

The women went through the front doors and out onto Main Street. Katherine put an arm around Maria's shoulders. "Listen, Maria," she said, "best thing for you, right now, is go back to work. You need to be in a place where you feel strong. Go and get back into the numbers. It'll be all right."

Maria's mother said something in Mandarin and tried to pull her daughter away from Katherine's grip. Maria gave her mother a short answer in the same language, then turned to Katherine. "Maybe you're right," she said. "But not today. I'll go in tomorrow."

Katherine squeezed gently. "That's the way, kid," she said. She looked to Ellen and Dory. "Come on, they got the bastard. What say we get some lunch?"

Ellen blew out her cheeks. "I could use a drink. We can talk about being big shots in Katherine's all-woman, all-purpose company. Come on, Maria."

"I look awful," Maria said. Then her mother threw in some more Mandarin that made up her daughter's mind. "Count me in," she said. She disengaged her arm from the older woman's grasp and said a few words. Her mother left, talking to herself.

"What about you, Dory?" Katherine said.

"I have some things to do."   She stopped where her car was parked at a meter.

Katherine let go of Maria and stopped beside Dory. She felt like fishing. "Seems like a nice guy," she said.

Dory unlocked her trunk and put the notebook computer in it. "What?"

"The cop, Harry. Seems nice."

Dory's voice tightened. "He's pushy. He's trying to control me."

Katherine shrugged. "I'd say he's a pussycat."

Dory opened the driver's door. "You don't know men the way I do."

"Maybe," Katherine said, "but I know that particular man has got it bad for you. Why don't you give him a chance?"

Something softened in Dory's face, just for a moment. For the first time, Katherine Tower got a glimpse beneath the cool businesslike exterior that was the consultant's armor. *That's the thing the policeman sees*, she thought.

Then the Dory Novello she was accustomed to took charge again. "I've got to go," Dory said. Seconds later, she was insulated by glass and steel and heading downtown.

Katherine watched her go, then turned to Ellen and Maria. "Ladies," she said, "let's do lunch."

#

The rain had eased up, and there were even some breaks in the clouds by end of shift. A miserly ratio of sunlight was leaking into the squad room as Harry typed up the paperwork on the line-up. Mack came in carrying the hardcopy file on Morris Shaeffer. She took it to her desk and spent a few minutes absorbing what it had to tell her. Then she closed the folder, laid it in the middle of her desk and said, "I just don't think so."

Harry looked up. "What?"

"Shaeffer. I still don't like it."

"You don't like what?"

"I don't like Shaeffer for Mr. Three-piece."   She tapped the file. "He doesn't fit."

"He fits fine," Harry said, and went back to the typewriter.

Mack got up and came over to sit on the corner of Harry's desk. "Look at the guy. Three counts indecent exposure. He goes on probation, takes a program, he's clear for four years."

Harry let the typing go. He said, "You look. He dodges me at MacroFiber Industries. He skips work today. And when he sees us, he runs. He's got a mustache. And two of the witnesses pick him out of the line-up."

"You come after me like that, I'd probably jump a fence."

"You're not buying all that bullshit, flashers never go on to more challenging outrages?"

"No. But I just don't see *this* guy coming on like some raping robot."

"Yeah?   Give him a knife and let him tie you to a bed for an hour. See how he looks then."

She stood up, walked a few steps away from the desk, then turned back. "Are you sure it's not that you just want it to be Shaeffer?"

"I'm sure."

"I don't know, partner. I've seen you drunk and I've seen you sober. I've seen you do first-class police work, and every now and then I've seen you go nuts over a case. Now I'm wondering if the reason you want to wrap this one up in a hurry is cause Novello's in it."

Harry got up and walked around the desk. He took Mack by the shoulders, gently turned her around and mimed the notions of frisking a suspect.

She laughed. "What the hell are you doing?"

He turned her around again. "Just wanted to see if you had a psychiatric degree concealed on your person."

"Least you didn't call it feminine intuition," she said. "For that you'd get a smack."

He went back to the desk and switched off the electric typewriter. "Come on, you modern, gender-neutral police person," he said, "it's quitting time."

"It's nice to see you happy," Mack said. She reached for her purse. "I still don't like canceling the extra patrols."

Harry put on his coat. "If you stop talking about this, I will buy you real coffee and something with calories in it."

They went to a place Mack liked, out on West Broadway, where people ate bagels and muffins and fancy breads while sitting on hard wooden chairs around small wooden tables resting on bare wooden floorboards. It was all very good.

Harry looked at the decor. "*De gustibus non disputandum est*," he said.

"Which means?" Mack said, around a mouthful of almond croissant.

"There's no accounting for taste. My old partner used to say that."

Mack swallowed. "That would have been Zip Metcalfe?"

"Uh huh," said Harry. "A scholar and a gentleman."

Mack sipped from her cup of Sumatran Mandeheling. "This would have been the same Zip Metcalfe who got his nickname when he was a kid because he could stand in the balcony of the old Lux theater, squirt a jet of urine onto the seats below, and be zipped up and sitting down again before it landed?"

Harry paused his basic Colombian halfway to his lips. "Who told you that?"

"Zip Metcalfe."

"Where did you..?"

"At that beer parlor where all the retired cops go. The one where the naked ladies pretend they really get off on shiny metal poles."

"You went to the Pit?   That dive?"

Mack took another nibble from the croissant. "I gotta wonder what they think about while they're working," she said. "I mean, what the hell *do* you think about when you're rubbing your crotch on chrome steel?"

"Why'd you go to the Pit?"

"I heard Zip Metcalfe hung out there. I wanted to meet him. My partner's old partner."

"So you met him."

"I met him, bought him a beer, talked shop, talked Harry."

There was a window next to their table. Harry looked out of it. "And?" he said.

"And, funny thing, he didn't use any of those Latin expressions. Occam's razor never came up even once. But, you know, he told me," she paused for a sip and for effect, "he told me that you had more books than anybody he'd ever known."

Harry said nothing, watched the rush-hour traffic on Broadway.

"What'd you do with all the books, Harry?"

"Jeannie's got them. They're in boxes in her basement."

She waited for him to say something more. Nothing came. When the silence had run on for nearly a minute, she said, "So how come?"

"No room for books at my place."

"Not the books. How come the act?"

He flicked his eyes over her, then looked into his coffee cup. "Who says it's an act?"

"Zip says."

"Okay, so I read some books, so I know how many parts Julius Caesar divided Gaul into. So what?"

"Zip says you had a ...a different kind of upbringing. Private school."

"You want to do an interrogation, they got a nice room back at the department."

His right hand was resting on the table. She put her left on top of it. He was a little startled, but he didn't move. "It's not an interrogation, Harry," she said. "I need to get to know you better."

He looked out the window again, then back to her hand on his. "Okay," he said. "I had a different kind of upbringing. My mom and dad were classical musicians. She played violin, he was a pianist. Dad was from Seattle, and she was Canadian. They met when he came up to play a series of concerts with the Vancouver Symphony. I was a surprise. They were almost middle aged, pretty set in their ways, and suddenly they had a baby. They took a year off and stayed home -- that was down in Seattle -- when I was born, but their real life was traveling and performing, all the time, all over the world. When I was little, they took me with them, but when I was ready to go to school, they sent me to this place in Switzerland. Boarding school."

"And?"

"And then one year, I was eight, they were on a train in Italy, coming to see me, and it derailed, and they died."

"So who raised you?"

"The school raised me. There were no aunts or uncles, only my mother's parents, and they were really old. They adopted me, and arranged for dual citizenship. I used to go to their place in Victoria for Christmas and the summer. But then they got too old, and when I was eleven they died, so I just stayed around the school. The teachers, the staff, they were my family."

"Poor kid."   She increased the pressure on his hand.

"Nah, it was okay," he said. "They were good to me. It wasn't till I came back to Canada to go to university that I found out how different I was."

"What do you mean?"

"Well, it was a very conservative school, very big on Greek and Latin. No TV, no movies, no radio, only the classics. The other kids, they got time off at holidays. But I was there twelve months a year. I kind of grew up in the eighteenth and nineteenth centuries. I can quote you whole chunks of Shakespeare and Byron -- he was my ideal -- but nine out of ten rock stars, I've never heard of them. When O.J. Simpson got in trouble, I didn't know he used to play football. I even had to learn how to speak ungrammatically. A girl said I talked like a dictionary."

"Let me get you another coffee," she said. She went to the counter and got them refills. When she was sitting down again, she said, "That is a different kind of background for a cop."

"Yeah, but it works. Occam's razor is as good a tool for cutting through confusion as anything in the psychobabble books down at the drugstore."

She took his hand again. He looked into her eyes, and realized, not for the first time, that there was something there for him if he wanted it. He looked away.

"That explains some of the weirdness," she said. "But what

about the rest of it?"

He ducked his head slightly. This conversation was going somewhere he didn't want to get to. "What rest of it?"

"Why you can't forgive yourself. Those teachers, did they tell you *you* had to be perfect?   Everybody else screws up, they learn to live with it -- but you have to be Sir Galahad, the true knight."

"Now comes the psychobabble," he said.

"No."

"Yes."   He took his hand from under hers to lift up his coffee cup. It made a barrier between them. "Let's put old Occam on the case, reduce the equation to its simplest terms. A man is supposed to take care of people who depend on him. He fails to do it. Those who depend on him suffer. So he suffers, too. It has an elegant simplicity."

"That's what's wrong with it," Mack said. "It's too simple. You're too complex a guy to be caught in such a simple trap."   She touched her fingertips to the wrist of the hand that held the cup. "Too nice a guy."

Her touch was warm. He knew that, if he let her, that touch could thaw parts of him that he had long ago put into deep freeze. For the first time, he felt a temptation to reach for that warmth.

The cell phone in his pocket beeped. He broke the contact between them to pull it out, flip it open, answer it. As he listened, Mack thought the lines in his rumpled face somehow deepened.

He said, "We'll be right there."

"What?" Mack said.

He closed the phone. "You were right about Shaeffer, looks like," he said. "Mr. Three-piece hit Katherine Tower's place again."

#

Katherine had brought Maria home with her. The alternative was to turn her over to her mother's ministrations. Maria said her mother was mostly kind, but she had strong opinions and believed implicitly that her views should be shared by her children. They had stopped at the younger woman's house only long enough to pack a few things and listen to a continuous stream of Mandarin from the elder Mrs. Chen.

Katherine's key opened the lock. "That goddamn woman still hasn't changed the locks," she said. When she saw Maria's sudden agitation, she quickly followed with, "Don't worry, kid, we'll put a chair against it. It'll be okay. The couch folds out into a day bed. I'll take it and you can have the bedroom."

The reassuring speech was enough to get Maria through the door and settled on the couch, her suitcase resting against her leg like a friendly dog. "Sit tight and I'll make us some coffee," Katherine said.

The kitchen was dark. Katherine flicked on the light and took the carafe out of the coffee maker. She had already half filled it from the sink faucet when she noticed the object on the counter.

The carafe shattered in the sink, the water sweeping the smaller shards into the drain. Katherine backed slowly toward the doorway. Maria came running.

"Get my purse," Katherine said. "That cop's card is in it."

Seconds later, they were in the elevator, dropping down to the ground floor where the building manager lived. They left the door to Katherine's apartment open, left the water running in the sink, left the marble and Lucite paperweight resting on the counter -- the award that her attacker had taken, and which had now come back, with a white carnation nestled against its base.

    #

The rain had washed the air mostly clean. There were even a few stars shining above the glare of the city's lights. They were in Mack's little red Geo, passing under the art deco arch of the Burrard Bridge, the ranked towers of the West End waiting to absorb them. Harry was on the phone to the assignment NCO.

"I don't care what it does to the manning allocations. Give some young guys a double shift, with overtime."   He listened, then cut off the voice from the phone. "Look, everything that Inspector Mason authorized then canceled is now *re*authorized. I'll call Mason and get his rubber stamp working."

The NCO said something more, and Harry snapped, "Just do it!   Anybody gets a rocket up the ass it'll be me!"

Mack swung them off the bridge and made an illegal left turn onto Pacific. The horns of oncoming cars called the Geo nasty names, but the sounds were mostly drowned by the squeal of the little car's tires as Mack careered onto the seaside boulevard, fishtailed around a double-parked cab and accelerated down the straightaway.

"I want each of these addresses checked, and I want a car in front of them until I say different." He read off the street numbers of Dory Novello's, Ellen Wiens's and Carla Gonsalvez's homes, then switched the phone off to cancel the desk man's protests.

He immediately turned it back on and dialed Dory's number. It rang twice, then Dory's recorded voice came on, saying, "This is Dorcas Novello. I can't take your call right now, but please..."

Harry swore and hung up. He found a number for Carla Gonsalvez and dialed it. He let it ring twelve times before he gave up.

The only space open on Katherine Tower's block was a fire hydrant. Mack angled the Geo into it and put a *VANCOUVER POLICE* sign on the dash. She got out and rushed toward the front door.

Harry got out too, but he stayed at the curb.

"Give me your keys," he said.

Mack stopped but made no move to comply. "No," she said. "Right now, the job is here. Come on."

His face worked. His right fist lightly smacked his left palm three times. "The keys," he said.

She came back down the walkway to him. She put her hands on his arms and said, "No, Harry. I can see what's going on inside you, and I feel for you. But *this comes first.*"

"I have to know she's okay," he said.

"The car you sent is probably already there. If you can't get her, you can call the guys in front of her house."

A patrol car with its lights flashing slid to a stop in the middle of the street. A male and female pair in uniform got out and approached the two detectives.

"Come on, partner," Mack said. "The job has to come first."

The uniforms waited, bouncing on their toes, looking up and down the street. The male said, "Sergeant? What do you want us to do?"

Harry blew out a long breath. "Apartment 1504," he said. "Secure it till we get there. Don't touch anything."

To Mack he said, "I'm calling first thing."

"Fair enough."

The detectives went inside and found the manager's apartment. Katherine Tower was pacing the living room, somewhere between angry and frightened. Maria sat on the couch; she looked just plain scared.

The manager, a dry-eyed woman with frizzled red hair, was truculent. It was the wrong attitude to take with Harry, but he was glad to have a target.

"You get those locks changed tonight," he told her, "or your life will take a massive and sudden turn for the worse."

The woman sucked on a slim filtered cigarette wrapped in dark paper. "You don't scare me," she said.

Harry leaned in close. "Well, I would if you had the brains God gave algae," he said. "The owner of this place will get calls from the building inspector, the fire marshal, the city engineer and the health department before lunchtime tomorrow. And somehow your name will keep cropping up."

The manager remembered that she had the number of an all-night locksmith. She went to the phone.

Harry and Mack took statements from Katherine and Maria, then went upstairs. The award sat where it had waited for Katherine Tower to come home. The apartment was otherwise untouched.

The two uniforms reported that they had searched it and found it empty before taking up positions outside the door.

"Too bad he didn't do a Goldilocks," Mack said. She was referring to a stalker who had become famous the year before. The man had gone to his estranged girlfriend's house, intending to lie in wait for her and her new boyfriend under the bed, and to jump them with a baseball bat when they were at their most vulnerable.

It turned out to be a longer wait than he had counted on. Meanwhile, the ex-girlfriend's fridge was full of beer. When the couple came home, they were alerted to the ambusher's presence by the sound of snores and a miasma of beer farts.

After the man appeared in court, the morning tabloid reported the story under the headline, "The Brew Was Just Right," and dubbed him "Goldilocks." He got probation and left town.

Harry told the patrol officers to take Katherine and Maria to a hotel and stay with them. He arranged for an evidence team to recover the award and the carnation and to recheck the apartment for fingerprints. While he waited for them to arrive, he asked Mack to recanvass the neighbors, to find out if anyone had seen a man come or go that day. Then he got on the phone again.

The cops at Ellen Wiens's house had talked to her. She was

all right, and nothing seemed to have occurred at her home.

The two at Dory Novello's house reported no lights, nobody home. They'd tried the front and back doors, shone flashlights through the windows, listened at the mail slot and come up empty. Same with the other half of the duplex, although there was some light behind a frosted window that was probably a bathroom. They took Harry's cell number and said they would call if anything happened.

The officers who had attended at Carla Gonsalvez's house in Richmond gave the same report. But they said a neighbor had seen her arrive home, and her car was in the carport. They wanted to know what to do.

"You thought you heard somebody faintly calling for help," Harry said, "so you forced an entry. Do it, then call me back."

He shut off the phone and it immediately buzzed. It was the two uniforms outside Dory Novello's place. She had returned home.

"We told her you wanted us to watch the place," said the cop on the phone. "She doesn't like it."

"Is she there now?   Put her on," Harry said.

"She went inside," the cop said.

Harry hung up and dialled Dory's number. It rang twice, then the recorded message came on. Harry waited for it to run its course. As soon as he heard the beep, he said, "Dory?   It's Harry Lukovitch. I know you're there. Please pick up."

He heard the handset being lifted at the other end of the line, then Dory's voice. "Hello," she said.

"Are you all right?"

"I'm fine, Harry," she said.

"I'm having two men stay outside your house tonight."

"I don't need them."

Harry's hand was sweating. It made the phone slippery. He switched to the other hand. "Listen," he said, "it now looks like the man you identified is not the right one. The real attacker is still loose!   He's been inside Katherine Tower's apartment!"

The voice on the other end of the phone was calm. "It's not my concern."

Her coolness made him want to scream. It was like watching a deer standing on train tracks, frozen in the light of an oncoming freight, and being unable to make the animal move before the onrushing metal smashed its naive innocence into bloody meat and splintered bone.

He found himself shouting into the phone. "You can't deal with this situation by just ignoring it!   This guy is not going to go away just because you don't think about him!"

"I'm not going to let my life be run by anyone," she said. "Now, it's been a busy day and I need to sleep."

"Please, Dory," he said.

Her voice softened a little. "It's nice that you worry about me," she said. "But I'm all right."

"I want to come over," he said.

"No."   She was firm again. "I don't want you to. I'm going to sleep. Goodbye."

The phone clicked in his ear. He stood in Katherine Tower's kitchen, looking at it. For an instant, he wanted to throw it against the wall. Fitzgard and his crime-scene crew arrived and indicated that they'd prefer to see him out of their work space.

Mack came in to tell him the neighbors had nothing to report. She put a hand on his arm. "You okay?" she asked.

Before he could answer, his phone buzzed again. It was the cops at Carla Gonsalvez's place. They'd found her taped naked to her bed, a carnation petal between her breasts.

Chapter 6

Dory Novello rewound the tape on her answering machine. There were no messages, but because she had picked up the phone after it had beeped, it had recorded her conversation with Harry. She listened for a few seconds, but the sound of her own voice made her feel strange.

She reset the machine and went down the hall to the bedroom, unbuttoning the gray woolen jacket that was just right with the knee-length black skirt. She made sure that the bedroom curtains were completely closed before she took off the top and tossed it on the bed. She unhooked the skirt and let it slide down her hips, then gathered it up and dropped it onto the jacket.

She was very tired. Sleep was pulling at her like an undertow, drawing her away from shore, into the dark, warm depths. The conversation with the policeman had upset her; she couldn't stand conflict or tension, knew it might make her lose control.

In her underwear, she went into the ensuite bathroom, turned on the light and examined her face in the mirror. The gray eyes that gazed back at her seemed to convey an undefined vulnerability.

She sighed and reached for the cold cream, scooped some onto her fingertips and rubbed it into the make-up. For the umpteenth time, she wished she didn't have to wear so much make-up, but as always, she avoided following that thought to its conclusion.

She dampened a face cloth and began to wipe away the cream. With its removal, something else left the face that she saw in the mirror. The vulnerability about the eyes disappeared; they seemed to narrow slightly. The softness of expression that characterized the lips withdrew into a harder, more self-indulgent cast. The jaw tightened and the brow drew down.

It was a combination of several small changes that created a whole greater than the sum of its parts. The hands that belonged to the face splashed cold water on it and on the short hair. A towel roughened the skin and dried the hair into spikes, which were then laid flat by a bristle hand brush.

The face that looked from the mirror was no longer Dory

Novello's. She had gone away, gone to sleep, gone to her corner of the mind that she shared with the man who now walked back into the bedroom and pulled the brassiere off over his head.

He removed the breast prosthetics from the cups and laid them on the dresser. Then he put Dory's clothes on hangers and hung them in the closet. Finally, he stripped off her panty hose and panties, and removed the buttock-shaping bustle he had bought from a mail order catalog. He left the underwear to soak in the sink, and put on the long robe that hung on the back of the bathroom door.

Yawning, he reached in through the parting at the robe's front and scratched his testicles. Then he belted the garment, turned off the bathroom and bedroom lights and walked down the hall of Dory's duplex.

The canvas suitcase was in the closet where Dory had dropped it. The man picked it up, then opened the closet door. He knelt and reached into the bottom right corner, found the finger-sized hole and pushed the thin panel sideways. He stepped through the opening, into the closet on the west side of the duplex, and slid the panel closed behind him.

He left the suitcase in the hall beside the bedroom door, having first removed the notebook computer that was in it. He fished his keys out of the robe pocket, unlocked the basement door and went downstairs.

He put the notebook on the desk, then contemplated the flow chart on the drafting table for a moment, before taking a pen and crossing off two boxes that read *APR 15, TOWER, RETURN AWARD and APR 17, GONSALVEZ*. He went to the desk, powered up the notebook, and made some notations in one of its files. Then, satisfied, he switched off the computer, left it on the desk, and went upstairs.

He locked the basement door behind him, picked up the suitcase and carried it into the unlit bedroom. From the bag he removed the suit, mask, shoes and knife, arranging them in the closet as before. The last item in the suitcase was a copy of the morning paper, its whole front page given over to the headline *3-PIECE NABBED?*

He tossed the paper on the bed, dropped the suitcase in the bottom of the bedroom closet, then plucked the carnation from the suit's lapel. Smiling, he sniffed the blossom, and as he did so, he became aware that another scent lingered in the room. He sniffed. It was a familiar fragrance.

He stood very still, listening. He heard a small liquid sound from the bathroom. He reached for the knob, turned it slowly and opened the bathroom door a crack. Soft light and warm humid air reached out for him, and the young woman lying in a froth of candle-lit bubbles that filled his bathtub looked up.

"Surprise," she said. "Want to scrub three thousand miles from a lady's back?"

He opened the door the rest of the way. "Monica?   Didn't you get my message?"

She sat up in the tub, the bubbles sliding down her slight, small breasted torso. "Oh yeah, I got your message. Whatta you mean, too busy for a couple of weeks?   You're working too hard again, aren't you?   Poor baby, I can see it in your face. Why don't you come and slip into something warm?"   She slid down in the tub and parted her legs. "I brought some of that bubble bath you always like."

"How did you get in?"

"I found the spare key to the back door hidden in the carport."

"But I didn't leave a key there."

"Well, okay, whoever lived here before must've left it there. Doesn't matter. What matters is I'm here and we haven't seen each other for three months."   She put her hands on the sides of the tub and began to rise. "So I need a really big hello."

He backed out of the door. "Just a minute," he stammered. "I think I left the front door open. I'll be right back."

He closed the bathroom door, stepped to the closet and grabbed the suit and shoes. He turned and ran from the bedroom, then spun on his heel in the doorway and added the tabloid on the bed to the bundle in his grasp.

As he turned into the hall, one of the shoes slipped from under his arm and fell to the carpet. When he stooped to pick it up, the ornate dagger slid from the suit's pocket and hit the floor.

"Honey," came Monica's voice, "are you all right?"

He made a small noise at the top of his throat, and grabbed the weapon. Crouching to hold the bundle to his middle, he scuttled down the hall to the closet and elbowed the louvered door open. He dropped the rapist's paraphernalia to the floor, then reached down and yanked open the sliding panel.

He heard Monica's voice calling for him again. He crossed over into the other half of the duplex, gathered up the suit and shoes and paper, dropped the mask and grabbed for it, then finally wadded the whole mess into a ball and ran for Dory's bedroom. There he flung it into the bottom of the closet and rushed back to the front hall.

He was back on the right side of the sliding panel and had it closed just as Monica came into the hall from the bedroom. She wore only a big bath towel, but she didn't wear it for long.

As it fell to the floor, she rotated her slim hips in a passable bump and grind and said, "Okay, lover, I need what you've been keeping for me."

He closed the closet door and went to put his arms around her. She took the tremor of his hands on the small of her back for the effects of passion.

Fifteen minutes later, in the dark bedroom, she said, "It's okay, lover. I've read that some men don't react well to surprises. I guess I come on a little strong sometimes."

"I told you I was working pretty hard on a big project."

She pulled his arm around her and laid her head against his chest. "Is that perfume?" she said. She reached to turn on the lamp. He blinked in the light, and she sat up to examine his face.

"What's this?" she said, and ran a finger down his neck. She rubbed her finger and thumb together. "Feels like cold cream."

He said nothing.

"What's going on?   What are you up to?" she asked.

"It's for taking off stage make-up. I'm... I'm acting," he said.

She laughed. "You're acting?"

"Yeah. You know I always wanted to. I'm in a little theater group. We're doing a play."

"What play?"

"Just something one of us made up."

"What's it about?"

"It's kind of hard to explain. There's a monster, and some women. A lot of symbolism."

She was interested. "Cool," she said. "What part do you play?"

"Different parts. Sometimes I'm the monster. Sometimes I'm one of the victims. We kind of improvise scenes."

"Could I be in it?   That would be so fun."

"I don't know. It's a pretty close-knit group."

"Could you ask the, whoever, the director?"

"I guess."

"Excellent," she said and snuggled back down against him. "I'm too jet-lagged to sleep," she said. "Talk to me."

"About what?"

"I don't know. Anything. You and me. Work. This place. Did you buy this place?"

"I lease it from a management company, and sublet the other half. With what I get from the tenant, I can live almost rent-free."

She ran her fingers up and down his bony chest. "Mmmm. I like it that you know how to handle money," she said. "Cause I like money and that means we'll always have lots. So who is this guy?"

"What guy?"

"Next door, your tenant."

He yawned. "He's a she."

Her fingers stopped. "I don't know about that, having a woman next door. What's she like?"

"I hardly know her. We don't talk."

"Well, is she young, is she pretty?"

"She's not my type. One of those tough career women, all suit and briefcase. Works a lot, only comes home to change her clothes."

"You know what?" Monica said. She sounds like one of those high-priced call girls."

"Come off it."

"Bet she is. I'm gonna keep an eye on her."

He twitched. "Can we go to sleep?"

Monica stretched, and began trailing her fingers again. "I'm not sleepy. I want to hear about the hooker next door."

"She's not a hooker!   She's just... I don't know, she's okay, I guess."

"I thought you didn't like her."

"I hardly even know her!"

Monica deepened her voice. "I sense a mystery here," she intoned.

"Let it drop. Please."

"Michael, come on. What have you got to hide?"

He turned on his side toward her, slipped his hand between her legs. Her thighs opened and she moved her fingers down his belly.

"Aha!" she whispered. "It's alive."

She stroked him a little, said, "That'll do the job," then climbed on top of him. "Tell you what," she said. "Let's pretend I'm the fancy hooker and you're the greedy landlord. Here's your rent, mister."

She rotated her hips. He made the sound at the top of his throat again, but she took it for evidence of pleasure.

#

Mack lived in Maple Ridge, a bedroom community way out in the Fraser Valley that sat on what had once been some of the best farmland in the world. It meant a fifty-five minute drive to work every morning, even when her shift assignment let her travel outside of rush hour, but at least she could afford the mortgage on a townhouse.

Most mornings, she swung off the freeway at the Willingdon exit and zig-zagged north a few blocks to pick up Harry, then took the Lougheed Highway and First Avenue into town. Today, as she inched along over the Port Mann Bridge that divided the suburbs of Surrey from Coquitlam, her cell phone buzzed.

"Don't pick me up this morning," Harry said.

"What's up?"

"I got to do something before work. I'll see you when I get in."

"You don't sound so good," she said.

"Didn't sleep much."

"That's probably The Mystery Turtle barking all night." It was a weak joke, but she thought he sounded pretty down.

Harry made no reply.

"You're not sleeping with Jack Daniels again?" she asked.

"Uh uh. Not sleeping with anybody. Not sleeping much at all."

"Okay," she said. "I'll see you later."

"Not too late." He hung up.

An asshole lane-changer cut in front of her. If she'd been six miles further west, over the Vancouver City line, she could have made his day memorable. As it was, she called him things his mother never thought of, and was sourly glad that he took her mind off Harry.

#

Down in the unfinished basement, Michael worked feverishly. He rubbed eyes that were already red from insufficient sleep as his felt tipped pen slashed through whole sequences of the flow-chart's boxes, and drew shaky connections between elements of the plan that had formerly been widely separated.

Eventually, he put down the pen and sighed. The elegance was gone, but the essential idea remained. It still ought to work. He switched off the clamp light, took the notebook computer from the desk and went upstairs, locking the basement door securely behind him. There would be no spare key lying around. He had installed this lock himself, and both keys were on the ring in the pocket of his robe.

Monica was sleeping with her mouth slightly open. The fingers of one hand were curled about the edge of the covers. She smelled of sweat and sex, with a lingering tinge of bubble bath.

Michael crept into the bathroom and put on jeans, a tee-shirt and his windbreaker. He hung the robe on the back of the bathroom door then crossed the bedroom floor to the hallway without waking her.

He went to the kitchen, wrote a note and left it on the coffee maker. Then he went to the hall closet, opened its sliding panel and crossed to the other side. He put down the notebook computer to ease the panel closed, and realized that he had left the keys in his robe pocket -- on the back of the bathroom door.

He went back for them, and almost made it again. But the jingle of metal seeped through the sleeping woman's consciousness. She was instantly awake.

"Where you going?"

He turned in the doorway. "Work. Got things to do."

She threw back the covers. "Did you eat?   You never eat." She levered herself up. "Let me make you some breakfast."

He was beside the bed very fast, hands on her shoulders, pressing her back down, pulling the covers up over her. "No, no. It's a breakfast meeting, don't worry. You just rest, get over the jet-lag."

He patted her on the shoulder and was gone.

In the hallway, he sprinted to the front door, opened it an inch then closed it firmly so the sound would carry to the bedroom. Then he stepped into the closet and through its open back, closing the west-side closet door and the panel quietly after himself.

He was hurrying now. A glance at his watch told him that time was short. He pulled off his jacket and yanked the tee-shirt over his head on the way to Dory's bedroom. He stripped naked and piled the clothes on the bed, then quickly began to mine drawers for Dory's things.

He put on the butt-shaping bustle and pulled panties and pantyhose over the padded form. He put on a bra, fastening the back hooks in front, then twisting it around before slipping his arms through the straps. He slipped the breast prostheses into the cups and adjusted them to hang right.

He sat at the dressing table and began to work with the cosmetics. Foundation, powder, blusher, eyeliner, mascara, lipstick, lipliner. One by one the elements of Dory's face came together, and as her face gradually appeared in the mirror, she awoke behind it.

She pulled down a lid and peered at the reddened eye disconsolately, shaking her head. She thought about sunglasses, but that was impractical. She put the finishing touches to her make-up, then combed a small amount of gel through her hair. She teased it into rivulets and chasms, the severe look she preferred, then pronounced herself as satisfied as she was likely to get.

Eyes averted, she took Michael's clothes from the bed and threw them into the closet. She vaguely registered that there was some more mess on the floor, but she avoided looking down. She took clothes from hangers and dressed quickly in the cream jacket and black skirt combo that she liked. She tied her favorite scarf around her neck, got her purse, and went to the living room. She was surprised to find her notebook computer on the floor in front of the closet. She picked it up and opened the front door.

The sight of the two policemen in the patrol car angered her, though she wasn't sure why. One of them waved as she came down the walk, and she nodded curtly in reply. Her car was parked behind the police vehicle. As she walked between them to get around to the driver's door, Harry Lukovitch got out of a beat-up, brown Datsun parked at the opposite curb. He looked as if he hadn't slept.

"Dory," he said   "I have to talk to you."

She opened the car door and got in. "Please, don't pressure me, Harry. I've got enough to deal with as it is."

She made to close the door, but he put his hip in the way.

"Where are you going?"

"To work."

"I want to know where you're going to be today."

She wouldn't look at him. "Let me go."

He bent down and lowered his voice. "Dory, for god's sake, a man may be stalking you right now!"

She stared straight ahead. "I told you, I can't deal with any of this!   I can't worry about what this guy or that guy is doing!"   She turned to him, and he saw that lost look in her face. "I've got all that I can handle, and I can't do any more!   Please, I have to go."

Harry backed away. She shut the door and started the engine, pulled out around the police car and drove to the corner. Harry watched her go. Before she made the corner, he saw her head turn toward the rear-view mirror, and he knew that she was looking at him standing there in the street.

He got into the Datsun. He thought about tailing her, dogging her around town, making sure she was okay. He knew it was a dumb idea, but he still had to fight the urge to follow her.

Mack's right, he thought. *I'm becoming obsessed.*

He started the car and headed toward the traffic flowing downtown on Oak Street.

　　#

On the west side of the duplex, Monica watched through a slit in the living room curtains as the patrol car did a u-turn and followed the little brown car.

Unable to go back to sleep, she had gotten up a few minutes after she had the front door close. She was still on eastern time, so that to her it was three hours later than what the clock radio on the bedside table said.

She had gone to the kitchen, poured herself a cup of coffee, then wandered down the hall to see if there was a morning paper on the doorstep.

She'd been about to turn the knob when she heard the door close next door. Curious, she went to the living room curtains and parted them enough to peek through. The first thing she noticed was the cop car at the curb. Then she checked out the woman who was going down the walk. Monica only saw her from the back, but that was enough to make a quick and favorable estimation of the value and style of her clothes.

Something going on here, she thought. *Maybe she is a hooker.*

She sipped her coffee and watched the worried looking man get out of the Datsun and cross the street. By then, the woman was in her car -- Monica had missed getting a look at her face -- and there was some kind of argument going on. Then, one, two, three, they all drove away.

Monica had always been curious about the lives of strangers. It didn't take much to start her speculative engines humming, and the scene she had just witnessed provided a rich mixture of fuel.

She went into the hallway and put her ear to the common wall. Silence. Then she opened the front door and found the morning tabloid. It's front page carried the headline *3-PIECE TERROR.*

She took the paper and her coffee back to the kitchen. Later on, she would examine the carport more closely. Maybe there was a spare key to the other side.

    #

The Marine Building had been the last gasp of the frantic prosperity that had swept Vancouver in the 1920s. Its twenty-five stories had been intended by its designer to represent a crag rising from the sea, an impression he augmented by having the stone of its lower facade carved into a frieze of sea flora and fauna, tinted in sea-green and gold. It was the last great monument to the art deco movement still standing in Canada, and its refurbishment in the late 1980s had restored it to its original pre-Depression glory.

Dory Novello parked her car in one of the parking spots across Burrard Street. She locked her notebook computer in the trunk, and hurried across to the ornate three-story high entrance, and through its revolving doors of wood and brass. Her heels clicked on the black and white zodiac mosaic that formed the lobby floor, a space that might have been transported whole from a 1930s Bogart movie. A vintage elevator -- double-starburst design worked in brass on its outer door, decorative wood inlay inside the car -- swept her up to the twelfth floor.

Here the look was up to date, the original plaster walls and windowed doors having been replaced by particle board and solid panels of wood. But the old-style wool carpets, with seahorses worked in blue and aqua, had been restored. Dory walked swiftly to a side corridor and a door that carried a sign reading *NOVA CONSULTANTS*. She opened it with her key and went inside.

The single room behind the door was spartan: only a desk and a chair -- not a plant on a windowsill or a picture on a wall. On the desk was a computer monitor with an oversized display screen, and on the floor beside the desk was a stacked system with enough RAM and clock speed to impress even the most jaded teenage hacker. Dory entered and locked the door behind her, switched on the computer, then unlocked the top drawer of the desk.

She paused and looked into the drawer. She couldn't think why she had opened it. An odd sense of detachment came over her, as it often seemed to lately when she was in the office.

It was as if she receded, somehow, as if she stepped back from herself. She watched from a distance as her hands did things of their own accord. Now it was happening again.

Best not think about it, a voice said.

The drawer contained a few bank statements, a checkbook and a pad of deposit slips. Ignoring these, she removed the drawer entirely, then reached into the very back of the space it had occupied. Taped to the underside of the desk's top was a small manila envelope. She pulled it free, unsealed it and carefully took out a compact disc.

The disc had no commercial label. It had been bought blank, and all the data on it had been burned in later. Dory waited for the computer to finish booting up, then inserted the disc into the CD-ROM drive and tapped some keys.

The monitor displayed an unbroken expanse of impassive blue. She typed a nine-digit code and the screen responded with the word *Access:* in the top left corner. Dory typed a twelve-digit combination of upper and lower case letters and numbers. A tool bar appeared at the top of the screen and a row of four icons, each one an identical stylized flower.

Dory used the mouse to click on the first flower. A digitized color photograph quickly washed in from top to bottom: a man wearing the mask of a little girl and sunglasses. He held a long, two-edged dagger. He was doing something sexual to the other person in the picture.

Dory moved her eyes away. *Don't look*, said the voice. *Not for you*. She moved the mouse to put the cursor on to the modem icon on the bar at the top of the screen. Then she reached over to plug a telephone cord into the jack on the back of the computer, and double clicked the mouse control.

A window appeared in the monitor's display. The word *TRANSMITTING* blinked on and off in the middle of it, while a rectangular space below the word gradually filled from left to right with a bar of solid blue. When the space was filled, the word *COMPLETED* appeared below the bar and the window disappeared.

Dory clicked on the second icon. Another image filled the screen but she kept her eyes fixed on the tool bar above the picture as she activated the modem again. She repeated the process two more times before the chore was finished.

Then she systematically closed the image files, the graphics interface and the master program that contained them. She withdrew the cd from the drive and returned it to its hiding place. Then she locked the drawer and turned off the computer. She left the office, went downstairs and retrieved her notebook from the trunk of her car.

Its diary file said she had an appointment with Maria Chen. She started the car, then looked back at the Marine Building. For a moment, she experienced a vague sense of unease. Something was tugging at the edge of her mind, something not nice. She pushed the feeling away, and drove away. Her tires made a little squealing sound.

#

The Taguchi Kawamura Merchant Bank occupied two floors of Cathedral Place, a newly built tower of gray stone and glass at the corner of Hornby and West Georgia. Maria Chen's office was on the side that faced out onto the dark granite walls of the Hotel Vancouver. If she looked up, she could see one of the hotel's carved gargoyles. Its grotesque presence used to provide her with an obscure sense of comfort, as if it were a tutelary spirit keeping its chiseled eye upon her. Now it was just another piece of stone.

The bruises on her jaw had deepened their color. She had tried knotting a silk scarf in various ways, but nothing provided complete coverage, and eventually she came into work barefaced.

Katherine Tower kept telling Maria to place herself where she felt strongest and draw from that strength. Her office, where she coolly weighed and formulated recommendations for the investment of tens of millions of dollars, was that place.

At five minutes to nine, her secretary, Bonnie, put a cup of fragrant black tea on Maria's desk beside the monitor of her computer work station. Maria nodded her thanks, and continued to stare at the unuseful gargoyle.

At nine o'clock, Bonnie returned and suggested she drink the tea. "It will do you good," the woman said.

Maria sighed and shivered. She picked up the cup and sipped the cooling liquid. The warmth and familiar taste soothed her. She turned on her computer.

The monitor blinked into life, but instead of the usual display that identified the bank as the registered user of a comercial software package, the screen remained blank. After a few seconds, it displayed the words, *Good morning, Maria.*

"What's this?" Bonnie said. Maria stared at the letters; a coldness crept up her back. She said nothing.

The cursor prompt kept flashing just beneath the greeting. "I guess you're supposed to answer it," the secretary said.

Maria transferred the teacup to her left hand. The fingers of her other hand moved reluctantly over the keyboard. On her screen, the word *Hello* followed the prompt. She touched the enter key.

A new line of type appeared under her response: *How are you?*

Maria typed <u>ok</u> and hit enter.

Very slowly, with a two-second delay between each word, the screen displayed *Well, take a look at this.*

It was a digitalized picture taken from a cheap pornographic video. It showed a naked woman on her hands and knees, her wrists bound in front of her. She was being penetrated from behind by a kneeling man.

Another image had been roughly superimposed on the woman's face. Maria recognized it. It was the same photograph that had accompanied the announcement of her promotion to senior financial analyst at Taguchi Kawamura the year before. She had been smiling confidently into the camera.

The man's face was also obscured -- by the mask of a

grinning, cartoon-featured little girl. Where his hand rested on the small of the naked woman's back, a graphic of a long bladed knife had been interpolated.

The image washed in from top to bottom, very rapidly. When it filled the screen, the figures began to move, the man thrusting himself energetically into the woman. There was a soundtrack. A woman's voice said, *Oh, oh, oh,* repeatedly; a synthesized male voice said, *Let's get together again soon*. It, too, began to repeat.

Maria stared at the screen. The teacup dropped from her hand. Her whole body began to tremble. She swiveled sideways in her chair, half-rising as her stomach convulsed and retched up the tea and her breakfast.

Her secretary grabbed the wastebasket and put it into position as the young woman sank to her knees beside the desk, her now empty stomach gripped by dry heaves. Between spasms, she moaned, but not loud enough to drown out the continuing soundtrack from the picture on her screen.

"Goddamn him!" whispered Bonnie. She held Maria's forehead with one hand while the other dialled 911. "Goddamn him to hell!"

Chapter 7

Mack Sinclair watched the masked man silently humping the bound woman over and over again. The digitalized video sequence had been looped so that it repeated endlessly. "This is a whole new order of weirdness," she said.

Maria's secretary had already turned down the volume on the work station's external speaker to a background murmur. Now Harry reached past Mack and switched off the monitor. "I want this asshole," he said.

A uniformed cop knocked on the door of Maria's office. "Those people you wanted are all in a conference room down the hall." He looked at his notebook. "Except for Gonsalvez. She's still in hospital. But we sent a man over to watch her."

"And they all got a message like this?" Harry indicated the dead monitor.

The cop nodded. He'd already seen it. "Soon as they logged in on their computers this morning."

"Shit," Harry said.

"Oh," said the uniform, "and that Mountie from commercial crime is here."

"Get him."

Ted Fisher came through the door. He was tall and thin, with the kind of stoop that RCMP sergeants usually drill out of lanky new recruits in their first week at the paramilitary training barracks in Regina. He wore faded corduroy slacks, a tweedy sports jacket and a generic striped tie, and carried a much scuffed leather briefcase. He would have blended inextricably into the crowd at any computer trade show.

He had been the Vancouver RCMP detachment's data security expert for four years, moving up to corporal's rank and the number two spot in the federal police force's commercial crime detail for all of British Columbia. Harry and Mack hadn't met him, but Fisher's reputation for offbeat insights into the increasingly nebulous world of computer crime had got around.

His social skills were perfunctory. He said his name, shook hands, looked around the office and said, "What have we got?"

Harry turned the monitor on and the sound up.

Fisher went to Maria's chair, sat down and started tapping keys. "Interesting," he said. He tapped more keys, saw that nothing changed. "Very interesting."

Harry called in the uniformed cop. "Ask the victims to come in."

The cop left and returned in less than a minute, bringing Dory, Katherine, Ellen and Maria. Maria's face was the color of unpasteurized cheese; she leaned on her secretary, and when she saw the image on the monitor, she looked sharply away.

"Kill the picture," Harry said.

"Huh?"   Fisher looked around. "Oh, sure," he said, and turned off the monitor.

"Ladies, this is Corporal Fisher of the RCMP. He's a computer crime specialist. He's going to see what he can do."

Fisher waved without looking up. He was extracting a notebook computer from his briefcase and linking it by cable to the work station.

Dory stepped past the others and put her hand over the notebook's keyboard as Fisher switched it on. "Hold it!" she said. "This station is part of a multi-million dollar management information system. You shouldn't be playing around with it."

Fisher looked up at her. "Who are you?"

"Dorcas Novello. I'm a data security consultant, and this bank is one of my clients."

The computer Mountie searched his internal data banks. "Novello. Didn't you do a paper on hardening up twelve-digit access codes?"

The question caught Dory off guard. "What?"   She blinked, then answered. "Yes, I did."

She turned to Harry. "Look, before we go monkeying around, I think we'd better get Wally Yaminski up here. He designed this system."

Harry looked at Fisher. The corporal shrugged. Harry told the uniform, "Find him."

Katherine Tower said, "I don't need to see this. I had the same kind of crap on my system this morning. If you need us, we'll be back in the conference room."

"I'll go with you. We need your statements," said Mack. She led them out.

Fisher asked Dory to stay. "I'd like your views," he said.

She looked irritated. "I have other things to do," she said.

"It's your client's system that's been violated," Fisher said.

Her flinch was visible to all of them. Fisher leaned back in the chair and considered at her. "You write a good paper," he said.

Dory looked away. "Thank you."

The Mountie scrutinized her face. "Funny, I thought you'd be older," he said.

Dory said nothing. At that moment, the uniformed cop returned with a large man in his late fifties, who wore a wrinkled suit, a tangled salt-and-pepper beard and an expression of perpetual wonder. He introduced himself as Wally Yaminski, the bank's chief data officer.

"Found him hanging around the fire stairs," the cop said.

Harry started to speak, but Yaminski went straight for the computer, leaning over Fisher's shoulder to switch on the monitor. He looked at the still-running pornographic display. "Interesting," he said.

"Isn't it?" said Fisher.

"May I?" asked Yaminski. He reached over the policeman's shoulder and rattled his fingers over the notebook's keyboard. The notebook replied with a list of programs and a query. Yaminski gave it another flutter of his fingers.

Man and machine conversed this way for several seconds. Then Yaminski said, "There it is."

The two detectives and Dory craned to see what was on the notebook's liquid crystal screen.

"There is what?" asked Harry. All he saw was a list of alphanumeric symbols, with one of them highlighted in flashing reverse face.

"It's masquerading as a batch file, but it's way too big," said the data chief.

"What's it do?   What's it doing there?" Harry wanted to know.

Yaminski blinked at him. "Can't say."

"What do you mean, 'can't say?'"

Yaminski handed it off to Fisher. "He means," the computer cop said, "we found the intruder program, but we don't know what it's a program for."

Fisher looked to Yaminski. "Want to try cracking it?"

Yaminski looked to Dory. She shook her head. "I'd leave it alone," she said.

The data chief weighed it up. "Wouldn't hurt just to give it a poke, see what happens."   He rippled across the notebook's keys again, but when he saw what came up on the screen he said, "Ouch! Now we back right off!   Don't touch anything!"

"What is happening?" Harry wanted to know. The techno-verbiage on the notebook meant nothing to him, except for the words *WARNING, POTENTIAL IRREVOCABLE DATA LOSS* that were now flashing rhythmically on the Mountie's machine.

"Worm," said Yaminski.

"Worm?"   Harry looked to Fisher.

The computer cop leaned back in his chair and regarded the flashing screen. "Worm, virus, logic bomb, dataphage, whatever. It's a self-feeding program that eats its way through a whole system, erasing and scrambling data at an exponential rate. The intruder program says it's got a worm in it, and if we poke it again, it'll sic it on us."

"Can it do that?"   Harry said.

"Only one way to find out," Fisher said.   "Want to try it?" he asked Yaminski.

The beard moved emphatically from side to side.

"Then that's all she wrote."   The Mountie disconnected the cable linking his notebook from the work station.

"So what do we do?" Harry said.

Fisher put his mouth through a brief contortion. "Right now, nothing," he said. "The intruder program is keyed only to this terminal -- which is pretty fancy work. And it doesn't seem to be linked to anything else in the company's data system."   He turned to Yaminski. "It's not showing up in your TA's, right?"

"No, they're clear."

"What are TA's?" Harry asked.

"Treasury Accounts," Fisher answered. "Direct access to banks. Where they keep the big bucks."   He closed his notebook and put it back in his briefcase. "I'll go round to the other companies, check their systems, but I'm betting we find the same set-up."

He picked up his briefcase and made for the door. Harry put a hand out to stop him.

"Wait a minute! Aren't we going to do something?"

"Like what?"

"I don't know," Harry said. "How about tracing this thing back to where it came from?"

Fisher and Yaminski looked at Harry from a great height.

"You're assuming it came from outside. Could be an inside job," said Fisher. To Yaminski, he said, "No offense."

"None taken."

"But the same program's in the computers of the other companies," Harry said.

"That makes it *probably* an outside job. A remote terminal connected through phone lines." To Yaminski, he said, "How hard is your access barrier?"

Yaminski looked at Dory. She was gazing out the window at the gargoyle across the street. "State of the art," he said.

"Not any more," said Fisher. "Ms. Novello, are you on line with all your clients' systems?"

She didn't turn around. "I have to be," she said.

"Open link or dedicated?"

"Dedicated."

"What does that mean?" He was starting to think he needed language lessons.

"Her system's linked to theirs by closed-circuit. She doesn't call them up on an open phone line," Fisher explained. "Does anyone else have access to your computer?"

"Of course not."

Fisher said nothing, just looked at the wall for a long moment.

"So?" Harry asked.

The Mountie did the thing with his mouth again. "So, who knows? Closed circuits can be tapped. We'll check Ms. Novello's office lines, maybe spot something. Good day."

He was halfway out the door when Harry got a grip on his sleeve. "Wait a minute," the detective said. "I need more than this."

Fisher frowned as he removed Harry's hand from his sleeve. "Right now, Sergeant, there isn't any more. Inside, outside, we don't know. What the program does, we don't know. Tell you one thing, it takes up one hell of a lot more room than you need to print an image on a screen. Tell you another thing, it's a brilliant, wacko piece of work. Brilliant because the perpetrator hacks into five heavy-weight data systems, past every security barrier. Wacko, because he then totally ignores the treasury and data files. Seems like a hell of a lot of trouble to go through just to scare some women."

"So what do we do?" Harry said.

Yaminski coughed. "If I can say something?   The size of the program means it has to do more than generate some dirty pictures. Right now it's just sitting there. So maybe it's got a timer that tells it when to start running, or maybe your perpetrator has to log on and start it up himself. Either way, all we can do is wait."

Harry slammed his hand on Maria's desk. Dory jumped, and the two computer men were startled. "We don't just fucking wait!" the detective shouted. "I'm tired of being two steps behind!   I want to move!"

Fisher put up a placating hand. "We'll move," he said. He mulled it over for a moment, then said, "One of the victims is in hospital, right?"

"Right."

"Well, then, best guess says he's not going to do anything till they're all back at work, where he can torture them."

Harry thought about it. "You're right," he said. "It's Friday. Earliest they would all be at work would be Monday morning."

"That's good," said the computer cop. "Gives me the weekend to check out the other companies' systems, link them all to a central command post. Monday morning, he comes out to play, we're waiting for him."

It was enough for Harry. "All right. In the meantime, we put the women into a hotel and keep them secure."   He slapped his palms together. "Let's do it. "Call me when you've checked the other companies."

"Yeah," said Fisher.

Harry asked Yaminski to get a key to Maria's office and lock it up. Then he went down the hall to the conference room.

"Why should I hide like a rat in a hole, while this bastard's playing his chickenshit games?" was Katherine Tower's response, when Harry broached the plan.

They were sitting around the Taguchi Kawamura conference table. It was of rich dark wood that matched the paneling on the walls and the plush upholstered chairs. The other furnishings were a pair of heavy mahogany cabinets and a carved Victorian sideboard that stood on iron eagle's claws. Pictures of strangely elongated horses galloped across the walls. Harry had never seen the inside of a stuffy Englishman's club, but this was pretty much how he imagined it would be.

"I don't see any necessity..." Dory began, but Katherine interrupted. Even as she'd voiced her own anger, she had seen the cringe deepening in the set of Maria's shoulders. "On the other hand," she said, "maybe it's not a bad idea at that. We could order up room service, have some laughs. How about it, Maria?"

Maria's answer was almost too faint to hear, but the nod was more relief than assent.

Katherine swung around to Ellen. "Want to do some girl stuff this weekend?"

"Yeah, what the hell."

"That just leaves you, Dory," Katherine said.

Dory shook her head. "I have plans."

"Ms. Novello, please," said Harry. "I think there is real danger here."

"No, I've made plans to go away. I don't want to change them now."   She gathered her purse and notebook and pushed back her chair.

Harry followed her out to the elevators. "Dory, I'm really worried. Let me drive you home."

She pushed the call button. "I have my own car," she said.

"I'll follow you home, make sure it's okay."

She turned on him then, but he saw unhappiness behind the irritation. "Will you just leave me alone?   I can't handle this!"

Harry put a hand on her arm. "You can't handle this, but you think you can handle a man who's raped four women and already tried to get you?"

"I'm not letting my life be turned upside down by this!" she said. "I can't stand being hemmed in by other people's concerns!"

"And I can't stand the thought of anything happening to you!" He tightened his grip on her arm. "For god's sake, Dory, be reasonable!"

Her nostrils flared. "Let go of me!"

"Please."

She shook off his hand with a speed and strength that

surprised him.

"You're strong," he said.

"Yes, I am!" she said. "And I don't want to be crowded or controlled!   I've spent my whole life buried under other people's lives. Well, now I'm out, and I want to stay out!"

Harry sighed. "I can understand that, I think. I know what it's like to be buried alive."

She turned away, jabbed at the call button again. He touched her elbow. "I can't help doing this, Dory."

Now it was her turn to say, "Please."

He saw a glistening light reflected from beneath her closed eyelids. "Okay," he said. "Let's not talk about it yet. Maybe you can't handle a man-woman thing right now. Hell, maybe I can't either. Let's just see where it goes."

"Please," she said again. "I don't know what to tell you."

The elevator arrived. "Just tell me you'll be careful over the weekend. Stay in public places and don't be alone."

She got on the elevator. "I like that you care about me," she said. "I'm just not used to it."

The door closed. Harry was left with the picture imprinted on his brain of the expression on her face. It was the strangest look, he thought.

\#

After the police left, Monica took a shower and got dressed. She ate breakfast in the kitchen while she read the paper, then took inventory of the house. It was a plain, utilitarian two-bedroom place, and the east side looked to be no different. A thorough inspection of the carport turned up no key to the other unit.

She made fresh coffee and installed herself on the living room couch with a magazine she had picked up at Pearson Airport in Toronto. But she was too restless to follow its idle tittle-tattle about entertainment and sports celebrities.

She switched on the television and flicked through the cable channels. The soap operas didn't interest her: she'd worked steadily since high school, and had never developed the daytime habit. She didn't care for the game shows, either, with the audience going *ooh* and *aah* over things she could never afford.

She watched a syndicated talk show for a while, but the stuff they talked about was creepy. The people who sat in the guest chairs, smirking as their tawdry private lives were dissected for entertainment, were just the kind of low-lifes she liked to avoid. Eventually, she put the tv on the rock video channel, turned the volume halfway down, and thought about what she was doing here and now.

Coming out here was a desperation ploy; she had no problem admitting that to herself. She could not afford to let this relationship slip from her grasp -- there might never be another prospect this good. Not for the first time, she felt a distant twinge of guilt: was she that much different from the trash she'd just seen flouncing around on tv, the manipulative tramps and strutting studs who dumped and lied and cheated?

She put that thought aside. *You're a practical girl*, her mother had always said. *You won't make the same mistake I did.* Mama's mistake had been to marry her high school sweetheart, a soft, sweet-natured schmuck who put everything they had into a drywalling business, and lost it all because he thought everybody he dealt with was as honest as he was. When reality had finished squeezing the pulp out of him, he'd saddled up a bottle of rye whisky and ridden it straight to the morgue -- leaving Monica and Mama to the bankruptcy receivers. Mama didn't live much longer.

At seventeen, Monica quit high school for the first dead-end job that would buy groceries. Ten years later, she was still walking into GreenGro Organic Foods in Markham, Ontario, every morning to spend another eight hours packing alfalfa sprouts. Eight hours on aching feet, taking handfuls of crisp, green and white stalks and slapping them into five-ounce baskets -- four ounces for those flavored with garlic or spice -- until she had put twenty-four baskets in a cardboard flat, and she could then reach for another flat and start again.

Occasionally, she was allowed to assist Cathy, the owner, in the growing room, scattering seed onto trays of organically certified soil, then stacking the trays in vertical racks made of black plastic plumbing pipe. There had once or twice been talk of training her for the office, but Cathy's thick-legged daughter had waged effective war against that notion from the beginning.

Packing sprouts had eaten the rest of her teens and half of her twenties. She knew what she needed: a man she could work with, a man with some potential, a man who just lacked the right woman to bring him along.

She started looking at nineteen. At twenty-four, a veteran explorer, she accepted that the pickings were thinner than she'd first hoped. Oh, there were plenty of guys: guys she met in bars, guys who drove the trucks that picked up the sprouts, guys who came in to fix a pipe or rewire the lights in the grow room.

Some of them were nice, some were sexy, some were fun. But those guys were going no further than the next paycheck, the next hockey game. She wanted a man who could climb above the go-nowhere, be-nothing existence. All he need have was the brains or the talent; she'd provide the ambition. And when he climbed out of the clouds into the clear mountain air, she'd be riding high.

She found him at twenty-six. On a rainy November night in Markham, she'd been driving home when her damned old Rabbit had died. She'd just turned a corner onto a main arterial, and everything stopped: engine, lights, heater, even the wipers.

With blinding rain streaming down the windshield, she'd nudged the car over to the curb, shifted to neutral and prayed that it would restart. But when she turned the key, she got nothing but a tiny click somewhere in the steering column.

She tried again, then pulled the hood release and got out. The rain smacked against her head, nailing her hair to her scalp in seconds. She peered into the engine compartment as if that would somehow help. She had no idea what was wrong, and if she had known, she had even less idea what would fix it.

The rain splattered on the upraised hood. She looked at the unfathomable mass of metal and rubber that was crammed into the small space and despaired. She remembered her dad, when she was a little girl, showing her what was under the hood of his old Nova. *This is the carburetor. This is the distributor cap.* If any of that was under the Rabbit's hood, she couldn't identify it.

Then she looked up and saw the man standing under the overhang of the bus shelter, just standing there holding his bus transfer. She said, "Can you help me, please?" and he came over.

If she'd seen him on the other side of a bar, she'd have written him off right away. He was a lightweight, fine-boned and delicate featured, with a coltish hesitancy in the way he moved; he reminded her of the actor who played the radio psychiatrist's brother on tv. Not a guy to climb on.

Nor the kind of guy who would know his way around an engine compartment. But he looked at the Rabbit's innards for less than ten seconds and said, "It's your coil -- plug's popped out." Then he reached in, did something, and the lights and wipers came back on. "Should be fine now," he said, and closed the hood.

He went back to the bus shelter. A little chime sounded in the back of Monica's head. "Would you like a ride?" she said.

"No thanks, that's all right," he said. He sounded shy.

"Please. You got all wet doing that for me."

So he said yes, and she gave him a ride, and once she had him in the car she said, "Tell you what, why don't I make dinner for us?"

"You don't have to," he said.

"I want to," she said. "I get tired of eating alone."

She drove to her basement apartment, took him inside and said, "You should get out of those wet clothes. I've got a robe you can wear while they're drying."   She gave him the robe and left him in the postage-stamp-sized living room while she went to the even tinier bedroom to get out of her own wet things.

Then, before she had even undone a button, she did the stupidest thing. She marched back out of the bedroom, her wet blouse still plastered to her body. He was standing there, jacket off, one leg out of his pants and the other leg raised, a look of surprise on his bland face.

She kneeled down in front of him, totally matter of fact, pulled the pants away, tugged down his boxer shorts, opened her lips and took his penis into her mouth.

He gasped but didn't say a word. He was hard in seconds. She put her hand on the shaft, stroked it up and down while her lips closed tightly. She swirled her tongue's broad muscle around the ridge at the base of the head, and flicked its pointed tip against the sweet spot just below. Her other hand slid up his inner thigh and her nails brushed his balls.

And all the time she was thinking, *Stupid, stupid, stupid -- you don't even know his name*. Then she thought, *You're totally blowing it*, which almost made her giggle, except right then she felt his cock flex and spasm, and the warm, salty fluid shot onto the back of her tongue.

She swallowed and drained him -- it seemed to go on a long

time -- while his legs trembled and his knees bent. Then she let him go and wiped her mouth with her fingers.

She looked up at him, still silently berating herself. His face wore an expression she couldn't read. His lips were open, his eyelids half closed. *Shock*, she thought.

She stood up. "I don't know why I did that," she said, truthfully. "I never did anything like that before." Which was almost true -- she preferred it when men pleased her.

He didn't reply, just put his arms around her and pulled her to him. *God, he's strong*, she thought, finding flat, hard muscle on the thin frame.

She gently pressed her palms against his shoulders until he released her. "I've got to get some dry clothes on," she said. "You too, or we'll get pneumonia."

He still didn't say anything. She went into the bedroom and changed hurriedly, shaking her head at the total idiot she saw in the mirror on the back of the door. She would not be surprised to come back to the living room and find him long gone, running like hell from the crazy slut in the basement.

But when she opened the door, there he was, in her robe, sitting on her couch, his hands folded in his lap like a well trained choirboy. "You must think I'm awful," she said.

His voice choked a little. "I think you're wonderful."

She made them spaghetti. She found out his name was Michael and pulled a life story out of him. He was a couple of years younger than she was, an only child estranged from his parents -- he didn't want to talk about them. He'd always wanted to be an actor, but his father had put a stop to that.

He had a flair for computers, had recently graduated from Ryerson and was now a systems analyst with a well established consulting firm -- Monica wasn't exactly sure what that was but she bet it beat packing sprouts. He was specializing in data security, which he explained to her so she felt she almost understood it. He was just starting out, he said, but he made good money, and his prospects were wide open.

She listened all through dinner, prompting him when he dried up. Then she made them coffees with Dream Whip and a healthy slug of Kahlua. They sat on the couch and he told her that he spent a lot of his time working out on Nautilus equipment. He didn't have a girlfriend. She believed him. He also told her that no girl had ever done *that* for him before, and from the way he blushed, she believed that too.

She laughed at his jokes, tossed her hair, touched his arm and his knee, and looked up at him from under lowered brows. She felt that at last here was something to work with. At eleven o'clock, she phoned Cathy at home to tell her she'd sprained an ankle and would have to rest it for a day. Then she led him to bed and didn't let him loose until she was completely sure.

She was still pretty sure now, as long as she could get close to him, keep him motivated. It wasn't cold blooded manipulation -- not to her -- just that he needed to be kept on track. His mind had a tendency to wander off into daydreams: he'd see himself making millions from some brilliant insight, buying a remote island, becoming a famous theater impresario. He could soar away from solid earth to cloud cuckoo land -- she heard Mama's voice there -- faster than any man she'd ever known.

But when she was there to keep him focused, he was okay. Maybe he spent a little too much time with his damned computer, like a solitary kid with his toybox, but that was where the money came from. Not that she minded a little neglect, once she realized that his almost total lack of sexual experience was coupled with a sometimes insatiable appetite. She was a healthy girl, but he could wear her out.

They had lived in separate apartments in Markham. She only went to his place a couple of times; he didn't like people in his rooms, touching his stuff. He also didn't like to go out, so mostly they stayed in at her place, while he talked about all his dreams and plans, inbetween wanting to get her into bed or tongue-twistingly asking her if she would suck him.

It had gotten pretty stable, Monica thought. She'd even raised the subject of marriage a couple of times, just tangentially, and he hadn't run for the door. So she'd started tapering off the sex -- *got a headache, got my period* -- because it was time to get him thinking how awful it would be if he didn't have Monica's hands, Monica's vagina, Monica's mouth, whenever he craved them, time to get him aching, get him hungry again.

It worked fine for a couple of weeks. Then suddenly, around the end of January, he told her he was moving to the west coast. His boss was sending him on some big new assignment, to run his own show, make some real money.

"You want me to come with you?" she'd asked.

"No," he said.

She didn't like the way he wouldn't look straight at her. "I could get some time off," she said. "Could be like a vacation. Like a honeymoon."

"Uh uh," he said. "It'll be all work, all the time. I'll be going gangbusters, setting up the branch office for Ms. Novello, getting clients. There'll be a lot of late nights, weekends."

"Well, how long will you be gone?"

"Three months," he said. "Maybe four."

She moved in closer, ran her palm up his inner thigh. "That's a long time," she said. She kneeled down and unzipped him. "What if you forget all about me?"

He was always quick when she used her mouth. But this time she stopped before he was finished and looked up at him. "I think I should come with you," she said.

He groaned. "I'll send for you as soon as things quiet down," he said. "May at the latest."

"Hmm," she said. "Okay. But you got to write me and call a lot."   She ran the tip of tongue up his penis from bottom to top. "I don't want you to forget me."

"I won't," he gasped. "I promise."

"Good."   She took him back in and paid him off.

And it had worked, at least for a while. Through February and into March the regular phone calls had come, and the occasional postcard of the big steel crab outside the Planetarium or the Lions Gate Bridge. Then, as March moved toward April, the calls became fewer, the conversations not so bright and cheerful.

Over a few weeks, he seemed to fade. She felt as if nobody was really there on the other end of the line, as if he'd been replaced by one of those pod people from the old movie. Even when she talked dirty to him, described things she wanted him to think she was doing to herself while they were electronically linked, she could sense something missing in his response.

So when April came and she hadn't heard from him in a week, no replies to the messages she left, she spent a big portion of her meager savings on a seat-sale standby ticket to Vancouver, and came out to rescue the plan. She'd told Cathy's daughter where to stick the sprouts, then put all her stuff in storage. There'd be no going back.

Now, here she was lying on a couch in his duplex, listening to the rock music and taking stock. It didn't look too bad. She'd had her antennae out for guilt -- lacking any illusions, she'd never had trouble sussing out infidelity in a man -- and she hadn't picked up any telltale signs. There was no trace of a woman about the place; that was the first thing she'd looked for when she went through the house.

It was true that last night he hadn't been as randy as before, but that could be from a combination of overwork and sudden surprise. He'd responded in the end, although he'd finished with a grim intensity that was different from his usual gasping helplessness.

Now that she was here, her confidence was rising again. *Just so long as nothing's going on with that bitch next door*, she thought. She went into the hallway and put her ear to the wall. There was only silence. She wished she knew what kind of woman was living so close to her man.

He'd said he'd be back after noon. She decided she'd better clean up. She knew he didn't like people messing with his things. She went into the kitchen and washed her breakfast dishes and the coffee cup, putting them away in the spotless cupboards. Then she pulled the sheets off the bed, and ran them through the piggyback washer and dryer in the kitchen.

While they were drying, she unpacked her two bags and her make-up case, and put her things away in the bedroom closet and under the bathroom sink. She aimed to make her presence as unobtrusive as she could.

The empty bags took up a lot of room in the bottom of the bedroom closet, so she hauled them down the hall to the front door. She opened the louvered doors wide, and tossed the cases into the closet. They hit the back wall with an odd sound.

"Oh shit," she said. She was afraid she'd done some damage. He wouldn't like that; it had been bad enough the time she'd rearranged the order of his shaving gear on the bathroom counter back in Markham.

She took a worried look at the back wall of the closet, and saw the crack where the panel had not quite slid all the way closed.

She put her fingertips to the edge of the board and pressed. It slid back a few inches, and she peered into the closet next door.

She opened it a little wider, put her head through, and listened. There was only the hum of a refrigerator. She waited almost a whole minute, ears straining for the faintest sound. Then Monica opened the panel all the way and stepped through to the other side.

Chapter 8

The hallway was empty. Monica crossed it to the living room, moving very fast, then went through to the kitchen, looked out the back door. She couldn't stop her head and eyes from constant motion. She was terrified and simultaneously filled with a glee she hadn't known since childhood.

Her mind was working at triple speed. *This is great. This is scary. Oh god I've got to pee right now.* The kitchen led into the hallway. There was a bathroom in the between the two bedrooms, the layout of the rooms a mirror image of the other side. She pulled down her pants and squatted on the toilet, and the relief was delightful.

There were no towels here. The dust on the counter top argued that no one had used this room in months. She dried her hands on toilet paper and flushed it away. Then she looked into the triple-paned mirror and told herself it was time to get a grip.

She went back into the kitchen, investigating now, probing. The cupboards and drawers were empty, with nothing but a box of solidified baking soda in the refrigerator. Dust was everywhere.

It was the same in the living room. She saw where a finger had recently traced a line through the gray deposit on the top of an end table. The line was now filled in by a lighter film of dust. She noticed that the answering machine was on.

She went out into the hall, looked into the closet where she had come across from the other side. A blue wool coat hung from the bar, next to a black raincoat and a woolly Cowichan sweater. On the floor was one pair of thin rubber galoshes, the kind a woman would pull on over her shoes on a slushy day. She wondered if Vancouver had slushy days.

The basement door was unlocked. She opened it, flicked on the light and went halfway down the stairs, saw right away that the unfinished space below was empty.

She went next to the master bedroom, and here she found something to feed her curiosity. There was a dressing table with a padded stool and a rim-lighted adjustable mirror on a stand. The top of the table was half buried in cosmetics containers. She read the labels on some of the bottles and jars -- there were several different brands for each type -- opened a few and sniffed the contents.

She noticed the pictures taped to the wall above the mirror. They were a sequence of head shots of a blonde woman that had been clipped from a magazine: it was a make-up makeover feature that gave step-by-step instructions on how to build up from foundation to final gloss.

Monica opened a couple of the dressing table's drawers; they were as empty as the kitchen cupboards. She looked at the bed, saw that it had a quilted coverlet snugged tight around the mattress. When she worked one corner loose, she found that there was no bedding beneath.

She is a hooker, she thought. *This place is only for turning tricks. Or maybe just for phone messages and a place to put on make-up.* That didn't make sense, but maybe there were men who had a thing about heavy make-up.

Her eye fell on the closet door. *Or costumes*, she thought. Her hand touched the closet doorknob. What would she find inside: black lace? leather and whips? a schoolgirl uniform? She turned the knob.

It was then that she heard the *snick* of a key unlocking the front door.

Monica froze. A cold shiver went down her belly. Suddenly she needed to pee again, a really bad need. She heard the front door open and close. Her knees shook. She felt at once the worst embarrassment of her life, and a stark fear.

She looked at the window. It had some complicated locking mechanism of notched levers. She thought about just running full tilt out into the hall, through the kitchen and out the back door, maybe screaming all the way. But then she'd have to turn around and try to get back into the locked unit next door.

She pushed down on the head of a hysterical giggle that wanted out of her throat. She bit her lower lip. But now she'd waited too long. She heard the swish of clothing. The woman was coming right this way, right now.

Monica's hand was still on the closet doorknob. She turned it, stepped inside and pulled it silently closed after her. A second later, she heard the rustle of clothing again. She held her breath.

The closet floor was uneven. She was crouched to fit under the bar, standing on a little heap of clothes and shoes. Her legs had already begun to ache, and the giggle was trying to reassert itself. She shuffled her feet around, trying for a more comfortable stance. She felt them sink into cloth, that had something hard underneath it.

Still, very still, she told herself, while she silently begged the woman, *Get in the bathroom, you bitch, you whore; take a shower, take a pee, oh god I've got to pee again.*

She heard water running in the ensuite bathroom and opened the door a crack, but then the water stopped. It was just the hooker coming back with a damp face cloth.

Monica saw her from the back, still in the morning's cream jacket, before she eased the crack in the door closed. She stood there trembling, praying, one hand pressed to her groin while her bladder rejected any concept of being empty.

She heard the whisper of moving fabric and the rasp of a zipper. *Getting undressed*, she thought, and willed the bitch to go straight to the shower. Then came the scrape of the stool's feet on carpet, followed by the sound of a jar lid being unscrewed.

Now she heard only the little noises of the make-up removal, punctuated now and then by deep sighs and full-bodied yawns. Through it all, Monica chanted to herself, *Shower, shower, shower, shower.*

She heard the scrape of the stool again. *Okay, Monica, hang in there*, she thought. *We hear that bathroom door close and we're gone. But if she opens this closet I don't know if I'm going to laugh or cry.*

As it turned out, she screamed.

Michael yanked open the door. He was still wearing the bra and pantyhose, but the features under the brushed-back hair were unmistakable. The lower half of his bland face fell to almost inhuman lengths, and he was forced back by the howl that blasted unbidden from Monica's mouth.

When the last reverberation of her scream faded, they stood and stared at each other, the moment suspended forever. She recovered first, and her impulse was to shove him bodily out of her way so she could run for the passage back to the other side of the duplex.

He staggered, and the force of her push shook the paralysis out of him. She went to brush by, but one foot was tangled in the wad of clothes at the bottom of the closet. She tripped and sprawled headlong on the bedroom floor.

"Oh shit!" she said, flailing her legs to clear her feet from whatever bound them, her eyes on the door and getting the hell out of here.

"Monica!" He recovered and knelt, reaching for her, but she at last got her feet free of the cloth wrapped around her ankle. She kicked at him hard, a self-defense move she'd seen on tv.

He said, *woof!* and went backwards. Monica came up on her fingers and toes like a sprinter in the starting blocks, and she was out of the room, in the hall, through the closet and next door, while he was still sitting on the bedroom floor holding a hand to the sharp pain in his ribs.

He could hear, from next door, the clatter she made as she dragged her suitcases from the hall closet, and stomped down to the bedroom. Then he heard the sounds of hasty packing, all punctuated by a steady stream of profanity.

Then the initial shock faded, and he began to assess his situation. His face registered a shifting pageant of emotion: first apprehension, then calculation. For the next moment, a peculiar blankness overcame his features, then the inertia was in turn replaced by a concentrated expression of feral violence.

But he fought down the monstrous aspect that had attempted to seize control. If the problem was only on this side of the double house, he believed he could resolve it. He stood up, wincing at the stabbing hurt in his side, and scooped up the suit and mask.

The dagger fell out of its pocket, and he picked it up. The feel of its cold, hard weight in his hand triggered another eruption of the contained force within him. But again he shoved it deep, and complemented the mental effort by cramming the attacker's paraphernalia under the bed.

He quickly stripped off Dory's undergarments and pulled on the jeans from the bottom of the closet. Then he went after Monica.

When he came through the closet to the other side, he could hear her swearing and bumping around behind the closed bedroom door. His first move was to check the door to the basement. It was still locked, and the key was in his jeans pocket. He doubted she'd gone down there.

He drew a long breath to compose himself. Then he opened the bedroom door. Her suitcase was on the bed, a jumble of clothes spilling out of it. Monica came out of the ensuite bathroom with an armload of cosmetics, cleansers and a big bottle of bubble bath liquid.

"You stay the fuck away from me!" she said,

"Monica! There's an explanation!" He moved toward her.

She threw the bottle of bubble bath at him. It hit his leg and left a small damp mark on the cloth. He stepped back and stood in the doorway.

"Please listen," he said.

She cocked her arm, ready with another missile.

"Out of the way!" she warned.

"If you want to leave, I won't stop you."

"You bet you won't! Fucking pervert!"

"Will you let me explain?"

"Sure. Just get out of the way." She zipped up her bags, slung one from her shoulder by its strap and picked up the other two by their handles.

He backed away as she came to the bedroom door. "There is a perfectly good explanation for this."

"Uh huh," she turned into the hall and made for the front door.

He followed her. "Monica, I can't let you go like this," he said.

"Wanna bet, asshole?" She put down the cases, got her coat from the closet and put it on. She looked through the open back into the other side, and for a moment the thin shell of calm over her rage and disappointment broke. "Jesus Christ!" she spat. "The time I wasted!"

"Let me explain," he said.

She picked up the bags. "I already got an explanation," she said. "You're some kind of transvestite drag queen hooker!"

"I'm what?"

She rounded on him. "Don't give me your fucking innocence routine! Christ, I should've seen though that one a long time ago." She mimicked his voice, "'Nobody ever sucked my cock before, Monica.' Yeah, right, but how many did you suck, sweetie? Or do you like to take it up your ass? Christ!"

She fumbled for the door, the bags in the way. He stared at her, open mouthed.

She dropped the make-up case to reach for the door handle, then a new look of horror washed the color from her face. "Oh my god!" she whispered. "Oh my god, I never used anything but my diaphragm and jelly with you!"   She threw the other suitcase at his feet, making him jump back, and her voice went straight up to a shriek. "You son-of-a-bitching, twisted bastard!   Did you give me AIDS?   Did you?"   She put her hands to her stomach. "Tell me, you fucker, have you had a test?"

He shook his head, held out his hand to her. "Monica," she said.

"Tell me!" she screamed. "Are you infectious?"

He was laughing now, from relief. "No," he said. "I don't have AIDS. I'm not a drag queen."

"Yeah, right!" she said. "And all that stuff next door, that's for your little theater group!   Fuck you!"   She flung open the door, stooped to pick up the suitcases.

"Monica," he said. What you saw in there, it has nothing to do with sex. It's about money."

She stepped out onto the porch.

"A lot of money," he said. "Millions."

She stopped at the top step. Then she put down the suitcases and turned around. A war was being waged across her face. "Millions?" she said.

"Ten, twelve million, easy. Maybe twenty."

Her face was still white and her eyes were narrowed like the slits in an armored car. "No AIDS?" she said.

"No AIDS. You want to come in, I'll tell you about it. You don't like it, I'll call you a cab."

She stepped through the door, left the suitcases in the hall. "I'll make some coffee," he said, and closed the door.

     #

The squad room was duller and grayer than Harry had ever noticed. He looked up at Mack. She was collating copies of Three-piece's victims' statements. Inspector Mason had asked to be copied in triplicate on every development in the case.

"Is this place always like this?" Harry said.

Mack didn't look up. "Like what?"

"I dunno."   He groped for the word. The best he could come up with was, "Crappy."

Mack nodded. "When it's not illuminated by your scintillating presence," she said.

"Scintillating," Harry repeated. "Oh," he said, after a moment, "that was sarcasm."

"Must be catching," said Mack. She patted the pages into three stacks and reached for the stapler.

Harry got up and went to the window. A pigeon on the ledge outside regarded him with indifference. He watched the latinos in the thin sunlight at the corner of Hastings and Main go through the complexities of establishing, defending and extending turf. He went back to his desk.

He sat down and stared at his phone. "Shit," he said. "I give up."

Mack looked up and blinked at him. "Just when you were winning, too," she said. But she softened the dig with a smile.

Harry picked up the phone and punched four buttons. "Get me records," he said into the mouthpiece. Three seconds later, he said, "This is Lukovitch, Serious Crimes. I want to know if CPIC has a file on a Dorcas Novello." He spelled it. "There's probably no criminal record, but check with the feds to see if they ever did a security clearance. And can you get it to me today?"

He listened to the reply, then made the kind of face people often make when they deal with bureaucracy. "Well, first thing Monday, for sure."

He hung up. "The System," he said in a tone that put the capital on the word and imbued the rest of the message with a gravity that would not have been out of place if he had been announcing the Queen's choice to replace Prince Phillip, "is 'down for quarterly file reorganization.' Where do we get these people?" he wondered.

"They fill in questionnaires on the backs of matchbooks," said Mack. She leaned back in her chair. "So you're checking up on her? An' you told me you was a gen'lmun."

But Harry had to know. Dory had appeared in his deliberately sparse and simple existence like a hidden door suddenly opening in what had looked like a blank wall. Through that door, he sensed, were mysteries and secrets that tugged at parts of him whose existence he had forgotten.

"There's something there, it's making me crazy," he said. "I have to know whatever there is to know."

"Might be better to leave a little mystery," Mack said. "Some women, they like men to come at them with all their appetites cranked up to maximum. I'm a little like that. Others, you press just a little too hard, and <u>bang!</u> they're up in the trees and they don't come down till you're gone."

"I have to know," Harry said.

#

Monica sipped the coffee and crooked her neck, trying to follow the text that scrolled slowly up the notebook on the kitchen counter. They were sitting side by side on stools.

"I still don't get it," she said. She frowned at the look of exasperation that drew his eyebrows together and down. "No, I get the part about you dressing up like your old boss. I think I even get the part about breaking into   computers. I just don't get it about the money."

He sighed. "It doesn't matter. What matters is that it will still work, even though I had to change the plan when I found out you were coming. I wasn't sure you'd want to be a... a criminal."

She straightened up. "Well, it's not like we're really criminals, is it?" she said. "I mean, everybody knows these big companies, they gyp each other any time they can, right?   And they screw ordinary people like us every day."   She sipped the coffee. "Okay, yeah, it is stealing, I guess,   but it's not like we were hurting anybody, is it?"

He smiled. "At worst, it's embezzlement. White collar crime. And you hardly have to do anything."

She looked around, as if somebody might be listening. "Are you sure it's okay?"

He shut down the notebook, and closed it up. "It's totally fine," he said. "It's just that when you told me you were coming, I sort of telescoped two weeks of the operation into two days."   He stretched. "But it'll still work. Except now you have to do this one little thing."

"Okay, I guess."

"It's no big deal. It's just that, Monday morning, it would really help if I could be in two places at the same time."

"I'm scared," she said. "Just a little, you know?"

"You'll be fine," he said. "Just keep thinking about the

money."

She couldn't help smiling when she thought about that part of it. And the giggle wanted to come back too.

"Now you know what I'd like to do?" he said.

He was still wearing just the jeans. She slid her hand along his leg. "I'll bet I do," she said.

He looked blankly at her, then said, "Oh, yeah, that too. But I was thinking we should get out of town for the weekend. There's a real nice resort out at Harrison Hot Springs."

She continued to run her hand over his thigh. Now that all the fuss was over, she was feeling a little horny. She wanted to celebrate all the money she'd soon have. But, again, he didn't seem to be responding.

She pulled down the zipper on his jeans and undid the metal button. She reached in, stroked and cupped. "Ah, now we're waking up," she said.

He squirmed a little on the stool. "I really want to get away from here," he said.

She let him go. "Sure," she said.

He stood and zipped up. "We can do that when we get to the lake," he said. "Nice hotel room, hot tub."

She considered him. Straight sex or the occasional blow job had always been enough to keep him coming back. Maybe it was time to broaden the repertoire. She didn't want to lose him now.

"Okay," she said. "Maybe we could even do something different, you know, a little kinky. I know!   Why don't you bring along your make-up and a couple of outfits?   See if anybody tries to pick us up?"

An odd look crept over his face. For the first time, she couldn't quite read him. "Come on, lover," she crooned, "it'll be fun. You'll be my boyfriend and girlfriend all rolled into one."

She could read him now. The proposition made him uncomfortable. *Time to reel him in a little*, she thought. Also, he deserved a smack for lying to her and upsetting her so much. "Oh, come on!" she said, letting a touch of iron seep into the coaxing, "if you really want my help on Monday, you can do this for me!"

The discomfort did not leave his face, but the resistance did. "Okay," he sighed. He headed for the hallway to get packed.

Monica laughed. "I wonder if I'll like her," she said. His back was to her. She didn't see the expression that came over his face.

#

There was a white-out in Winnipeg and freezing rain in Toronto, but Saturday in Vancouver was one of those April days the rest of the country can only dream about. An offshore wind blew the smog out to sea, leaving the North Shore mountains as sharp-edged as a Hollywood backdrop. On the beach at English Bay, the sand was warm enough to lie on, and the sun was strong enough for its oiled worshipers to pretend they were getting a start on their tans.

Harry woke early and fast, fighting his way up and out of a bad one, the same bad one. He lay in his own cold sweat while his heart slowed, listening to the perpetual Lougheed Highway traffic, then tried to burrow back into sleep. But someone had locked the door, and left him out here in reality.

After a while, he got up and made coffee and sat in his chair. The Mystery Turtle was bumping its nose against a corner. Harry wondered if it was really that dumb, that it would keep on battering a blank barrier, or was there some purpose behind the persistence? Maybe it was hunting spiders or carpet beetles -- he didn't know if it ate other things beside greens and junk food.

At eight he phoned the hotel where Katherine, Ellen and Maria were staying, and was relayed to their suite. A policewoman answered. The victims had made the best of it, she said, watching pay-per-view comedies and cleaning out the mini-bar. No one had talked about why they were there until they were watching the closing credits of a movie starring that English actor who had got in trouble over a hooker a few years back. Maria started to cry. Ellen got very quiet and Katherine swore and threw the tv remote at the couch.

Harry said he would check back again later and hung up. He called Fisher at the RCMP detachment and was patched through to another number. The Mountie said he was setting up a command center in a convenient place. He didn't say where, and the detective had to make a point of asking before Fisher would divulge the exact location. Harry said he'd check back through the day, to see how things were going.

"There's no need," the computer cop said. "We're all copacetic."

"I'll talk to you later, anyway," Harry said.

He called Carla Gonsalvez's watcher at St. Paul's, the big hospital downtown. She was feeling better. They were talking about moving her to the hotel where the other three women were.

He called Mack.

"Just try and relax, take some time away from the job," she said.

"Can't do that."

"You want me to come over, maybe go out, get some lunch? I'm not doing anything."

"I gotta make another call," he said.

"Get back to me, if you feel like doing something," she said.

"Maybe, okay."

He hung up and called Dory's number. He listened to her voice repeat the recorded message, then put the phone down before the machine could beep at him. An hour later, he did the same thing again, then three more times before dark.

He didn't like what he was doing, but he couldn't stand not doing it.

#

Monica enjoyed Harrison Lake. The hotel was old but comfy, the food good, the scenery a welcome change from the generic North American street scenes of Markham. The big hot tub, fed by underground pipes from the natural volcanic spring at the west end of the lake, was bliss.

They had a long lunch followed by a muscle-melting soak, then she took him back to the room, a whiff of sulfur on their skins, and gave him what he liked.

Again, she noticed a difference. He'd always been pretty passive in bed; *he'd rather be the do-ee than the do-er*, was how she thought of it. He was still mostly that way. But occasionally she saw flashes of something new; it was as if somebody else was crouched behind him, reaching around to get some of her. That somebody was less patient, more forceful. He didn't want to wait for dinner to be cooked -- he wanted it *right now*, raw and bloody.

She did him twice in the afternoon. The first time, she rode him the way he'd always liked it, straddling him and reaching around and under herself to squeeze and bobble his balls. He lay there, as usual, eyes closed, scarcely moving as she ground against him, his palms flat on her thighs.

All at once, with no build-up, his fingers dug into her flesh, with that surprising strength he never used. His eyes opened and locked on hers, a hard stare. Then he rammed himself up into her, no more than a half a dozen times, and came, silent except for the air whistling from his nose.

His eyes closed as he finished, and when they reopened after a few seconds, the hardness was gone from them. His hands were inert on her again.

She stroked his chest. "You okay?" she asked.

"Uh huh." His face was bland, sleepy. She searched his features. They were as placid as the surface of a pond, but she was beginning to sense that something other lived in the depths.

They pulled the sheet over themselves and slept in the warmth of the afternoon, the April sun streaming across the foot of the bed. Monica woke up when the light as beginning to yellow. She looked at her sleeping boyfriend, saw that his eyes moved beneath the lids. *Dreaming*, she thought, and decided to give him his favorite.

Often when he dreamed, Michael would grow an erection. Once, for fun, she had stroked him as he lay dreaming. He had gotten very hard right away. She had curled her fingers around him and gently pumped. In moments, he had been panting and his pelvis had begun to jerk. Then he'd said something indistinct and a gush of semen had arced out of him onto his belly.

It was only then that he woke up, confused, trailing the clouds of an intensely erotic dream. She told him what she'd done. He had begged her to do it again, anytime she saw him asleep and erect.

She'd complied a couple of times since, making it a special rare treat. Now, in the heat of the hotel room,   he lay with his mouth open, and she saw the flickering movement beneath his eyelids.

She got up and found a little jar of hand cream in her make-up case, smeared some on her fingers and rubbed it onto his semi-erect penis. It smelled of roses.

At her touch, his cock stiffened and angled up off his stomach. She pumped it slowly and firmly, not squeezing too hard. Too brisk or intense a sensation would wake him, she had learned. *Slow and steady wins the race*, she thought, wondering where that came from.

He began to move, his hips rotating. He smacked his lips and made a sound that might have been a word. A muscle twitched in his inner thigh and he grew harder; she could feel the veins swelling in her loose oily grip. *Pretty soon*, she thought, and upped the rhythm slightly.

Her attention was focused on his cock, on carefully maintaining the right speed and pressure. The hand on the back of her head caught her by surprise. She turned her head, saw that his eyes were open, with that same hard glare -- it was like being stared at by stones.

He forced her head down to his rigid penis. She sighed and opened her mouth. He tasted like salt and flowers. She sucked and he came, just like that, his fingers gripping her hair -- *that hurts!* -- to drive her head up and down.

When his grip loosened, she straightened up, reached for a tissue and spat his stuff into it. Swallowing it always made her throat burn. She wiped her lips and looked at him. He was asleep, his eyes flickering again under their thin shields of skin.

#

Harry put in a call to Treleaven and got the psychiatrist's answering service.

"Is it an emergency?" said the woman on the line, in a Jamaican accent. "If it's an emergency, I can connect you."

"No," said Harry, "no emergency. Just ask him to call me at home when he can."

"Will he know what it's about?" asked the operator.

"Just about work, tell him that."

When the sun was almost down, he microwaved something that came in a box and ate it, sitting on the couch and holding the hot plastic dish under his chin. He turned on the tv and watched some news, then flicked over to an old comedy rerun halfway through.

The Mystery Turtle had finished its work in the corner. It clumped across the floor toward him, then stopped at midpoint. *Diem perdidi*, he told it.

It regarded him blankly.

"Look it up," Harry said. He clicked the remote and came across the closing credits to an English sitcom on one of the cable channels. The background theme was Schubert's Trout Quintet, one of his mother's favorites. He hummed along with it for a few bars, but the music got him thinking about things he didn't like to dwell on, so he grabbed his jacket and went out.

#

"You look really good," Monica said. "You look... genuine."

She wouldn't have believed it, but there was no arguing with what she saw. You took a nondescript man, put him in the right clothes, filled in here and there to provide the bits that nature had left out of the recipe, added some make-up and gave a little attention to the hair, and out came a convincing woman.

It had taken some persuasion on Monica's part to get him to go along. But she was fascinated to see what he had been trotting out for strangers the past few weeks. She wouldn't have thought him capable of fooling anyone who could go out without a white cane. But here it was.

Dory touched up her cheek with the blusher, blending the pigment imperceptibly into the base.   "You really think so?" she said.

Monica said she really did. It had been a strange thing to watch. As the clothes and equipment went on, something seemed to happen to Michael. *No, not to him, it happened* inside *him.*

Then as he applied make-up, and with a remarkably skillful hand for a man, it was as if he awoke some other part of him, some feminine part, that filled out the shell he had created, made it live and breathe as a woman.

"You know how you always talked about wanting to act?" Monica said.

Dory looked wistful. "Yeah."

"Well, you could have. You should have. You've got something, some kind of talent."

Dory liked this Monica. She seemed to know her but couldn't quite place what their relationship had been. There was a history of some kind, but she shied away from thinking about it.

"You're sweet," she said, then put a hand on her stomach. "I'm starving. Let's go eat."

"You've been working up an appetite all day," said Monica.

Dory looked puzzled. "I'm sorry?"

Monica laughed. "I get it. You're in character, right?"

Dory looked confused.

"Okay, okay," Monica said. "It's just Dory and Monica, and we'll play it by ear."

Dory smiled. "Good. I like that."

They went down to the dining room and turned a few heads. "It's those boobs," Monica said. "God, they look real."

Dory was a little flustered. "I don't like being stared at," she said.

Monica tossed her hair. "Hey, you wanna be in show business, sweetie-baby-honey, you got to give 'em what they're paying for."

The maitre d' wanted to put them by the window, where they would have been practically the centerpiece of the room. But Dory insisted on a quiet table in the back corner.

They ordered the best the menu offered, and Monica called for champagne. Then they put their heads together over dinner and talked about everything.

For the first few minutes, Monica kept snapping back into focus, reminding herself that a couple of hours before, the woman across the table had been a man and had pushed her mouth down onto his penis. But the reality of Dory was so plainly evident that, try as she might to see her boyfriend's face across the table, she couldn't. Michael had faded completely into this warm, bright woman with the sadness in her eyes.

They had the crême brulée for dessert with Spanish coffees. Monica was already tipsy from the champagne, and Dory had loosened up. Her eyes were bright and her cheeks were glowing with more than make-up.

Monica looked beyond Dory to a nearby table, then leaned in to whisper conspiratorially, "Don't turn around, but there's a couple of guys over there want to jump our bones."

Dory's smile froze. "We should go back upstairs," she said.

Monica laughed. "Oh, come on. You think they're gonna come over and ravish us on the table?" She laughed louder. "Whoops, one of them would get a surprise, hey?"

She sipped the liqueur-laced coffee. "Oh, shit," she said. "They're making their big move." She giggled.

They were a matched pair, if you thought of the thumbs-up/thumbs-down movie critics as natural companions. One was tall, lugubrious and balding. The other was plump with a sensual mouth and glasses.

"Hi," said the tall one. "hope we're not intruding, but, you know..."

"We're not interested," said Dory. She hadn't looked at the men. She stared straight ahead, her jaw clamped.

The fat one put his palms on their table and leaned over. "Listen, honey," he said, "we're just trying to be friendly."

Monica was watching Dory's face. The woman she had just spent a happy hour with was dwindling, fading out like a distant signal on the car radio late at night. Someone else was homing in.

There was a steak knife on the table, pointed and serrated. Dory's hand closed on it as the fat man spoke. Monica heard Dory growl -- it was an actual growl, an animal sound.

"Hey, ladies," began the skinny one, "let's be reasonable..."

The knife was suddenly quivering in the table, between the spread fingers of the fat one. He lurched back, and bumped into a tray-laden waiter. Dishes clattered to the floor and the fat man skidded in spilled food and did a bent-knee splits. His companion helped him to his feet.

"No need for that," the thin one said to Dory.

"Fucking dykes," said the other one. He winced; he had pulled something in his groin. He limped after his companion to their table. They signed the check, then left.

The maitre d' came over, summoned staff to clean up the mess. He looked at the steak knife that pinned the tablecloth to the wood beneath. "Is everything all right?" he asked.

Monica let out a breath she hadn't known she'd been holding. But Dory spoke first. "Just fine, thank you. Would you ask the waiter to bring us a couple more of these Spanish coffees?"

Dory noticed the knife stuck in the table top and briskly pulled it free. She smiled at Monica, and said, "I'm feeling really good tonight."

Monica stared at her. For a moment, she didn't know who was looking back.

Chapter 9

Fisher had established his command post in an empty building at the rear of an industrial park in suburban Burnaby. A year earlier, the RCMP corporal's commercial crime team had neatly foiled a California-based fraud crew who had targeted a manufacturing firm belonging to the man who also owned the industrial park.

The Mounties had bagged the scammers when they came north on a Friday to take delivery of several hundred thousand dollars worth of electronic components. The equipment was manifested for the San Francisco Bay area, but the truck it was loaded onto was heading instead for Mexico. It would have been untraceably gone when the bank draft offered in payment (and vouched for by one of the gang when the electronics firm's sales manager called to confirm), was found to be a forgery the next Monday.

Fisher's team, working with Canada Customs and Excise officers, had stopped the shipment at the Douglas border crossing and arrested the fraud ring as they were about to board a United flight at Vancouver International Airport. The successful police operation saved the electronics entrepreneur several hundred thousand dollars, and the grateful businessman had said that if there was ever anything he could do to repay the benefit, the Mountie need only call.

Fisher made that call as soon as he saw that the same intruder program had been inserted into the data systems at each of the companies where the victims worked. He knew he would need space in which to set up for a few days. He also knew that requisitioning space through the RCMP bureaucracy -- which still operated more like a creature of the nineteenth-century British Empire than of near-twenty-first-century Canada -- would have taken a week, even at maximum emergency rush.

He'd also been able to make an unofficial request of the data security chief at BC Tel, the province-wide phone company. A special crew had arrived Saturday morning to augment the empty building's communications. Now Fisher had high-speed, high-capacity fiber-optic connections linking him directly to Hamilton

Lynch, MacroFiber Industries, Taguchi Kawamura, Fat Choy Developments and Nova Consultants. The phone company had also lent him the prototype for a top-speed broad-band switching system that had been nothing more than an engineer's dream twelve months before. It was, the security chief said, the "bleeding edge" of data transmission nodes.

By late Saturday night, Fisher was feeling like a cat that had settled comfortably outside a mouse hole: he was confident that when the curtain went up on Monday morning, it would be for Mr. Three-piece's last performance.

He had had his team put their equipment on low platforms made of shipping pallets -- the concrete floor was too cold -- and now they were scattered around the building's dark, echoing space like wooden islands. The archipelago's shirt-sleeved inhabitants crouched over work stations they had set up on sheets of particle board laid over saw horses. Their fingers clicked on keyboards and computer mice, or sorted through skeins of cable as they connected deck to deck, their faces lit by the quiet glow of monitors.

Today, Fisher and his people had ironed out almost all the wrinkles from the linked components of the system they had established within the building. Tomorrow, they would initialize the LAN software that would link these computers to all of the victims' invaded systems, creating a unified local area network. On Monday, when the bad guy so much as nibbled at any one of the systems he had cracked, Fisher would be on him.

The Mountie took a print-out from one of his people and ran his eye down the numbers. "Looks good," he said. It was about time to tell his crew to wrap it up, and be back for phase two in the morning. Then he saw Harry Lukovitch coming across the concrete toward him.

"Hey," said Fisher. "How's it going?"

"I thought maybe I could help."

"Maybe. Know anything about LAN protocols?"

Harry shook his head. "This all gonna be ready on time?" he asked.

Fisher yawned. "Oh, yeah. Got good guys here. We got this piece of the puzzle built. Tomorrow, we add in the victims' systems and make sure we're all sining in the same key. Monday morning, we're on-line and ready to rock and roll."

A Mountie brought the corporal another print-out. He chewed his lip as he scanned the figures.

Harry looked around at the flickering monitors and the bare cinderblock walls. "I really want this guy," he told Fisher.

Fisher checked a number on the print-out against a technical manual spread-eagled on a make-shift table. "Me too," he said.

"No, I mean I really want him," said Harry.

The tone made Fisher look up. "You should get some sleep," he said.

"Later," Harry said.

#

Sunday morning was cooler, a stiff breeze whipping up wavelets on Harrison Lake and slapping the tops of the evergreens about. Monica didn't notice the weather; she was learning about the money.

"But why the Mariana Islands?" she asked, as they walked along the shore. Nobody else was braving the early chill.

"Because that's where the bank is," he said.

"The bank's on an island in the Pacific?   I don't get it."

"Actually," he said, "the Marianas are a whole bunch of islands. It's where they used to test atomic bombs in the fifties. Bikini Atoll."

Monica scratched her chin. "But when we go there to get the money, why won't they just arrest us?"

He laughed. "We're not going there."

"Well, that's what I don't get."

"I'll tell you again," he said. "It has to do with the banking laws. Now, banks in Canada and the States are governed by a lot of laws and regulations, right?   Like the law that says if the cops show up with a court order, the bank has to open its books."

"That much I understand, sure."

"Okay. Here's the thing about the Marianas. They're an American protectorate -- that means they come under most American laws, but not American banking laws. Their banks don't have to tell anybody anything."

"But they'll know when you ship the money there. They'll be watching the airports or something."

"You're not listening. It's all done by phone lines and satellite relays. It's like when you use a bank card in the supermarket. One second the money's in your account; the next second, it's in the store's account."

"But they can trace that, right?"

He shook his head. "Most transactions go on leased lines that belong to the big national consortium of phone companies. I had a talk with the phone company's computer."

Monica stopped at a wood and concrete bench. She sat on one end, turning her back to the wind off the lake. "Okay, so we send the money to this island, electronically. And then we don't have to go to there to get it?"

His face was blandly passive. "The accounts are all set up. The money bounces right through the Marianas bank, then it splits up and goes to the Bahamas, the Grand Caymans, Panama, a couple of other places. Nobody's ever going to trace it."

"But how do we get our hands on it?"

He showed her in the hotel room. She sat on the bed with him, the notebook between them. This wing of the hotel was very quiet, the guests sleeping in before a leisurely brunch in the dining room.

The colored screen showed a list of numbered files. Monica watched Michael manipulate the cursor control. His hands were always very sure when he used a computer.

"Watch this," he said, and moved the cursor down the list. "These are the accounts." He closed the window and opened another. "These are the access codes. You just open an account in a regular North American bank. The branch transit number is on the bottom of the cheques they give you. Then you dial up one of these," -- he reopened the accounts window -- "and tell it to transfer funds to the new account. Couple of hours at the most, the money's there for you to withdraw." He exited the program and closed the computer.

Monica stroked the notebook's hard plastic surface. "It's like having your own personal cash machine," she said.

"Yeah. Except you don't even need a card. Just a phone and the codes."

"Will it really work?"

He stretched out on the bed, out his hands behind his head and smiled at the ceiling. "It will really work," he said.

She sat beside him and thought about it for a while, then she said, "Want me to do anything for you?"

His eyes were unfocused. "No, thanks," he said.

"You okay?"

"Yeah," he said. His voice somehow sounded far off, as if he were receding slowly into the distance.

She thought about the money again. "Know what I'd like to do?" she said.

"Hmm?"

"I'd like to go shopping with her."

"Who?"

"You know, *her*, the lady I had dinner with last night."

He closed his eyes. "You guys really get along," he said. "Okay."

A stillness stole over his features. He might have been dead. Then the eyes popped open. "Just give me time to change and get my face on," said Dory's voice.

She came off the bed with fluid strength and went to the closet, began flicking through the outfits hanging there. "I need something new," she said.

Monica joined her. "Something with pizzazz," she said.

\#

The Jamaican woman put the call through to Treleaven's office at eleven o'clock Sunday morning. "Harry," said the psychiatrist, "how are you?"

"I've been better," said the detective. "I'll be better again when I catch this asshole."

Even as he said it, Harry knew this was not like the previous times when he had become obsessed with cracking a case. He was concentrating on Mr. Three-piece to take his mind off what Dory Novello was doing to him. But he wasn't going to tell that to Treleaven.

"It's not about the bad guys, Harry," Treleaven said.

"It's always about the bad guys, Doc -- especially this one. What can you tell me?"

Treleaven got a file from the stack in the corner of his desk and opened it. "I've been thinking about this guy," he said. "The mask. Maybe it's not just fixation. Maybe he needs the mask so the victims don't recognize him."

"We're already assuming he knows them. He has access."

"Exactly. Which means they must know him."

"Yeah, so?"

"So, when you know somebody, a mask is not much of a disguise. Little things give you away, gestures, body language."

"But none of the victims has picked up on anything."

"Right. So either this guy's a hell of an actor, or..."

"Or what?"

"Or we could be dealing with dissociative disorder."

"What's that?" Harry said.

"What we used to call multiple personality disorder. When the psyche fragments into different personas."

Harry sniffed. "I thought most shrinks didn't subscribe to that one."

Treleaven made a face. "A lot of us don't, until we encounter one."

"I thought it was just in the movies. Three Faces of Eve." He'd seen the flick on a four a.m. late show.

"It's actually pretty common. A matter of degree, mostly. We're all at least partly subdivided inside our heads. Who do you think drives your car when you're listening to some talk show on the radio? Who leaves your keys where you can't find them?"

"How does this help me catch him?"

"I don't think it does, per se," the psychiatrist said. "But it seems to me if we're dealing with DD, the perpetrator's situation has got to be inherently unstable."

"So?"

"So it won't last. If we're dealing with multiple personalities and multiple rape, I think we can expect conflict."

"What conflict?"

"Well, think about it. It would be hard enough having a monster like that in the family. Imagine having one right inside your head."

Harry thought about it. Treleaven was not giving him much help. He said so.

"Well, maybe I'm giving you hope, Harry."

"No, you're not," said the detective. "But thanks anyway."

#

Dory and Monica came back early Monday morning, and went into the east side of the duplex. The light was flashing on the answering machine in the living room. Dory pushed the button and the tape spool rewound.

"Dory," came Harry's voice. "It's Harry. Please get in touch as soon as you come home. I need to know you're okay."

Monica saw Dory's face change as she listened to the man's voice. "Who's Harry?" she said.

Dory's expression became cool and businesslike again. "Some crazy man," she said. "I don't have time."

In the cupboard under the kitchen sink she found rags and a spray can of furniture polish. She gave them to Monica. "The whole place, both sides," she said. "Anywhere and anything you might have touched. Then pack. The car's in the carport."

Monica took them. "Okay," she said.

"You know where you have to be and when you have to be there?"

"Yeah. I'll see you later."

"Good." Dory looked at the answering machine and sighed. "This'll soon be over," she said. "Then we can put it all behind us."

"Don't worry," Monica said.

Dory took one last look around, then she left.

\#

Fisher's command post was ready. His team had arranged five work stations in a crescent on trestle tables made of sawhorses and sheets of particle board. Each was connected to the office work station of one of the victims, and would mirror whatever happened there. Between the horns of the crescent, the RCMP corporal sat at a sixth work station, tapping the middle finger of his right hand on the table's rough surface. Beside the computer was a speaker phone and a digital travel clock on the table read 8:56.

One of his team told Fisher that the conference call was set up. The Mountie noted that the hold button on his phone was now flashing, nodded and continued to tap.

Harry had been there since before seven o'clock, crowding Fisher's elbow, getting under the computer cop's skin. Now he made room as Treleaven arrived and took a seat behind the computer cop.

"Thanks for the invitation," the psychiatrist said.

"I thought your professional skills might come in handy," Fisher replied. He glanced at Harry. "We're ready," he told the detective and pushed a button on the speaker phone.

Harry leaned forward and spoke into the speaker phone. "Ms.

Tower? Can you hear me?"

Katherine Tower was in her office at Hamilton Lynch. A uniformed policeman stood behind her.

"Loud and clear," she said. There was only the tiniest quaver in her voice.

"Good," Harry said. "How about you, Ms. Wiens?"

"I'm here," said Ellen. She asked the constable in her office to close the door.

"Ms. Chen?" said Harry.

"Yes."

Katherine heard the strain in Maria's voice over the conference line. "Don't worry, honey," she said. "You're safe."

"Ms. Gonsalvez?" Harry said.

Carla Gonsalvez's customary smile was gone. Her voice came from some place far away. "Go ahead."

Harry leaned closer to the phone. "Mack? What's happening?" he said.

Harry's partner was watching Dory power up her computer and insert the phone jack into the modem card. "Just about ready here," Mack said.

While Dory watched the computer run through its boot sequence, she spoke over her shoulder to the detective. "We're on line. Would you make sure that door is locked?"

Mack double-checked the locks. While the detective's back was turned, Dory quickly touched one function key on the keyboard.

"Door's locked," Mack told Dory, then spoke into the phone. "Harry? Let's do it."

"We're waiting for it now," said Harry. "Everybody sit tight." He punched the phone's hold button.

Treleaven cleared his throat. "Professionally speaking," he said, "I wouldn't recommend having the victims participate."

Harry shrugged. "We need them." He watched the clock. The numbers had reached 9:04.

"Anytime now, I'll bet," Fisher said.

"Yeah," said Harry. "They come in, get their coffee, get ready to work..."

"Harry," Treleaven said quietly, "I'm concerned about the effect this case is having on you."

"Don't be."

"You were my patient. I have to be."

"Not now, Doc."

"Let me say one thing, then I'll keep quiet. Your basic problem relates to power, not guilt. What happened to your wife made you feel powerless to protect her. This three-piece creep you're after, he's all about power."

"Some other time," said Harry, but his voice had too much breath in it.

"He steals the power of the women he attacks," Treleaven went on, relentless, "takes their trophies and symbols of accomplishment. And that's a direct affront to you, because you're the one with the badge and the gun. You're supposed to have the power in this situation."

"Will you shut up?" the detective whispered.

One of Fisher's work stations gave a discreet *beep*, and its screen cleared.

"We're on," said the Mountie.

The other four monitors blanked, then each displayed the message, *Good Morning*, followed by the name of the victim to whom the system belonged. After a ten-second pause, the screen displayed, *Press C to continue.*

Harry looked at Fisher. The computer cop nodded. "All right," Harry said, "let's do it."

Katherine stabbed the C on her keyboard. Ellen touched hers. Maria hesitated, then complied as if the key were slimy. Carla mechanically followed suit. Mack watched Dory nervously press the key.

The screens cleared, then displayed, *Enter your birth date -- year, month, day.*

Harry put the conference call on hold. "He wants to make sure it's them."

Treleaven said, "It's also a dominance ploy. He's forcing them to give up personal information."

Harry hit the hold button. "Go ahead," he said.

Mack watched as Dory typed in the information. The screen cleared, then displayed, *Mother's maiden name?*

Dory entered the name "Veitch," and touched the enter key.

At the command post, Fisher watched the screens clear as each of the victims answered the intruder program's prompt. He tapped a couple of keys on his own keyboard and said, "Definitely not an outside link. The program is resident in the victims' systems. And it's a lot busier than it needs to be to do what it's doing." He tapped more keys and studied the information that came up on his own screen.

The victims' blank screens now displayed a single line of type at the bottom. It read, *What's the scariest thing in the world?*

Treleaven put his hand over the grill that covered the speaker phone's mike. "He wants to hear that he is," he said.

Harry spoke into the phone. "The answer is 'you.'"

As Ellen Wiens typed the three letters and pressed *enter*, Rhys Maitland opened the door of her office and tried to push past the policeman. "What's going on here?" he demanded.

"Who the hell is that?" Harry said.

Maitland raised his voice to answer the speaker phone, while the constable kept him out of the room. "This is Rhys Maitland. I want to know..."

Harry cut him off. "Mr. Maitland, this is a police investigation. Please do not interfere."

Harry was sure that the president and chief executive officer of MacroFiber Industries was not used to being spoken to in that manner, and that he would not be pleased by the novelty of the experience.

"I demand to know what's taking place in my office," came the voice from the speaker phone.

"A police investigation of a serious crime," Harry said. "You can watch, but do not interfere."

Maitland fumed, but the policeman in the doorway was a wall of meat and bone. The CEO craned past the man's shoulder to read what was appearing on his executive assistant's screen: *I can reach you anytime.*

Video images began to wash in on the crescent of monitors in front of Harry. He looked from one to another: each showed a bound woman being sexually used, each with a victim's face superimposed on the video. A mask covered the heads of the men in the different pictures, and each scene contained a prominent representation of a knife.

A line of unused blank screen remained below each picture, and in that space the words, *Want another visit?* now appeared.

Harry spoke into the phone. "The answer is 'no.'"

Each woman typed the two letters and touched the enter key.

The images disappeared from the screens, and a new line of type said, *Then here's what you have to do. Enter "yes"*.

Fisher was getting excited now. "We're there!" he said.

Harry hit the hold button. "Where?   What?"

The computer cop's fingers dashed over his keyboard. "We've fingered the intruder program!   We can watch it work!"

"Can we trace him?"   Harry said.

"No," Fisher said. "It's definitely not an outside link. He's put this thing in and let it run itself."   He tapped more keys. "Jesus in Japanese, will you look at that!   He's got all five company systems on-line with each other and wide open!   Bank accounts, personnel files, the whole megillah!   What a piece of work!"

Harry put the conference call back on-line. "Ladies, whatever he tells you to do, do it. We've gotten into his program, and it's going to help us catch him."

He hit the hold button and turned to Fisher. "It is going to help us find him, right?"

Treleaven spoke up. "He has to be connected somehow, otherwise he can't watch and enjoy the effect he's having on the victims."

"It would have to be a passive link," the Mountie said.

"If it's there, can you find it?" Harry asked.

"Maybe," said Fisher. "Let's see what happens."

What was happening then was that each of the victims was receiving individual instructions from the intruder program, and the instructions were detailed. Katherine Tower's screen had split into two unequal parts: the bottom portion, only a few lines deep, displayed the intruder's instructions; above, the main part of the screen showed the system's security gateway to protected files.

At the bottom of Katherine's screen, the intruder ordered her to *Open account PTM-00217*. Katherine used the cursor keys to highlight the identified account in the list on the main screen. A window appeared, displaying the words, *WARNING!   PRIORITY AA ACCOUNT -- NO UNAUTHORIZED ACCESS -- INPUT IDENTITY AND ACCESS CODES*.

Katherine tapped the keys, the warning window now displayed, *IDENTITY AND ACCESS CODES CONFIRMED*. Her main screen cleared, then displayed a list of credits and debits. At the bottom was, *CREDIT/(DEBIT) $2,406,775.23*.

Maria Chen's message told her to *Open account 4TS-24-01*. When she had cleared the security barrier, the credit and debit columns scrolled up until the bottom line read, *FUNDS AVAILABLE $1,572,904.68*.

"He knows these systems inside out," Fisher said.

Harry craned to see what was happening on the various work stations. "What's he doing?"

"Making them use their security codes to crack company accounts," the Mountie said.

"It's dominance again," said Treleaven. "The codes are an expression of the victims' power, which he's taking from them."

Harry looked back at the screens. "Fisher?   Is that right?"

But the Mountie was watching closely as the action on the five systems heated up. "Wait a sec," he said. "Look at this."

Carla Gonsalvez's screen said, *Transfer one dollar to MacroFiber Industries Account # CCA 8753879*.

"What's happening?" Harry asked Fisher.

"He wants her to move a dollar to Ellen Wiens' company," the Mountie said.

"What the hell for?"

"Power," said Treleaven. "Dominance."

"Shit," said the detective. Into the speaker phone he said, "Carla, do as he says."   He put the conference call off-line again and spoke to Fisher. "Are we getting somewhere?"

"Wait," was the answer. The computer cop rattled his keyboard, his eyes flicking from one screen to another.

Carla followed the instructions. The bottom of her screen said, *Good girl, Carla. Now transfer one hundred dollars to Taguchi Kawamura Account # BT-004*. She complied.

"Fisher!"   Harry watched the flicker of activity on the five screens. "What are you getting?"

The Mountie spoke without taking his eyes of the screens or his fingers off the keys. "Definitely an inside job!   There's a master program!   It's in one of the five computers!"

"Which one?"

"Can't tell yet. Christ, this guy is good!"

The five-fold flow of instructions from the intruder continued unabated. All of the victims were now responding to a succession of commands to open this file, close that one, open another, move a dime from here to there, then move it back again.

Mack looked over Dory's shoulder as the consultant struggled to keep pace with the changing directions. "What's going on?" Mack said.

"I don't know. It's happening too fast."

The speed picked up. "Wait a sec," Fisher said. "Who did that one?"

"What?" Harry said.

"Not sure. It went by so fast. It looked like there was another player." He called to one of his team, "Are we current on all of these transactions?"

The other Mountie shook his head. "Too many, too fast."

"I need to know what's happening here," Harry said.

Fisher worked his keyboard. "He's got them moving money all over, one account to another, through five complex data systems! Our system can't keep up!"

Harry stood up. The flickering flood of letters and numbers across the crescent of screens might as well have been hieroglyphics. But he felt a cold slug turning in his belly as he sensed that this operation was getting away from him. "Is he stealing it? Is that what this is all about?"

"It's dominance," said the psychiatrist, at ease in his chair.

"I don't know," said Fisher. "There's some big money on the table now. But it looks like it's just going round and round." He tapped his keys. "There. If it goes out of any one of the five systems, I should be able to trace it."

Treleaven said, "It's a power trip. He has to be tapped in somewhere, watching. He's probably masturbating."

Harry leaned in close to Fisher. "Find him!"

"If he's on a passive receiver, I might not see him. Peeping Toms don't make a lot of noise."

"Should we continue or shut it down?"

"If we shut down, there's no chance we catch him," the computer cop said. "If we stay up and running, we might find him somewhere in the middle of all this. We're looking."

Harry opened the line to the conference call again and told the women to keep cooperating with the intruder program.

At MacroFiber Industries, Rhys Maitland was watching the events with growing horror. As six and seven digit numbers began to move across his assistant's screen, he tried to push past the policeman. The cop held him back.

"Ellen!" Maitland called. "Stop this now!"

His voice came to Harry over the speaker phone. "Who the hell is that?" the detective said.

"Rhys Maitland! I refuse to allow this to continue! Ellen, shut down immediately!"

Fisher was peering at his screen. "Something's not right here." He called to his second in command. "How current are we?"

"We're out-powered by a factor of ten," said the other cop.

Harry was talking into the phone. "I'm speaking to the constable in Ellen Wien's office. Remove Mr. Maitland from the room. If he won't go, charge him with obstruction. Then lock the door."

He heard the spluttered protests as the executive was forced out. He chewed his lip and watched the computer cop sweat.

Fisher said, "I don't like this." His eyes flicked from screen to screen, his head snapping through short arcs, his shoulders hunched.

"Tell me, Fisher!" Harry said. "Talk to me! Where the hell is he?"

In Dory's office, Mack had been watching the avalanche of data flow across the monitor as the consultant responded to the prompts at the bottom of her screen. Although she considered herself to be computer literate, the transactions Mack was seeing were well beyond her experience.

"What's going on?" she asked, a couple of times, but there was no answer. Dory was intent on the interplay of command and response.

Harry had left the speaker phone live after ordering the constable at MacroFiber Industries to evict the company's CEO. She heard him badgering Fisher for an answer, heard the growing frustration in his tone.

"Do you know what's happening here?" she asked Dory. The consultant shook her head.

"Look, I need to know..." Mack began, but at that moment the doorknob rattled slightly. Then there came a hard *thump* on the door, the sound of something metallic slamming into the wood.

Mack drew her automatic and reached for the deadbolt lock. A second later, she had the door open. Her immediate view of corridor outside showed nothing. But still quivering in the door was an ivory handled dagger.

Mack stepped out of the office carefully, her pistol poised, her head and eyes moving. The side corridor in which Nova Consultants had its office was empty. She moved swiftly to where the passageway met the elevator landing, and came around the corner with her gun leveled.

A young woman waiting by the elevators jumped back, her eyes wide in shock. Mack lowered the weapon.

"Police officer!" she said. "Did you see a man?"

The woman was white faced. She pointed to the door that led to the fire stairs. "That way."

"Stay here!"   Mack told the woman, then she moved to the door, gun ready. She pushed it open. She looked up and down the stairwell, listened, then stepped through the door. It closed behind her.

Dory came down the corridor from her office, carrying a briefcase. "It's done," she said to the woman at the elevators.

"Then let's get out of here," said Monica. She had already pushed the call button. The elevator came and they got in.

As they descended, Dory set down the briefcase. She took off the white linen jacket she had been wearing unbuttoned, reversed it and put it back on; now she was in yellow imitation silk, buttoned to the chin.

She opened the briefcase and took out a long, brunette wig, a pair of sunglasses and a second pair of shoes. She put the first pair in the briefcase.

Monica had worn a calf-length, dark raincoat buttoned up over stockings and flats. Now she stripped off the coat and wadded it into the briefcase on top of Dory's notebook. Underneath, she had on a sweatshirt and oversized jeans with the legs rolled up to her knees. She quickly rolled them down to her ankles. Her collar length hair had been done up in a bun at the nape of her neck. She pulled the elastic loose and let it swing free.

The elevator's descent took less than twenty seconds. The two women who left it in the lobby went straight out through the revolving doors onto Burrard Street and turned south. They crossed with the lights at Pender and entered the Bentall Center complex of office towers and underground mall, walked through its corridors of shops to the SkyTrain station, and bought tickets from the automatic dispenser.

The eastbound train arrived within a minute. They rode it to the Terminal Avenue station beside the old British Columbia Pavilion at Expo 86, a steel geodesic sphere that now served as an interactive science center for children.

They crossed Main Street and cut through the little park to the massive old pile of stone that had once been the Canadian National Railway's main terminus -- back in the hey-day of rail -- but which was now downgraded to service as a mere bus depot. They retrieved the suitcases Dory had put in a locker that morning. The bus to Victoria was idling in its bay, loading passengers.

Chapter 10

Mack came back to the office of Nova Consultants, breathing hard, to hear Harry's voice calling her name and Dory's from the speaker phone.

"Harry!" Mack gasped. "Something's wrong!"

At Fisher's command post, Harry shouted into the phone. "What do you mean, she's gone!   Stay there, I'm on my way!"

Fisher stopped him as he headed for the door. In his hand was a sheaf of papers. "You'd better look at this," he said.

Harry tried to go around him, but the Mountie blocked his way. "Listen!   A lot of money is still moving around, but it looks like a big chunk went into one computer and never came out!   I can't find it!"

The slug in Harry's stomach rolled its sickening weight over. "Which computer?" he said.

"Novello's."

Harry knew something awful had happened. It had involved Dory Novello. And it had been his fault.

"Come on," he said, and turned the Mountie toward the door. "Let's go see how bad it is."

Treleaven watched the data flow across the screens. Once the accounts were opened, the intruder program had had no more interest in the victims. The program had run itself, leaving the women to watch helplessly as an alien force had played at will in what should have been their secure places.

The psychiatrist pulled his nose and stroked his chin. "Dominance," he said, to nobody in particular.

#

The weapon was still sticking in Dory's office door. Harry left it there while he examined it from several angles. It was a World War II German *Kriegsmarine* officer's ceremonial dagger. At the end of the war, returning Canadian soldiers had brought back thousands of such things. They were sitting in attics and the backs of granddads' junk drawers all over the country. The chances of tracing it were probably nil.

Fisher ignored the knife and went straight to the computer. He sat down at the desk and pulled on latex gloves.

Harry followed him into the room. "Can you turn it on?" he asked, eying the blank screen.

"It *is* on," said the computer cop. He tapped some keys. "But it's deader than bellbottoms."

He tried another combination of keys. "Zip," he said. "Wiped clean. Drive's been reformatted, and all the money is just microwaves. By now it'll have bounced through some off-shore bank and gone halfway round the world. The guy who did this is a genius."

Harry turned away and faced the wall. Its serene blankness should have been a comfort. It offered him nothing, drew him not at all. He wished it could flow out around him, enclose him in sterile isolation.

"Can't we cancel the transactions?" Mack was asking.

Fisher got up. "Nope. E.F.T. is legal, official and instantaneous."

"E.F.T.?" Harry said. He still faced the wall.

"Electronic Funds Transfer," the Mountie said. "Looks like that's what it was all about."

"Oh shit," said Harry.

#

The furniture in Dory's living room gleamed. All the dust was gone. Fitzgard's crime scene crew were not finding any latent prints.

What they had found was an empty house behind an unlocked door, the rooms quiet except for the constant whir of traffic up and down Oak Street.

Mack went to talk to the neighbors, came back shaking her head. "Either side don't speak much English -- or they just don't want to talk to any cops," she said. Recent arrivals from Hong Kong brought longstanding attitudes with them: police were people of low status who could only cause you trouble and cost you money.

"The woman across the street remembers a visitor late one night last week," Mack continued. "The description fits you."

Harry put his hands in his pockets. His shoulders slid down. Mack put her hand on his arm. "Take it easy," she said. "We don't know what's happened."

"That's what's worrying me," Harry said. "What about the landlord?"   He motioned with his thumb to the hallway and the common wall.

"Nobody home," said Mack. "Mrs. Eagle Eye across the street says he's the quiet type, keeps to himself. Only been here six months or so. Same as Novello."

Harry knew what his partner was thinking. "You think they were...," he began.

Fitzgard entered from the hallway. "Harry," he said, "you need to take a look at the closet."

They looked, then they went through, emerging into the other unit of the duplex. Harry sniffed. The smell of furniture polish was just as strong on this side.

"Cozy," Mack said.

Harry put on plastic gloves, went down the hall, opening doors.

Fitzgard came through from the other side. "We found it!" he said. "Mask, suit, gloves, the whole thing!"

It seemed to Harry that the world suddenly got larger, while he got smaller. The hallway appeared to go on into an immense distance.

"They were under the bed," Fitzgard said.

"Her bed," Harry said, mostly to himself, but Mack heard.

"Looks like she already had a boyfriend," she said. It was the kind of thing cops said when things went wrong, the hard-ass jokes and one-liners that get them through the bad moments. But it was also the wrong thing to say. Mack knew it even as the words came out and smacked into Harry. She saw something sag in her partner's face. His eyes closed and stayed closed.

She said, "Harry, I'm sorry."

The eyes opened. "Let's just do the job," he said.

#

The intercity bus was always the first vehicle onto the Victoria ferry at the Tsawwassen terminal, south of Vancouver near the American border, so the bus passengers were always at the head of the line in the on-board cafeteria. Nerves had kept Dory and Monica from eating that morning, but now that they were in flight, the notebook tightly snugged under Dory's arm, they were suddenly famished.

The man behind them was a frequent ferry traveler; he made some remark about how it didn't matter what they ordered, because the burgers and chicken strips and sole Neptune were all passed through a giant flavor extractor at the BC Ferry Corporation headquarters. But Monica loaded up her tray -- salad, soup and a teriyaki burger -- and it all tasted great.

They ate fast, then got double-strength cafe lattes in disposable cups from a machine in the forward lounge and took them out onto the upper deck as the now loaded ferry pulled out.

"That's the Roberts Bank Superport," said the food critic from the cafeteria line-up. He indicated a man-made peninsula off the ferry's starboard side, where immense conical heaps of black stuff surrounded something that looked like a lightweight roller coaster. "It's for loading Japanese freighters with coking coal from the Kootenays. Conveyors are fully automatic. Three or four guys can run the whole thing."

"Very nice," Dory said and moved toward the stern. Monica gave the man a smile that said, *I'm just being polite; please go away*, and followed her.

"Funny thing about Tsawwassen," said the man, tracking them along the rail. "It's at the lowest end of a rain shadow gradient that starts in the North Shore mountains and declines until you get down her to Boundary Bay. So it can be pouring in North Van, drizzling in Richmond, but bright sunshine right here -- like today."

He was an odd man, middle aged with eccentric whiskers and a pony tail that spiraled like a ringlet, and he was talkative. Eventually, they threw their half-finished lattes into a waste bin and ducked into the women's washroom to be rid of him.

Dory went to the mirror and opened her purse, brought out a blusher and touched up her cheeks. Monica watched. "I'm still amazed," she said.

"At what?" Dory put away the blusher and took out eyeliner.

"At all this, how authentic you look. It's not just the clothes and the make-up. It's like you've changed from the inside out."

Dory put away the eyeliner and snapped her purse shut. "Let's not talk about it."

Monica heard the finality in the tone, and let it drop. "What do we do when we get to Victoria?" she asked.

Dory looked around. There were no feet under the toilet stalls. "Michael's got several bank accounts under different names at different banks. As soon as we get to a phone, we can transfer money directly to them."

"Good," said Monica. It was weird, hearing Michael talk about himself as if he were somebody else. But somehow it was so natural when he was being Dory. "I need to go shopping."

"That'll be nice," Dory said.

They went out on deck again. The ferry's rapid speed sent a stiff wind flying back along the exposed parts of the deck, but there were sheltered areas with rows of seats. They jumped when the ship's whistle blared: the ferry was nosing through a narrow passage between small wooded islands. Vacation cottages were scattered along the shore, and here and there tiny farms had broken clearings through the mixed forest.

"We're actually in American waters for the next few minutes," said the talkative man, sitting down beside them. "Right over there is the island where they had the pig war in the 1850s. U.S. infantry on one end of the island, British Royal Marines on the other, faced each other for, I dunno, months, because some farmer had shot a pig that belonged to another farmer."

He couldn't remember whether it had been an American or British pig that had been shot. "Didn't matter. Whole thing came to nothing in the end. But the officer commanding the American troops was Picket. He led Picket's charge at Gettysburg?"

Monica could sense that Dory was growing increasingly anxious. She remembered the two men at Harrison Lake, the knife in the table. She put her hand on Dory's arm, felt the ridges of tensed muscle. "It's okay," she murmured. "He's harmless. Will we be there soon?"

Dory stared straight ahead and said nothing. After a while, they noticed that the man had gone away.

#

Harry and Mack got back to the squad room at four, to find an internal correspondence delivery waiting for them. Harry unbent the metal holder that sealed the manila envelope and shook out the contents.

It was six faxed pages. At the top of the cover sheet were the words, *Security Clearance -- Dorcas Paula Novello*. Beneath was a date of birth in the late 1940s, and a Toronto address and phone number.

Harry ran his eyes down the sheet. The Dorcas Novello it

described was a married computer consultant pushing fifty. She'd had her own firm for twelve years, and its only office was in the financial district of the country's largest city, almost three thousand miles from Vancouver.

He flipped the top sheet over. Underneath, a four-page detailed resume told how this Dorcas Novello had made her entry into the computer world as a keypunch operator, then grown to become a highly regarded systems analyst with a client list of blue-chip corporations.

The final page was a faxed copy of a palm sized photograph. Even after being photocopied then broken down into computer code and bounced off the Anik 1 satellite, the picture still transmitted its subject's maturity, toughness and intelligence. It was also clearly not the Dory Novello Harry knew.

He went back to the cover sheet. There were phone numbers for home and office. He looked at his watch, added three hours, and called the home number. The voice that answered was a deep, well modulated contralto.

He identified himself, then asked Dorcas Novello if a woman of a certain age and description had left the employ of Nova Consultants about six months before.

She wanted to know why. He told her that someone using the name Dory Novello was part of an investigation he was conducting, that she was not implicated in the case in any way, and that he could say no more than that. He repeated the description.

"Nobody like that has ever worked for me," Novello said. "Most of my employees are younger men -- they seem to infest the field." She paused, then added, "I did have to let one of them go -- I mean a young man -- about seven months ago. He was brilliant, but not focused too tightly on what the clients really need, if you know what I mean. One of those techno-dreamers."

"And that was why you let him go?"

There was a pause, then she said, "No." There was another pause. "I could have put up with the la-la land lapses," she said. "He was that good. But there was something else. One day he was having a hard time straightening out some lousy coding work that a client's own in-house people had done. He got really frustrated. So frustrated, he picked up a monitor and threw it through a wall. Ten seconds later, it was as if nothing had happened. There were a couple of other incidents. People got nervous."

"What happened when you let him go?"   Harry asked. "Did he make threats?"

"No. He just looked at me with the deadest eyes I've ever seen, took his severance cheque, and walked out."

"What was his name?"

"Taft. Michael Taft."

"Did he have a girlfriend?"

"I think so. He didn't talk about his social life too much."

"You wouldn't know her name?"

"Uh uh. Sorry."

"One last thing, Ms. Novello. Could you give us whatever you had on this Taft guy -- address, social insurance number, date of birth, any references he gave when he applied for the job. And a picture, if you have one."

"I can get my staff to dig it out, fax it to you first thing tomorrow," she said.

He gave her the squad's fax number. Then he called records and asked for anything they had on the name Novello had given him. The clerk said there'd be nothing before the next day.

While he was talking to records, Mack's phone had rung and she had answered it. Now she hung up and said, "That was Inspector Mason. He wants to see us."

Harry said, "*Morituri te salutamas*."   He stood up.

"Like your old partner used to say?" Mack asked.

"Like the old Roman gladiators used to say when they went out to fight: *We who are about to die salute you.*"

Mack looked apologetic. "You might as well know," she said. "That Maitland guy?   Seems he went to school with Mason."

"What the hell," Harry said. "Maybe they didn't like each other."

She put an arm around his shoulders and walked him toward the door. "Mori-tori-whatever," she said. "We'll die together."

"You're a good partner," Harry said.

"Hold that thought."

#

"We've got to get you changed into some proper clothes," Monica said.

"What do you mean?"

"Men's clothes. They'll be looking for you, and a wig is no kind of disguise."

The bus from the ferry had deposited them and their suitcases in downtown Victoria. Although it was still only early April, the streets of the old city around the inner harbor were busy with tourists.

"We need a place where you can change before we get a hotel," Monica said. She saw a building across the street, with a sign: *Royal British Columbia Museum*. "They'll have a washroom. Come on."

Dory held back. "I don't want to."

"We've got to," Monica said, taking her arm. "By now, there'll be a description of you circulating to police forces all over the place."

"No, there won't," Dory said. She resisted Monica's pull. "It'll be hushed up. It always is."

"Get real."

"I am real," Dory said. "Do you think this is the first time anybody's used computers to steal money from banks and corporations?"

"I've never heard of it happening."

"Exactly. The companies never want people to know they've been taken. If a billion-dollar corporation admits it lost a couple of million to people like us, it loses ten times that much as soon as the stock market opens."

"You mean the police aren't looking for us?"   Monica couldn't believe it. "We just walk away with all that money?"

"Yes."

Monica thought about it, then shook her head. "I'm not buying it. How much did we get?"

"About fifteen."

"For fifteen million, somebody is going to come looking. Maybe not the police, but somebody."

"Nuh uh. I'm telling you."

"You say so," Monica said. "But I still want you back to normal."

Dory looked uncomfortable. She stared at her hands that held the briefcase. She had not released it since she had left her office.

"I mean, this is fun," Monica went on, "and it's weird that it feels so natural, like you're a girlfriend. But don't you think we ought be more man-woman, at least some of the time?   Hell, most of the time!"

"I am kind of tired," Dory said.

"Well, sure, it's been a big day," said Monica. "Come on, we'll get you changed. Then we'll get the best hotel room in town, order up room service and live like pigs!"

Dory's face wore the look of a small child told to go to bed while the older children get to stay up and have fun. But she let Monica lead her across the street.

#

A busload of elementary school kids, all of them participants in the gifted children's program of a school district further up Vancouver Island, were touring the museum.

"Too much noise and fuss," Monica said. She led the way into a side gallery that contained artworks and crafts of coastal native cultures. Carrying their suitcases, they skirted a long wall of glass cases filled with brightly painted masks that represented deities and mythic figures -- bears, ravens, killer whales, frogs -- of British Columbia's aboriginal inhabitants. There had to be a washroom somewhere.

Monica didn't glance at the contents of the cases, but Dory's attention was abruptly caught by one of the exhibits. The printed cardboard sign behind the glass said it was a ceremonial mask of a First Nation with an unpronounceable name, all k's and w's. Whoever had set up the artifact had wanted the viewer to experience it fully, and had therefore installed a small electric motor behind it. The motor was connected to cables and a small cam mounted on an axis. On a fifteen second cycle, the rotating cam drew in the cables and caused the mask to divide in half lengthwise, smoothly opening and closing like a pair of church doors.

Dory could not move. Each time its two halves opened, the bland outer face of the mask was pulled aside to reveal the grimacing visage of a monster, seemingly lodged in its throat. The creature's blood-red pointed tongue, lolling between bared fangs, gave it an aspect of lazy ferocity. The black holes of its eyes, rimmed in fiery orange, stared back at Dory with a complacent appetite, as a cat might regard an exhausted mouse when the teasing torture draws to an end.

"This way!" Monica stage-whispered. She had gone on a few meters while Dory stood transfixed before the mask. "Come on!" she said.

Dory could not speak, could not move. The relentless cycling of the painted wood, from placid innocence through savage hunger, spoke to her. It was as if it endlessly repeated a tale of horror, a dire warning, but phrased in a language she could not comprehend.

Monica came and took her arm. "What are you doing? It's just a mask. Come on!"

The guards in the provincial museum are members of the Canadian Corps of Commissionaires, which recruits from the ranks of retired military and RCMP careerists. The commissionaire who was watching Dory and Monica was named Baggot. She had joined the corps after mustering out the Canadian Forces, capping a thirty-year hitch with the rank of sergeant major in the military police.

Sgt-Major Baggot expected a certain standard of decorum to be maintained at the Royal British Columbia Museum. Excited young women carrying suitcases and whispering to each other did not come up to that standard.

She marched over, heels clicking on the polished floor. For the thousandth time since leaving the service, she regretted the absence of a swagger stick tight in the blue serge of her armpit. "Is everything all right here?" she said in a voice that said it bloody well wasn't.

Monica jumped at the sudden bark behind her. Dory flinched and drew her shoulders in. She kept her face averted.

But Monica turned to brave the uniform and the permanent frown above it. "We're fine," she said. "We were just looking for a washroom. My friend's not too well."

Commissionaire Baggot's concern was with the suitcases. They didn't belong in her museum; made the place look like a train station.

"There are lockers near the front entrance where you can store those cases," she said, her head jerking sideways in a gesture that said, *move out!*

"We'll keep them with us," said Monica. She ignored the signal. With fifteen million dollars growing interest somewhere in the world, she'd soon have people like this jumping any time she raised her little finger. "Thank you very much," she said in what she meant as a dismissal.

The ex-military policewoman's professional instincts, cultivated through long years of dealing with recalcitrant soldiers, told her to pass up the little hard-nosed one. She went for the one who shrank away.

"How about you, Miss?" she barked. "We don't want to be lugging that big heavy bag all over the museum, do we now?" She leaned closer to Dory, who rotated a little to keep her eyes averted.

"Feeling poorly, are we?" said Baggot, pressing closer. "Why don't I just take that to the front desk for you?"

She reached for the suitcase, and exerted steady pressure to pull it from Dory's hand. She felt a limp resistance. "That's my girl," she said. "I thought you'd be reasonable."

As if the shrinking violet was a powerful machine that had suddenly been switched on, the handle of the suitcase was abruptly yanked from the commissionaire's grip.

"Here now," she began, but then her voice died away to a surprised grunt as the young woman smoothly turned to the ex-sergeant major the most frightening face she had seen in thirty years of military police work.

The commissionaire had seen crazies seized by a manic urge to destroy lives and property. She had seen deeply depressed soldiers who only wanted a quiet corner to be alone with their rifles. She had seen bad soldiers become brawling drunks and she had seen brittle perfectionists break into pieces.

Yet never had she looked into a face so devoid of feeling, so empty of affect, as was turned upon her now. It might have been taken from the wax museum down the street that the tourists still loved to visit. It might have been the death mask of a corpse, or the work of a soulless sculptor.

But it was not the absence of human warmth from the features that caused Baggot to take an involuntary step back. It was the lethal hunger in the eyes, the cold, blank craving stare that said, *I want to see you in pain; I want to make you weep with shame and agony; when you crawl to me I will delight in wringing out of you one more cry, one more droplet of anguish.*

It was there for only a few seconds. The monster had assumed control of the young woman's face as easily as the carved devil appeared in the bifurcated mask, and then had disappeared as quickly. But the ex-military policewoman had seen enough.

"Washrooms are just down there," she said, pointing with her chin. She turned away, clasped her hands behind her back, and watched from the corner of her eye as they went.

Monica had seen nothing. She took Dory's arm and led her to the small square room with tiled walls and stalls. When the door was closed behind them, she said, "Okay, quick now, get that stuff off your face."

Dory lifted her suitcase and laid it flat on the sink counter. She was moving very slowly.

"Gotta be quicker than that," Monica said. "Butch out there might decide to follow up."

"I'm so tired," Dory said. She took a jar of cold cream from her case and reached listlessly to the paper towel dispenser.

"Christ," Monica said, "this has got to be done fast." She took the jar and towels from Dory's limp grasp, lifted her chin with two fingers and began to smear the cream on the made-up face.

She scrubbed the paint away then wiped clean with a wet towel. As the cosmetics came off, the character of the underlying face changed. Dory faded, and was gone.

Michael emerged. When she wiped the last traces from his eyelids, she could see it was he who gazed back at her. She marveled at whatever untapped talent he had within him, that could make such a change.

She also saw that there was something different now. He had never been what she thought of as a strong personality -- she wouldn't have been interested in him if he had been. But there had always been at least the glimmer of a spark somewhere back in the far recesses of his eyes. And now it was gone.

The man with her in the museum's women's washroom was a stepped down version of the man she had picked up that rainy might in Markham. He had waned, somehow, faded like a pair of jeans that had been washed too many times. It was as if the little color that had once been in him had now been mostly leached away.

She wet his hair and combed it back. His eyes were unfocused; they seemed to look through her. "Are you okay?" she asked.

"Sure." The voice was inert.

Monica was not sure what to do. "Let's get you changed," she said, unbuttoning the reversible jacket and pulling it away. She worked fast, but without much assistance from her subject; it was like undressing a life-size doll, or working with a sleepwalker.

It took longer than she wanted, and she kept expecting the door to open, but eventually she had him dressed in jeans, a sweater and sneakers. The Dory clothes went back into the suitcase.

"Let's go," she said. She cracked the washroom door, checked that no one was nearby, and pulled him after her into the gallery of masks. The commissionaire was back at the entrance now, keeping tabs on the kids, studiously not watching the couple with the suitcases.

Monica returned the snub, walking by with her face averted. But the man beside her looked long and hard in passing at the ex-military policewoman, and while his gaze was on her, something hungry crept up behind the dullness and looked again through his eyes.

Out on Government Street, Monica sought in vain for a cab. Apparently taxis did not cruise this street lined with low-rise government office buildings, one of which had been converted into the provincial museum.

Monica walked toward the office towers downtown. Michael was beginning to worry her. He followed along like a robot, stopping when she stopped, crossing the street at her heel. He said nothing, contributed nothing to their situation.

He's stressed out, she thought. *Pulling it off has used him up.* "We need to find a hotel," she said aloud.

And then she saw the sprawling pile of weathered brick and Victorian glass that dominated the inner harbor of British Columbia's capital city.

"Is that that old hotel, the one where the grannies go for afternoon tea and crumpets?" she asked.

His eyes wandered toward where she was pointing. "That's the Empress," he said.

"It's fabulous. We got to stay there," Monica said.

They used her credit card to check-in. The clerk regarded her credit limit and said, "The suite is seven hundred a day, madam."

"Don't worry about it," Monica told him. "We'll pay cash." When she saw the man's eyebrows climb his overheight forehead, she added, "We won big on the lottery."

"Congratulations," said the clerk with a shallow smile, and rang for the bellman.

A little hairless man in an old fashioned uniform appeared out of nowhere, briskly scooped up the suitcases and headed for the elevators. He took them up to a well appointed set of connected rooms that looked out on the harbor, and showed them all the facilities that money can buy.

There were flowers on a delicate table, a tv discreetly confined to a cabinet, a locked refrigerator full of booze and goodies. You could get on the phone and order anything from an ice cream sundae to a full body massage.

The bellhop didn't stop the demonstration until Monica thought to press five dollars into his hand, at which point the small man touched his tiny hat, said, "If you need anything, just buzz the front desk and ask for Warren," and left them.

Monica went to the windows. The view was worth the price, she decided. She tried the plush couch in the sitting room, bounced on the four poster in the bedroom, and wondered at the gilded wall telephone in the bathroom.

She came back to the sitting room to find that he had not moved from where he had stood during the bellman's performance. "Are you okay?" she asked.

"Sure."

"Why don't you sit down?"

"Okay," he said, but didn't move.

"Come on," she said, and led him to the kind of chair she'd only seen in movies.

He sat. She sat on the floor beside him. "How long before we can get the money?" she asked. "Can we do it over the phone here?"

The technical question seemed to draw his focus. "Sure," he said. "We just have to plug into the socket."

"Well, let's do it."

"Okay."

She got the computer from the briefcase, put it on his lap and flipped it open. There was a phone on an end table beside the chair; she disconnected its cable and plugged the jack into the modem socket on the computer phone the way she'd seen him do it.

"Okay," she said, "show me."   She watched very closely.

Working with easy speed and precision, he powered up the machine, started the modem and called up the list of offshore banks where the money had been sent. He manually dialled to get an outside long distance line, then tracked the computer's cursor over to the first bank on the list and double-clicked it.

While the machine was doodling to itself with the dialing tones, he opened another window on the screen's desktop display, and put up the list of local banks in which he had opened accounts weeks before.

The computer beeped to advise that it was now at the E.F.T. security gateway of a bank on the Caribbean island of St. Lucia. He copied the correct code from a list that he called up from another file. As soon as the string of letters and numbers was received, the offshore bank's system welcomed the notebook and invited it to choose from a menu of transactions.

Michael's fingers rattled expertly across the keys and nudged the cursor around, and in a few more seconds the Caribbean bank had sent a long burst of ones and zeros to bounce off a geosynchronous satellite, then to be pulsed through a groundbased microwave relay and finally to become an organized sequence of photons rushing down the LightGuide fiber optic trunk that stretched from one end of Canada to the other.

The signal's total travel time, through all media, was less than a second. Its final destination was the foreign banking sub-system of a computer at the Royal Bank of Canada's main branch in downtown Victoria. Five seconds later, the Royal's electronic guardian accepted and acknowledged the transfer from St. Lucia. The Caribbean bank's computer told the notebook that the transaction was confirmed, and asked if it had any more banking to do.

Michael pressed escape and shut down the desktop program. He switched off the computer and folded it closed. "That's it," he said. He put his hands in his lap and his face became expressionless.

"We can get the money now?" Monica asked.

He stared straight ahead, and spoke as if he was reading from a teleprompter script unrolling on the wall. "Probably have to wait until the main computer gets around to updating the ATM system -- say an hour -- but then you can put the bank card into any cash machine and get some money."

"How much money?"

"Daily cash limit of two thousand," he said, "but the account totals about one hundred and twenty thousand."

"What if I need more?"

"Transfer money to another bank."

Monica looked at the mantelpiece clock above the sitting room's gas powered fireplace. "Okay," she said. "An hour. I think I'll take a swim."

He made no reply.

"Want to come for a swim?" she asked.

"No."

"You just want to stay here?"

"Sure."

"I'll put on the tv for you."

"Okay."

She took the notebook off his lap and put it on the french provincial desk. She turned on the television. Bob Barker came on in mid-sentence, talking about some prize package. She put the remote in Michael's hand.

She went down to the stores clustered in claustrophobic corridors beneath the ornate lobby, and bought a one-piece swimsuit and a robe. She wore them from the store to the hotel's indoor pool, which was deserted except for a stringy old man swimming endless lengths in slow motion.

Monica lay on her back in the warm water, watching the scalloped patterns of light reflected onto the ceiling, and letting her thoughts unwind into the future. After a while, she transferred to the hot tub, soaking in the opaque liquid warmth until every last knot and kink had melted away. Then she flung herself back into the shock of the pool and climbed out on full recharge.

She dried her hair with a towel and walked through the hotel, looking at the stuff in the gift shops. *Real fancy stuff,* she thought, *and I could have all of it.* She watched the well dressed, well fed people in the stores and in the lobby. *Bet I'm richer than you,* she thought, *or you, or you, even you.*

A store in the side corridor off the main lobby dealt in perfumes and toiletries. In one of the windows, they had mounted a display of Victoriana: a man's shaving set of soap in a mug, badger-hair brush and cutthroat razor; a woman's silver-backed dresser set of mirror, brush and tortoise-shell comb. At the back of the display window hung a picture of the old queen herself, looking generally disapproving.

Monica went in and bought herself a jar of bath oil that cost more than she'd ever paid for anything that small in her life. She returned to the suite to find Michael sitting in the same chair, the tv tuned to the same channel. Bob Barker was gone. Now it was a low-rent talk show, with a jeering audience that had nothing better to do than help trashy people to crow over their pointless infidelities.

His eyes were aimed at the screen, but they didn't move. He didn't respond to the boasts or whines of the guests.

"You hungry?" she said.

He didn't answer.

"I'm going to soak this chlorine off me, then we'll get something to eat, okay?"

Still there was no response. "What's up?   You okay?"

"I'm fine," he said.

"Well, do you want to go and eat?"

"I guess."

She came to stand in front of him, put her hand on his forehead. It was cool. "What's the matter?" she said.

"Nothing."

"But you're acting... weird."

He said nothing.

She knelt down beside him, put her cheek on his knee. "Is it, like, some kind of delayed reaction?   You scared somebody's going to hunt us down and take the money back?"

He shook his head.

She straightened up, peered into his sterile eyes. "Then what?"

When he still said nothing, she took his hands. "I want you to tell me what's wrong," she said. "Come on, tell me."

He sighed. "I don't know. I feel okay, just kind of blank. It's funny. When I was working it out, all the planning, it was good. When I made it all come together, even when I had to change a lot of it, that was exciting, scary but still good. Now... it's over, I don't feel much of anything. I just feel like I'm turned down to minimum... like I'm fading away."

She sighed. She regarded his passive form for a long moment, biting her lower lip. Then she unzipped and unbuttoned his pants. She reached into his shorts and fished him out, but he was as soft and inert as a stillborn puppy. She went to work, using her lips and tongue and teeth. After two minutes, there was no response.

"Boy," she said at last, "you really are down."

She leaned forward and kissed him on the forehead. "I know what you need," she said. "A real night out, a little celebration. That'll put you back together."

There was no response. She shrugged. "I'll go and get irresistible, then we'll find the best restaurant in town."

The bathroom was through the bedroom. She used the shower first, washing her hair with shampoo and conditioner that the hotel had left in a wicker basket full of little bottles, then shaving her legs and armpits with a disposable razor she found under the bottles. Then she filled the bath with hot water and poured in the oil she had bought downstairs. She luxuriated in the warmth, surrounded by a cloud of scent that was sweet and golden, the way honey would smell in heaven.

When she opened the bathroom door, Dory was sitting at the dresser in the bedroom, putting the last touches to her face. She turned and smiled, touching the long dark fall of hair from the wig.

"I think I should wear this more," she said. "I like what it does for my eyes. Do you?"

Monica stood in the doorway. "You're feeling better?"

Dory smiled. Her eyes were bright. "Yeah," she said. "I must've dozed off. But I woke up feeling great."   She put down the blusher. "You want to go eat?"

Monica shrugged. "Sure."

Chapter 11

"It could have been worse," Mack said. "Mason could've suspended us."

"He's a very colorful inspector," Harry said. "Mostly puce, shading toward a deeper purple around the jowls when he shouts."

Mack laughed obligingly, but there was no humor in her partner's eyes. She looked at the clock on the wall, said, "It's after eight. I'm going over to Hy's and eat a steak. Want to come?"

"No."

She sighed as she put her coat on. She couldn't help it; it just got away from her. He heard it.

"Sorry," he said. "I would not be good company. Hell, I'd need a personality implant just to get up to bad company."

"Harry," she said. "Don't do this to yourself."

He sat down at his desk and did not look at her.

"You're not the only one she fooled," Mack said. "A lot of smart people got sucked in."

"But I got sucked in deepest."

"We still don't know the whole story."

"Thanks for the straw. I'll try to stay afloat."

"Now, you're going right past tragic and over into maudlin," Mack said. She was heading for the door. "See you tomorrow."

Harry picked up the phone and dialled Treleaven's home number. When the psychiatrist answered, Harry didn't bother with a greeting. "So much for your psychological profile," he said.

"What do you mean?"

"What I said. You were wrong six ways from Sunday. It was all about money."

There was a silence on the other end of the line. Then Treleaven said, "You're not my patient any more, Harry, which means I don't have to be protective of your feelings. So let me tell you you're full of shit."

"I'm full of shit?"

"You were any more full of shit, you'd have to rent space for it."

"You're saying you were right about this three-piece asshole?"

"I'm saying I was totally right."

Harry took the phone away from his ear, looked at it, then put it back. "In what way were you right?"

"It was not about sex. It was not about money. It was always about power."

"Fuck you."

"Exactly."

"What?"

"When you say 'fuck you,' it's got nothing to do with sex. It's about power."

"That is cute bullshit. The guy stole millions, we don't even know how many yet."

"Harry," Treleaven said, "I don't always like you, but I've always respected that eighteenth-century brain of yours. Put it to work and you will catch this monster."

Harry said nothing.

"Come on, detective. You always liked to throw Occam's razor at me."

"What are you saying?"

"That the simple answer is usually right. The guy was swinging around in those corporate data systems like Tarzan in the jungle. He could do all the things he did, and he couldn't crack those women's access codes?   I don't think so."

Harry thought about it. "You're saying it looked like he was going after the money, but he was really after the women?"

"He tied them up, used them, stole their trophies, made them do tricks for him in the places where they had the power that he wanted to take away."

"Yeah,"   Harry said, his mind beginning to turn over. "Why all the complexities?   Why invest all that energy when there are women around every corner?"

"My guess is two things," Treleaven said. "Number one, this guy has a monstrous hatred for strong, capable women. I'd look for a domineering mother, weak father, that kind of scenario."

Harry made a note. "And the second thing?"

"I'm still thinking multiple personalities. It may be he had to fool parts of himself into believing it was about money, or those parts wouldn't have gone along with the monster that lived in their basement."

"No," said Harry. Suddenly the straw was a little thicker. "He had to fool the female accomplice. She had to think it was for the money, maybe she needed it for some good purpose, or she wouldn't have helped."

Now Treleaven said nothing.

"What do you think?" Harry said.

"It's possible."

"It's more than possible," Harry said. "It's probable. Because it's the simple answer." He knew he had been right about the woman who had called herself Dory Novello. She hadn't been cold-bloodedly fronting for a vicious psychotic. The vulnerability he had responded to had been real. *Mack's right*, he thought. *I don't know the whole story yet.*

"Whatever," said the psychiatrist. "The real question is what happens next. Think about that."

Harry did. His brain was back on line now. "If it wasn't about the money," he said after a pause, "then there's no reason it should be finished."

"Now you got it."

"He'll do it again."

"Almost certainly. He loved every moment of it. That part of him will be stronger now than ever before. Strong enough to overpower the more human parts of his psyche."

"Or a woman who's tied to him by some kind of sick connection. Maybe that's what's held him back so far," Harry said. And, inside, a voice said, *She's in danger.*

Treleaven said, "Maybe."

Harry knew what to do now. He needed to get all the information onto the RCMP's serial crime net. It was a two-hour job to fill in the paperwork. But once it was on the shared system, anytime Mr. Three-piece repeated his performance, at least if it was anywhere in North America, it would ring bells.

And when the bells rang, Harry would come running.

"I got to go," he told Treleaven, but before he hung up, he said, "Thanks."

"Apology accepted," said Treleaven.

Harry dug around in his desk drawers and found the multi-page RCMP form. He picked up a pencil and licked its tip, like a schoolboy facing a final exam, then he started filling in the blanks.

The late shift came in. Harry waved at the ones who said hello, and kept working. A half-hour later, his phone rang. It was Dorcas Novello.

"I couldn't stop thinking about it," she said, "I decided it shouldn't wait till tomorrow, so I phoned Eric -- he's my chief assistant -- and asked him to go down to the office and dig out that information. He just called back."

"And?" said Harry.

"And nothing. There is not one scrap of information on the guy anywhere in our shop. Not on paper and not in our data system. You can bet Eric got curious -- he ran different data recovery programs to restore anything that had been wiped, and still got nothing."

"What does that mean, data recovery?" Harry asked.

"Well, when you 'erase' a file on a computer, you don't actually rub it out. You just tell the computer to ignore it and to use the memory space it takes up as if it were empty. You sort of write over it the way you would record over a piece of used audio tape. But if that space has not been re-used, the original data will still be there, and you can tell the computer to stop ignoring it and it will call it up again."

"But your assistant couldn't do that."

"No," said Dorcas Novello. "Our friend had done some pretty fancy microsurgery on our system. Any data item that referred to him -- payroll, medical benefits, you name it -- was thoroughly expunged. The individual sectors of the hard drives had been targeted for irreparable damage. He must have done it from outside. I'd like to know how."

"Christ," said Harry.

"It gets spookier," said Novello. "Like I say, Eric gets curious, so he starts looking for information on this guy here and there -- credit checks, school records, voters lists. Nothing. He goes to the next level -- police information systems..."

"Wait a sec," said Harry. "Those are not for civilian use."

"Give me a break, Sergeant," said Novello. "We do data security for a living. We helped design some of the systems you guys use -- can we help it if we happen to remember how to talk to them?"

Harry shrugged. "Fair enough, I guess. So what did you

find?"

"I'll teach you a new word, Sergeant: *muk-woy*. It's Cree Indian. It means 'nothing.' And that's what we found -- nada, zilch, zippola. Not a byte, not a bit."

"You're saying this guy has covered his tracks."

"No. That would be like saying Michelangelo touched up the pope's ceiling. I'm telling you that our friend has done the near impossible -- he's made himself invisible. We can't find a single reference to him anywhere in any data system that we can access, and we can access more than a few, Sergeant."

She paused, and Harry heard her puff on a cigarette. Then she said, "When he joined us, we took his fingerprints and filed them with the RCMP -- standard practice. Eric went looking for them tonight. They're gone, whisked away."

"But he can't function without an identity," Harry said.

"As my daughter would say, 'well, duh,' Sergeant," Novello said. "My guess is, he's got a whole bunch of different identities, either borrowed from real people or invented from scratch. He'll have everything from passports to kindergarten attendance records." She puffed on the cigarette again. "He's not going to be findable."

It was not what Harry wanted to hear. "Let me think about this," he said. After a moment, he said, "What about the female accomplice, the one who pretended to be you?"

"Nothing we can do," said Novello. "We can unravel anything if we have one loose end to start with. But we don't have that loose end."

"Shit," said Harry.

"Same here," said Novello.

"I'm going to think about this some more," he said. "Can I call you back?"

"Sure."

After he hung up, Harry swiveled his chair around and looked out the window. The sky above the downtown was a featureless, luminous gray, like a cheap special effect in a low-budget movie. He stared at the overcast that was as dull as death, and let his eyes unfocus. Then he suddenly swung back to the desk and worked the phone.

"Ms. Novello," he said, "I think I've got your loose end."

"Shoot," she said.

"Ask your guy to find a small to medium-sized manufacturing firm somewhere in southern Ontario that went under during the hyperinflation of the early eighties. The man who owned it died soon after. Daughter of the family went into computers, took some course in data security."

"This would be the female accomplice," Novello said.

"Yes. It's the life story she gave me. Maybe it was based on truth. Is it enough to go on?"

"Oh yeah. I'll call my guy, have him start a search. Shouldn't take too long. Call you back."

"If I'm not here, I'll be at home."   He gave her his home number.

She didn't call in the next hour and twenty minutes, during which he completed the serial rapist profile. He took it down to the data processing section, where the night shift was doing manpower stats, and talked the supervisor into entering it into the system immediately.

When he got back to the squad room, Mack was sitting on the corner of his desk.

"I saw your car was still here, so I came up."

"I maybe got a lead on the accomplice," he said.

"I don't want to talk about the case, Harry."

"Then what?"

"I want to talk about us."

He sighed. "What us?"

"Exactly. What do you say we go somewhere?   Away from all these ears."

"I'm waiting for a call."

"Tell switchboard to forward it to your cell."

He said nothing.

"Harry, I'm going to say this one place or another!"

People were looking. "Okay," Harry said.

They went in Mack's car. She drove in silence, the tires *scissing* on glistening black pavement that reflected the colored signs of beer parlors and pawnshops lining the skid road section of Hastings Street. They followed the curve up the little hill at Victory Square, where the old main drag was starting to reclaim its respectability. At the big hole on Burrard where the customs house used to be, Mack jogged up to Pender and took it west to Georgia and the park.

She eased over to the right lane, letting the rest of the traffic stream along the causeway toward the Lions Gate Bridge and the North Shore. She took Stanley Park Drive. It paralleled the seawall, winding around past Brockton Point and then following the straight section to Lumberman's Arch.

She parked in one of the angled spaces near the old pool. Despite the slight rain, a few rollerbladers and pedestrians dodged each other on the asphalt. A kid with dirty blond dreadlocks was sitting on a bench and falumping his home-made drum. Across the harbor, the piles of sulfur scrubbed from natural gas deposits way up north were a ridiculously bright yellow against the dull bulk of the mountains.

She hadn't said a word yet. Harry stared straight ahead as the scattered drops randomly decorated the windshield.

"So," Mack said, after a while.

"Yeah," said Harry.

The silence lengthened. Mack leaned back and rubbed her nose. "I don't know where to start," she said.

"Maybe you shouldn't."

She nodded. "Oh, yes, I should. I have to. So, okay, the kid goes for broke."   She cleared her throat, turned and faced him. "You're a good guy, Harry, and I'm attracted to you. I always have been, and I think you know it."

"Mack."

"Shut up and let me say this. We've been partners now a couple of years, and during that whole time I figured we would never be having this conversation. Know why?"

"Why?"

"Cause you were dead, Harry. I didn't see much prospect of a relationship with a man who had killed himself and presided over his own funeral. I might as well have had a thing for your old friend Occam."

He said nothing.

"So I accept that. Day after day. And then, what happens? It's like one of those movies where corpses rise from the grave and start wandering around in shopping malls. All of a sudden, it's 'there goes Harry Lukovitch, the romantic cavalier, in hot and heavy pursuit of the blonde mystery woman,' and he's hanging out at her place and he's phoning her and wanting to protect her and he wants to talk about her -- *to me!*"   She took a breath. "And you know what I think?"

"What?"

Mack swallowed. "I think, well, that's okay. He's alive again, got a little juice flowing through the system. Sure, he's not aiming any of this at me, but what the hell, where there's life there's hope."

"Look," Harry began.

"Shut up," she said. "Just shut up. Because right in the middle of this big romance, Miss Blonde Superbitch turns out to be the bad guy's girlfriend. And that means Harry gets it in the nuts again, and there goes the life, and there goes the hope and we're right back where we fucking started!"

She loosened her seatbelt and leaned her head against the steering wheel. He listened to her breathing.

"Well fuck that noise, Harry!" she said to the dashboard. "I'm not just going to stand there while you go sliding down into your comfy little tomb again. You got hurt. So what?   Life's supposed to hurt. Get used to it."

"It's okay, Mack," he said.

She turned to him. "No, it's not okay, Harry."

"Yes it is."   He put a hand up to forestall the argument. "Listen to me. You're right, I've been a little crazy the past couple of weeks. I don't know what it was, the woman, the asshole in the mask, whatever... but you're right, something happened."   He watched the silhouette of a freighter ease into his view of the sulfur piles.

"And?" Mack said.

He sighed. "And I guess I came up from wherever the hell I've been since Jeannie and I... you know. And, sure, I did get whacked in the hoolihans by the whole thing with the money and the computers. But I'm not going back in the hole again."

"You're not."

"I'm not. Truth is, I feel okay."

"What about the woman?"

"I don't know. I can't help feeling that she didn't want to be a part of it. I can't believe that she would knowingly set up the victims -- her *friends* -- for what he did to them. But I just don't know."

"Well, I know something," Mack said.

"What?"

"I know I want *my* chance," she said. "I want *my* turn!   And if it doesn't work, okay. No blame. I'll get another boyfriend. I'll get another partner."

"Jesus, Mack."

"Jesus, nothing, Harry!   Bottom line is you *owe* me. I pulled you out of a bottle two years ago. It was a lousy, messy job, but I did it!   I did it because I thought you were worth keeping. I still do. I put in my time, partner -- now you pay me back my investment."

Her face was pale in the glow of the streetlights dotted along the park drive. But the look she gave him was level and steady. There was no vulnerability about her; she didn't want protecting or saving -- she wanted him on equal terms, an even trade.

"I don't know if I've got whatever it is you're looking for," he said.

"I'll take the chance."

He swallowed. "Okay. I've been crazy in a bad way enough times. Maybe I can try being crazy in a more productive vein."

"Good," she said. Then she leaned over and kissed him.

It had been a long time since Harry had been kissed, long enough that he couldn't really remember the last one. He knew it had to have been Jeannie, but then he thought that not being able to recall the actual event was maybe a good thing. Maybe it was a sign that part of his past was far enough behind to be left alone. Then he stopped thinking and concentrated on what he was doing.

"Okay," he said, eventually, "now what?"

She started the car. "Now you come over to my place, I make you some dinner, you eat the dinner, we go to bed. Just like real people."

"I don't know..." he said.

"Don't argue."

"But I don't know if..."

"If what?"

"If you can cook."

She backed the car into the park drive, shifted gears and hit the gas. "You don't know the half of what I can do," she said.

#

Dory was drunk, spread out on the hotel bed that seemed to move down and to the left every time she closed her eyes, but every time she opened them the bright spill of light from the bathroom stabbed her retinas. Monica was in there, running water and clunking things on the counter and humming the endless, maddening dance tune that the band wouldn't stop playing until Dory thought she was going to run screaming from the club.

After a hundred years, Monica finally came out of the bathroom, wearing the robe she'd bought downstairs. She sat on a corner of the bed, causing that side to dip alarmingly. Dory made a sound of weak protest.

"How you doing, honey?" she said. "Little drunk?"   She was tipsy herself but holding it well. "You should've danced. Burns off the alcohol."

"Um," said Dory. "I got to sit up."   She struggled to rise.

"Nah, stay there," said Monica. She pulled down the zipper on the side of Dory's black skirt, popped the button and pulled it off. The slip came with it, and the pantyhose were next. Monica got her hands under the waistband and began to tug them under Dory's buttocks.

"What are you doing?" Dory said. "Don't do that."   She batted at Monica's hands, but not fast enough.

"There," said Monica. "Now let's wake him up."

"Stop it!" Dory protested, as Monica's hands made her feel something she didn't want to feel. She knew she couldn't look, knew she had to resist, but she was too far sunk into the muzzy grip of the booze.

Something was happening that shouldn't be happening. Monica was throwing open her robe and shifting over to straddle her.

"No, don't!   Please don't!" Dory said. She looked down, saw the *don't look there!* and pulled her gaze away. Her head swam from the motion. She felt Monica's weight settle atop her, heard her grunt, then felt something warm and slick enclosing her -- *No!   You can't touch that!* -- and suddenly the black stuff came up from her neck, over her chin and mouth and nose, and when it reached her eyes, *thank God*, Dory welcomed it, and was gone.

    #

Monica got him inside her and started to rock her crotch back and forth with that sharp hunching motion that rubbed her where she needed it. He wasn't quite hard enough -- not at first -- and he protested and squirmed for a while, but she kept on. This one wasn't for him.

She thought about the man at the club where they'd gone after dinner. She'd clocked him all the way across the room. He was looking at her. When their eyes met, he bee-lined over to where she and Dory were sitting. The music was banging in Monica's head, and she'd gone right out onto the dance floor. No talking, no names, just straight into the rhythm and the heat and the smell of clean sweat coming from under his cologne.

He was a good size and well muscled, kind of a Jeff Goldblum thing working for him, and he never took his warm brown eyes of hers except to run them lazily up and down her body, so she could practically feel their touch on her breasts and belly and thighs.

She thought about those eyes and the way he moved, and she ground herself down harder on the man beneath her. Now something was happening. The wriggling had stopped, and suddenly he was fully erect inside her. Something was definitely happening; his body all at once seemed to pull itself into a new shape, all softness and hesitation gone. He grabbed her hips and thrust himself up into her, fast and powerful, lifting her off the bed, banging against her cervix.

"Oh God!" she said, and met him stroke for stroke, the orgasm like a eruption of hot steamy mud washing up from her thighs into her belly. She grunted again and followed with a voice-cracking moan.

She was still gasping when he rolled her over, staying tight inside her. His left hand grabbed her wrists with a fierce strength and pinioned them together over her head, while his right pulled her leg up until the ankle hooked over his shoulder. And all the time he drove himself into her, battered her insides with a rapid, machine-like rhythm, silently, with monotonous power.

She felt him come. He made no sound, and when he was finished, he rolled off her and lay face up on the bed, staring at the ceiling. She half sat up, felt her mound where his bony groin had pounded her. It was tender.

"Ow," she said. "That was pretty intense, lover."

He said nothing. His eyes were closed.

"Aren't you going to get that stuff of your face?   It'll be all over the pillow tomorrow."

He turned his back on her. She went into the bathroom to cleanse herself. When she came back, he was asleep.

#

Harry had to admit, it had been all right -- every bit of it: food, bed, and afterwards. She made good morning coffee and didn't push for morning conversation until he'd had some.

Her spare robe was much too small, so he wrapped himself in a comforter and they sat facing each other at different ends of her couch: he with his legs crossed, she with her feet tucked underneath her bottom. He remembered the curve of it, the firmness, and the memory brought a stirring in his groin. He rearranged the folds of the quilt and concentrated on the coffee.

"What is this, not Colombian?" he said.

"Kenyan," she said. "It's a little rough, but I like it."   Her eyes watched him over the rim of her mug. He noticed it had a light green stripe that almost matched her eyes.

He held his cup in both hands, resting it on his lap, feeling the warmth through the comforter. "So," he said.

"So," she agreed.

"So what do we do now?"

She stretched. "Go to work, catch bad guys, bitch at each other, argue -- the usual."

"So this doesn't mean..."

"This means a lot," she said. "But I didn't notice any magic wand last night. Just 'cause you begin something doesn't mean it's complete, zip, bang, like that. Happy ever after takes a while."

"Yeah," he said. "Okay. *Stillicidi casus lapidem cavat.*"

"What's that?"

"Slow and steady wins the race. That's just an approximate translation."

"Approximate does me fine," she said.

His cell phone buzzed. It was somewhere in the heap of clothes in the bedroom. "I can ignore that," he said.

"Nice," she said, "but we'll take the thought for the deed," then called after him as he went for the phone, "You ain't the only one can sling a quote, sweetie."

The call was from Dorcas Novello. Harry came back to the couch with the cell phone. "Anything?" he asked.

"Nothing," she said. "Eric found two possibles that almost fit the profile, but in both cases the kid in question was male. He traced them anyway. One's working for a video store in Hamilton; the other one's dead."   She paused, and he could hear her exhale the cigarette smoke over the mouthpiece. "I think I remember that one. I was living not that far away. About a year after the old man killed himself, a natural gas explosion blew to house to nothing. Took out the whole family -- mother, sister, and the kid who had the computer course. Wasn't enough left of them to bury."   Another drag on the cigarette and a exhalation of smoke. "Shame, too. Eric looked up the boy's marks -- he was going places."

"Huh," said Harry. He asked questions, took down the particulars.

"Anything more I can do?" Novello asked, when he was finished.

"Don't think so," Harry said. He thanked her and turned off the phone.

"No help?" Mack asked.

"No."

They sat in silence for a while.

"You want to talk about it?" Mack asked.

"About what?"

"Jesus, Harry!"

He looked at her. "I'm sorry," he said. "I don't know what to say."

"How about, 'I really felt something for her and it hurt when I found out she wasn't what I thought she was?'   That could be a beginning."

"Okay," he said, "but the thing is, I don't know what I felt for her. It was weird. I was weird."

He could say the word to himself. *Obsession*. But somehow, he didn't want to say it to Mack. It wasn't that he was ashamed of it. It was more like being astonished by it, as if one day he'd turned around and found another part of his body -- a second head or a set of wings -- that he hadn't known was there.

He tried to tell Mack about it. "It kind of challenged my whole idea of who I was. When I was with her, I found myself doing things and feeling things that weren't like me at all."

"I think I know what you felt," Mack said.

"Oh yeah?"

"Yeah. You felt like her big brother. Like you were going to protect her from all the bad stuff. Then it turns out she was bad stuff right from the git-go. That's gotta hurt. But you also got to let it go now."

Harry thought about it. "You're wrong," he said.

"Where?"

"She was not part of the bad stuff. I would've known. She was scared -- tough on top but scared underneath, I could sense that -- and she was trying to put distance between herself and the whole situation."

"Well, yeah," said Mack. "I mean, if I was mixed up with Mr. Three-piece, I'd want to put a continent in the way."

"Treleaven was right," Harry said. "He had some kind of power over her, and she couldn't get away from him. That's what I sensed, her helplessness; that's what pulled me to her."   He looked Mack in the eye. "And maybe still does."

Mack shook her head. "I don't buy it," she said. "Let me be blunt and rude, Harry. Your whole thing is about protecting helpless women. You're practically a cliche. You met the woman, you felt something for her. She made your dick a little hard, but these days you have trouble with that, so you had to transform her into Pearl Pureheart, someone you could play faithful guard dog for. Which she sure as hell wasn't."

"You're still wrong. I know what she was."

"A good girl mixed up with bad company?" Mack said. "Don't forget, we found that stuff under *her* bed, not his."

Harry sighed. "Okay, I don't know," he said. "Maybe you're right."

"It's not such a bad way to be, you know. Every woman likes a little Sir Galahad in a man."

"Actually, it was Lancelot who was the romantic knight, the one who had an affair with Guinevere. Galahad was really uptight, repressed, all business, chasing after the Holy Grail."

"I used to know somebody a little like that," Mack said. She leaned closer, put her hand under the comforter. "Now, you want more coffee, or do you want to take a shower?   With me?"

Harry said he would take the shower. It was what Sir Lancelot would have wanted him to do.

Chapter 12

There were bruises on Monica's wrist. She noticed them as she was getting dressed. There was another on her right calf, where he had gripped her last night. She chose a long-sleeved blouse and slacks from the growing assortment in the bedroom closet. Then she heard a knock on the outer door and a voice said, "Room service."

It was the little bald man who had shown them the room when they checked in. He smiled at her and wheeled the cart through the door, then began transferring dishes to the french provincial table while making encouraging remarks about the weather.

Monica signed the receipt and sat down to eggs benedict and coffee. "Breakfast!" she called.

Michael had been in the bathroom beyond the bedroom, showering and getting the gunk off his face. He came through now, scrubbed clean and wearing her robe.

"Do you want me to get you one of those?" she said.

He shook his head and sat opposite her, reached for a piece of toast, and bit off half of it. His cheeks bulged and the muscles in his jaws rolled in and out. He gulped coffee to liquefy the mass in his mouth and forced it down his gullet, then took the rest of the slice in one bite.

"Lost your appetite and found a donkey's -- that's what my mom would say," Monica told him.

He made no reply. His attention was entirely on the food. He lifted a dish cover, found crisp bacon and grabbed two pieces of it. It followed the toast. There was fruit -- melon balls and pink grapefruit segments in a bowl; he scooped some up in his fingers and pushed them into his mouth. The juice ran over his lower lip.

Monica watched him eat. She'd never seen him like this before. Something was different this morning, the way something had been different about last night. There was a new intensity, a crisp, sure speed to his movements; not a donkey's appetite, she corrected herself, more like a wolf's.

She had had enough of the eggs. She put down her fork and said, "So, what are we going to do?"

His head came up from his plate, the eyes hard and bright the way she'd seen them once or twice before. He made some kind of dismissive noise around the food in his mouth.

"No, come on, where do we go from here?" she said. "I mean, this is nice, I can get used to this, but we can't just sit around hotel rooms and go shopping for the rest our lives, can we?"

He stared at her another couple of seconds, then went back to eating. There was something missing from the way he looked at her, something that made her uneasy. She got up from the table and went to look out at the harbor.

"We ought to be investing the money," she tried again, "buying real estate, mutual funds or something. I'm no financial genius, but even I know that."

She waited for an answer. The only sound in the room was the noise of his eating. She came back to the table. "For Christ's sake, say something!" she said. "When you were planning this whole thing, there must have been something you wanted to do?"

His face changed from within, became the introspective young man she had picked up in the rain. He chewed and swallowed to clear his mouth. "I did used to think about opening a theater, maybe even a little repertory company, off Broadway."

She laughed at that. "Yeah, that'd be great!   You could get your picture in People magazine on opening night!   You could stick it up on the wall in your prison cell!   Come on, get serious, will you?   We're criminals!"

His face hardened again. He put his palms flat on the table and pushed himself up. The look he gave her drove the laughter out of her voice.

"Come on," she said. "Whatever you want to believe about corporations not wanting bad publicity, we can't just go and advertise ourselves. Be reasonable."

He froze. His teeth ground together; she could see the muscles clenching under his ears. He stood fully erect and pushed the table out of the way.

"What..." Monica began.

There was a knock on the door. She went to open it, quickly. It was the little bellhop. He bustled into the room. "Sorry," he said. "I forgot to take the right copy of the receipt for the catering manager."

It was on the wheeled cart where he had left it in the corner of the room. "If you folks are all finished, I can take the dishes now," he said.

"Sure," Monica said. "I think I'll just go down to the lobby."

The little man began loading the dishes from the table onto the cart. "Beautiful day," he said. "Beautiful city out there."

"Maybe I'll take a walk," she said. The door was still open. She grabbed her purse and went out.

"Anything else I can get you, sir?" the bellhop said. But the male guest had gone into the bedroom. *Newlyweds*, the bellhop thought. He'd seen a lot of them come through these rooms. He always tried to do a little extra for them -- not for tips, but because he liked to see young couples get a good start.

Later, he saw the man in the men's clothing shop in the hotel's lower arcade below the lobby. He was trying on a vested suit. *Snappy dresser*, Warren thought.

\#

Commissionaire Baggot thought of the entire museum as her theater of operations, but the holy of holies was a small cubicle off the cloakroom. Here she repaired for breaks and to undo any hurt that associating with civilians -- particularly underage civilians -- might do to her uniform.

The little room contained a desk and chair, a kettle and teapot, and a cupboard in which she kept a complete spare set of skirt, tunic and cap. The creases were knife-edged and the buttons burnished brighter than when they had come fresh-minted from the stamper at the factory.

At ten a.m., the commissionaire unlocked the front doors to the museum and took up her position in the foyer. At eleven, she began the first of her regular rounds of the galleries. At noon, she stopped at her cubicle for her lunch break.

The masked man was waiting behind the door. He hit her as she came in, a hard blow to the back of her neck that drove her to her knees. Later, she reported that while she struggled to get up, he struck her four more times, coolly and deliberately, before she lost consciousness.

\#

The story about the family that died in the natural gas explosion bothered Harry. "Fatal accidents that leave unidentifiable corpses always bother me," he told Mack. "What was the name of that OPP guy we had a drink with at the seminar in Calgary?"

Mack shuffled through her address book until she found the name and number. Harry called the man up, went through the *Hey, good to hear from you* routine, and got a referral to the Ontario Provincial Police detachment in Mississauga, where the gas explosion had taken place. Three minutes later, he was talking to the detective who had caught the case, a senior cop named Kapuschinsky. Mack listened in on her phone.

"Yeah, I remember that one," Kapuschinsky said. "The family business went blooie. First time I ever heard about computer hacking -- somebody stole every scrap of information on a big order and that sank the operation practically overnight. Next thing you know, dad's sucking on a twelve-gauge, leaves a note on the computer saying bye-bye, lotsa luck."

"On the computer?" Harry said.

"Yeah. Then, couple of months later, boom goes the house. They found some of the mother's body on the front lawn, blown through a window. The two kids, well, there were bits and pieces, but not enough to put in a grocery bag, you know what I mean? Time they got the fire out, they were cooked down to ash."

"Any insurance?" Harry asked.

"Some, not much. Went to some cousins. Nothing there." Harry heard what he thought was the OPP detective unwrapping a stick of gum, followed by the sounds of chewing. "Why?" Kapuschinsky asked. "You got some indication there was foul play? We didn't come up with anything like that."

"Any missing persons about that time, runaway teenagers, that kind of thing?"

The OPP cop snorted. "Just the usual weekly dozen. What's the deal here, Detective?   What's your interest?"

Harry said, "Just a maybe. Maybe the brother and sister didn't die in that explosion. Maybe they got rid of mom and dad and went into business for themselves."

He told the man about the impersonation of Dorcas Novello, the attacks against the four women and the looting of the corporate accounts.

Kapuschinsky looked through the file. "Their names were Michael and Angelina Kasparin," he said. "Not enough remains to do a dental records check. Coroner was pretty sure about the girl, though."   He read Harry some of the autopsy notes. "Not so sure about the boy. Main thing there was a partially recovered hand with the kid's high school ring."

"What about pictures?" Harry asked.

"Family album burned with the house," the OPP detective said. "Got high school yearbook pictures here in the file. Want 'em?"

"Can you fax them?"

"Better than that," said Kapuschinsky, "I'll run 'em through the scanner and attach them to an e-mail message. Way better quality than fax if you've got a laser printer. Gimme your Telnet address."

Harry looked helplessly at Mack. She spoke into the line, identifying herself and reeling off the Department's secure Telnet number for incoming files.

Kapuschinsky said, "Five minutes," and rang off.

"Let's go down," Harry said.

By the time they got to the data and communications center, the e-mail from Mississauga was in the system. Mack asked the duty operator to route the images to the high resolution printer. Twenty seconds later, the machine rolled the sheet of paper with two pictures on it into the out-tray.

Harry grabbed it. "That's her," he said. "That's Dory."

Mack took it. She saw a reasonably clear black and white of a pretty sixteen-year-old in a Farrah Fawcett hairdo. "It could be," she said.

She looked at the other picture. There was a distinct family resemblance. "Same eyes and brow" she said, "maybe a different mouth."   It was hard to tell because the boy's lips were bent into a knowing smirk.

"It's her," he said.

They went back up to the squad room. Harry sat at his desk and looked at the pictures. Mack sat on the corner of Harry's desk and watched him. He was getting that look again.

She tried not to let it get to her, but when he continued to gaze at the kid's picture, she knew she couldn't sit by while he settled back into the dream. She said, "I know what you're doing."

"What am I doing?" he said.

"You're looking at the innocent kid, and you're building yourself a story. She's the pure princess who's sacrificed herself to serve the evil ogre, the nasty brother she's sworn to protect."   She put the back of her wrist to her forehead. "Unwillingly, she aids his twisted plotting, hoping that in time the shining example of her goodness will win him back to the path of righteousness."

"Knock it off," Harry said.

"Oh, if only some noble knight could come riding over the hill. If only Sir Harry..."

"Shut up!" he said.

"Sure," Mack said. She stood up. "But you get out your medieval razor and cut yourself a slice of this one: whatever people do, it's usually pretty much the thing they *want* to do. If she's alive and helping him, it's cause she wants to."

"You're wrong."

"Well, if I am, I'll give you a big fat apology. And if I'm right..."

"What?"

"You go back to Treleaven, dig this crap out of yourself and come back to life. I care about you too much to see you wasted on a fairy tale."

#

His name was Littlemick. That was to distinguish him from his father, who became Big Mick. Littlemick was "born" one day when Michael was two-and-a-half years old. It was a day when his father came home from the plant with an oversized teddy bear -- a "just-because" present -- but his mother wouldn't let Dada give it to him, because he'd been bad again: he wouldn't eat the peas.

This time, Littlemick had been strapped into the high chair and left there for most of the afternoon. His SuperKid tee-shirt had not stopped the plastic restraint harness from rubbing the skin of his shoulders and waist raw. He had marks that looked and hurt like long cigarette burns.

It was after four o'clock. He'd been crying for almost three hours. He was out of tears and the moisture in his throat had dried out after the first forty-five minutes; he could only manage occasional short bursts of croaking between long periods of ragged, diaphragm-shaking breaths.

Littlemick saw his father come through the front door and down the hallway into the kitchen, the big brown soft thing in his hands. It hurt the boy to reach out his arms, and when he tried to say, "Down, Dada," he sounded like a little frog.

Big Mick would have let him loose, would have picked him

up and cuddled him and given him the bear. But Pearl said, "No, he can damn well stay there until he smartens up." So dad went upstairs to change out of the three-piece suit he wore to the plant -- "Got to show them who's boss," he always said -- with the carnation in the buttonhole.

When Big Mick came back down, he tried again. "Come on, Pearl," he said. "He's just a little kid. Be reasonable."

It was what he always said, but she never was. She rounded on him, letting loose the accumulated complaints of all the years they had been together, the disappointments never to be atoned for, the failures never to be redeemed, until Big Mick put his hands over his ears and walked away. He went into the den and turned the tv on loud.

Seeing his father turn and leave him, Littlemick *stepped aside* from the crying child in the high chair. He stayed in another place from then on, always nearby, but sometimes he came out for a little while, especially when the boy got older and went outside, where other people would make the mistake of trying to boss him. Littlemick was a strong fighter, very strong, and not afraid of anything.

The bear lived in the hall closet until Christmas, the boy forbidden to touch it. Then his mother gave it to Angelina, his little sister.

In time, his mother stopped them from calling him Littlemick; she preferred Michael. As the boy grew older, other parts of him occasionally became detached from the core. Some of them were short-lived and evaporated in a few months; others were absorbed by ever-hungry Littlemick.

When Michael went to school, Littlemick began to appear more often. His abilities were expanding, but his appetites had ...intensified. Sometimes, he got too enthusiastic. There was trouble.

Littlemick found it was best to remain in the background, most of the time, only coming out when the risk of discovery was slight. As he grew more aware of the differences between what he needed and what others would tolerate, he came to see that he would have to find a less restrictive environment than southern Ontario. Before he reached his teens, Littlemick realized that that would require substantial amounts of money.

He began to develop his plan.

Michael was attracted to computers. He picked up quickly what others were much slower to grasp. He persuaded his father to buy one for the company, and soon became its principal operator outside of school hours. But personal computers were new and costly then, and the business was not doing well. Michael's father said the boy would have to wait for a machine of his own.

Littlemick did not like to wait. Besides, owning a computer was a crucial part of his developing plan. By watching what Michael did, and learning what Michael learned, he discovered how to convert the information in the company's computer into money. He had Michael buy the best home computer on the market.

But then Big Mick found out about it. There was trouble again, more trouble than Michael could handle. Littlemick had to come right out in the open to clear things up.

After that, Littlemick kept to himself for a long time, surfacing only when he had to nudge Michael along. With a computer in Michael's room, to which Littlemick added capacity and peripherals as needed, the plan flowered. There were occasional obstacles to its progress, but Littlemick overcame them through Michael's ingenuity or his own direct action.

Michael's mother was not much of a problem any more, not since she began to drink heavily and grew fearful of leaving the house. But Angelina was becoming a complication. She was too smart, too observant. She liked to pry into things that didn't concern her -- such as Littlemick's directory on Michael's computer. Although it contained a large number of files, Michael somehow never noticed it.

Littlemick caught her in Michael's room, reading through a text file. "Just a story I'm writing," he had Michael say, but she didn't believe it. Michael got flustered, and pushed her away from the computer. Then the girl started shouting.

Things looked to be getting out of control, so Littlemick came out and hit her, the edge of the hand hard in the throat, the way the books said to do it. She fell down, and he watched her face turn different colors. She tried to crawl through the door, but he closed it.

After she stopped making the gargling noise, Littlemick realized that he hadn't much time to arrange things. Fortunately, he had worked out a number of scenarios for this kind of situation, although he had not expected to use any of them for several months.

But, under pressure, he could be adaptive.

While his mother was in the den, watching her "stories," Littlemick drove down to the place where the street kids hung out. He had Michael hire a runaway who wanted to sell sex and brought him home. He killed him in the kitchen, then put his clothes and his high school ring on the body.

He took the dead boy and girl down to the family room, where he loosened the fitting on the gas pipe to the glassed-in fireplace. He knew that, some time before evening, Michael's mother would go into the kitchen to put on the kettle for her herbal tea.

Then he downloaded what he needed from Michael's computer onto floppies and walked away. He already had enough of the plan in place to step into another existence. He began to work on it in earnest now.

Later, Littlemick was surprised to find that a piece of his dead sister had come with him. The persona had taken root far out at the edge of his awareness, where she was mostly just a collection of tag phrases heard in his head, things Angelina had used to say. He tried to dig her out once or twice, but somehow she always grew back.

The lack of success against the sister-thing frustrated Littlemick. He did not deal well with frustration, so he decided it was best just to ignore her.

In time, the continuing evolution of Littlemick's plan required that a new part be added to Michael, a female part. But when a space was created for her, it was the sister-thing that inflated to fill it. Irritated, Littlemick tried to uproot her, but she stubbornly hung on. In time, he gave up the fight; she tended to do what he wanted done, acting as if it were her own idea. Besides, the real girl's annoying curiosity had not come with her.

The plan was years in the growing, elaborating and complexifying itself in several directions, until it emerged full blown and ready to erupt from the basement of a duplex on West Sixty-Third Avenue. Littlemick was savagely pleased with the results, even after the last-minute changes that the arrival of Michael's greedy girlfriend had necessitated.

Now it was time to reap the rewards of all the planning and effort. Time to dispense with the unnecessary parts -- the last vestiges of Michael, the annoying Dory, and the money-hunting

Monica.

Then Littlemick would go to a place Michael had researched for him, a place where he could at last be purely, simply himself, could devote all of his time to providing for his own unique and special needs. The airline reservations were made: a first-class trans-Pacific flight, then a regional shuttle to a less restrictive country where fifteen million dollars bought privacy and the fulfillment of even the most sophisticated tastes. An agent was already negotiating for an estate in a province far from the capital.

#

There were seven banks within a three block radius of the Empress Hotel. It took Monica two hours to visit all of them; at each one, she opened checking and savings accounts in her own name.

The hotel suite was empty when she returned, the notebook computer where he had left it on the french provincial desk. She quickly connected the telephone cord to the modem jack and powered up the system.

She worked slowly and methodically, pausing at each step to remember what he had done. Tracking the cursor around took some practice, and the last time she had used a keyboard it had been attached to an old IBM Selectric in a high school typing class.

But by perseverance, she came through. She called up a bank in the Bahamas, matched the right code to the account and had it transfer an amount to one of the accounts she had opened during her walk. It took her longer than it had taken him, but eventually she was looking at a six-figure balance in her new checking account.

She steadily emptied the rest of the Bahamian bank's trove, routing the money, bank by bank, account by account, to her own constellation of balance sheets. Then she moved on to a bank in Manila. She intended to take half of the fifteen million, then leave a note.

She spun the cursor across the screen and brought it to rest on the security gateway of the Philippines bank. She was getting better at this. She thought she would get her own little computer and learn more.

Her fingers moved more quickly now. She put her tongue in the corner of her mouth and squinted at the screen. When she connected with the Manila bank's services menu, the machine beeped at her. As the sound faded, she heard the lock turn on the outer door.

#

Treleaven was homeward bound in the rush hour traffic on Southwest Marine Drive when he heard the five-thirty news summary on CKNW. He turned off into a side street, parked in front of a new megahouse that was under construction, and punched Harry's office number into the cell phone.

"Did you hear about the museum guard in Victoria?" he said.

"No, what?" Harry said.

"I think it's Mr. Three-piece again."

Harry said, "Let me check it, I'll call you back."

He had a couple of good contacts with the Victoria Police Department. The one he called had caught the commissionaire assault case, and gave Harry a quick rundown.

Harry called Treleaven's cell. "You're nuts," he said. "All we know is that the attacker wore dark clothing -- don't know if it was a suit or what. There was no mask, no knife, no sexual assault, no goddamn carnation."

"All of that was only surface noise," Treleaven said. "The core of the incidents is the same. He attacked a woman who represented power, and he stole the symbol of that power."

"What, you mean the spare uniform?"

"I mean the spare uniform."   Treleaven paused. "He's out in the open now. He's focused on the one thing that, for him, is everything -- power over the powerful, dominating the dominators, as long as they're female."

"We don't have a good description," Harry said. "The guard was hit from behind, never really saw him. There's just a ticket taker, got a rear view of the guy going out the front door with the uniform on a hanger."

"Tell your contact over there that there'll probably be more victims -- could be a female politician or somebody prominent in the community. Warn them."

"I will."

He hung up and told Mack what the psychiatrist had said.

"Tomorrow, we should go over and talk with your man at the Victoria PD," Mack said. "Maybe we can help."

"You think Inspector Mason would authorize the trip?" Harry asked.

"Right now, he'd authorize anything that gets you and me out of his sight."

"Well, you do the asking," Harry said. "For some reason, he doesn't seem to appreciate my qualities lately."

"I appreciate them," Mack said. "What say you trot them over to my place?   We could get a couple of steaks."

He said nothing. He picked up a paper clip and began to bend it into complicated shapes.

"I promise I won't mention the touchy subject," Mack said.

Harry threw the twisted piece of wire into the waste basket, and said, "Okay."

#

Monica moved fast. Before Michael was through the door, the notebook was off and closed, the telephone jack was out of the modem card and she was standing away from the desk, staring out the window. She'd been lucky, though. He had come down the hall with his hands full. Before he entered the room, he had to put down the shopping bags he was carrying, to free his hands for opening the door. The seconds he spent picking them up again were her time of grace.

She turned as he came in, tossed her hair back in a way she was pretty sure got to him, and said, "Oh lover, I'm sorry I was mean. Let me make it up to you."

He closed the door and stared at her.

She couldn't take those inert eyes for more than a few seconds. "What's in the bags?" she said.

She moved in closer and looked inside. The bags bore the names of men's clothing stores. She reached into one and pulled out a mass of dark cloth that was folded around a hanger. When she shook it loose, it became a narrow-lapeled suit with a vest, conservatively cut from good material.

"This is nice," she said. "Off the rack?   You're lucky you've got just the right build."

He said nothing, only watched as she delved into the other bags -- there seemed to be a lot of them -- and brought out suit after suit. They were all sedate, dark blues and grays, not a conspicuous check or stripe among them, each one just the thing for a well established businessman or professional.

She reached into the last bag. It looked like another navy blue suit, but when she got it out, the silvery buttons winked at her. "It's a uniform," she said. "Where the hell'd you get this?"

The shoulder patch said *Canadian Corps of Commissionaires*, and it had a skirt. She held it up against her chest and spun to see herself in the mirror. It was for a much stockier woman than she was.

"Is this for me?" she said. "A little costume party?"

His eyes narrowed.

"I'll go put it on," she said. She took the uniform into the bedroom and closed the door. She leaned against the old wood and let her breathing return to normal. *Just one more time,* she told herself. *One more and we're clear.*

She undressed and put on the uniform, with nothing underneath. The fit was very bad, but she didn't think she would be wearing it too long. She went into the bathroom and brushed her hair straight back in a severe style, then sprayed it heavily to hold it in place. *That ought to do it*, she thought.

She returned to the bedroom and stood for a moment in front of the closed door to the sitting room. Then she took a deep breath and reached for the doorknob. *Show time!* She flung the door open.

He had changed into one of the dark suits. It gave him a different look, leaner and simpler somehow, like a neatly assembled weapon that's designed to do one thing, and do it with complete efficiency. He'd plucked a flower from an arrangement the hotel provided with the suite, and was threading it through the buttonhole in his lapel. His eyes were no longer dead -- instead, they showed a fierce appetite.

Monica stepped into the sitting room and let go the breath she had been holding. "What do we do now?" she said.

Chapter 13

Dory fought her way up to consciousness, struggling to break free of a dream in which she was being smothered by a thickening layer of cold ooze. It was like being buried alive beneath the bottom of a stagnant pond. She sucked air into her lungs, and stared wildly around at the darkness. Her heart thudded several times before she recognized the hotel room.

There was a sharp pain somewhere. Her hands reached automatically for the part that hurt, then recoiled -- *don't touch! don't look!*

She sat up, ignoring the soreness. She was alone in the bed, and naked. The clock radio said it was nearly four o'clock. *The dying time*, she knew, *when people are at lowest ebb.*

She felt as if she was dying, as if all the life had drained from her, leaving only thin curd and sour dregs. Her arms hung heavily off her shoulders like tubes of meat sewn to her skin. Her chin was on her chest. It took a supreme effort to raise her hands and rub her eyes.

Her mouth was dry. She needed a drink. She slowly forced herself to stand and felt her way into the bathroom, ran water into a glass and drank it down.

The tap ran on. There was a voice in the gurgle of liquid running from the faucet and swirling down the drain. The words were indistinct but the message behind them was clear: hate and violence and futility.

She shut off the flow and fled the bathroom. The bedroom now seemed stifling, the air thick and soupy. Dory opened the window and tried to get a breath, but it had started to rain and now the voice was in the sound of the drops hitting the evergreen shrubs on the hotel lawn.

She backed away from the window, but the voice came in after her. Now it was in the whistle of her own ragged breathing and the thump of her own blood pulsing in her ears. She shook her head, said "No!" and tried to push the insinuating whisper away.

It sneered and chuckled and snarled, lashing at her with words that were now almost intelligible. The voice was telling her terrible things, things that would destroy her, dissolve her, if she let herself listen to them.

She closed her mind to the repulsive sound, tried to think of something else, something good, something that was for Dory.

She remembered, then, although it was hazy. She turned on the light. The furniture seemed to leap at her. She looked for her purse -- not on the table, not on the floor, not under the bed -- and finally found it in the back of the closet.

The detective's card was in her wallet. It was only when she saw his name in print that she remembered it. There were two numbers beneath the name: office and cellular. She turned it over and saw his home number.

She knew it was too late for the office. She fumbled for the phone next to the bed, touched the digit that opened a long-distance line, and dialled the home number. She heard the buzz of the phone ringing, far off in Vancouver, and the ugly voice crept into the silences between the rings.

It mocked her, threatened her, reviled her. She wouldn't let the words shape themselves into meaning but the hatred and contempt seeped through. She clutched the phone to her cheek as if it were a charm against an evil spell.

The phone rang and no one answered. She made a helpless sound, and disconnected the line, then tried the cellular number. The line hissed at her, the bad voice riding the static, then she heard the phone ring, again and again.

The voice pressed on her ears. It was breaking through the barrier. She moaned. And then another voice in her ear, sleepy and thick, said, "Lukovitch."

"Harry," she said. "Help me. He's going to kill me."

There was a silence on the other end of the line, then, "Dory? Where are you?"

"I don't know any more," she said. "A hotel room. Something's wrong with me. I can't remember. He keeps crowding me. Please, help me."

"Is he drugging you?"

"I don't know. Help me."

"I'll help you," Harry said, "but you've got to tell me where you are. I'll come right away."

He said more, but now his voice seemed to recede, like something heard in a dream. Dory struggled to hold onto the connection, but she became aware of being enclosed by vast pressure, forcing itself upon her, squeezing in from all around. It was as if the room had been plunged a thousand fathoms beneath the sea, and now the walls were besieged by an immense, bone-chilling force, a dense, black fist closing inexorably around her, to crush this little sphere of light and air into nothingness.

The phone on the night table seemed to draw back into an impossibly distant circle of light. A gelatinous darkness was drawing in, and Dory could only see as if through an elongating, narrowing tunnel. Harry's voice shrank and diminished, became no more than the creaking of an insect's wings. Dory saw her own hand, a million miles away, replacing the handset in its cradle.

She was almost helpless now. She was frozen, the smallest, most defenseless animal in the night forest, where something strong and implacable circled her burrow, snuffling up the scent of her unprotected warmth, thrusting its bristled snout into her hiding place.

The sussurating sound of the monster's voice kept telling her to give up, to fade through despair into oblivion, to be done with it and let it go. But she would not. She dragged her strangely distant body over to the bed and, though it quivered and squirmed, she made it lie down. She curled it around herself, and held onto consciousness as long as she could, thinking, *He will come.*

#

Harry sat on the edge of Mack's bed, the cell phone in his hand, still hearing the *click* of the disconnection.

"Was that...?" Mack said.

"Yeah," Harry said. He felt cold and sick. "He's after her. I got to find her. Where is she?"

"Christ, Harry," Mack said. He sounded like some lost little boy. She sat up. "Give me the phone. Get dressed."

The room was chilly, gray with predawn light. She turned on the lamp beside the bed and took the cell. She got a dial tone then pressed the asterisk, the six and the nine. The BC Tel computer came on the line and told her the number of the phone that had last called Harry's cell.

Mack wrote the number down, then dialled 1-604-555-1313. The computer's female voice -- recorded by an actress chosen for her warm and friendly tone -- answered and told her exactly what to do. She used the phone's keypad to enter the number she had written on the pad, and the computer was back to her in seconds.

Mack switched off the phone. "Victoria," she said. "The Empress Hotel, no less." The computer had even given her the room number.

She got up and padded barefoot across the hardwood floor to the window, the air of the unheated room raising bumps on her naked skin. The sky was clear outside.

She was thinking, while Harry threw on his clothes. "A guy I know has a float plane on Pitt Lake, couple of miles from here. He could fly us over, land right in the inner harbor."

"You think he'd do it?" Harry said. He was putting on his shoes without untying the laces.

"He wants me," Mack said.

Harry looked at her then. Four hours before, he'd been inside her, snug in the little cocoon of her bed. "I'm sorry," he said. "It's all happening again. It's not fair to you."

She reached for the clothes she had thrown on the floor, began pulling on her jeans. Then she paused. "It's okay," she said. "It's better we get to the end of this thing. No more mystery, no more what-ifs. We wrap it and go on."

She called the flyer. He agreed to meet them at the plane. He was only rated for VFR, so they could not take off until there was enough light to meet the standards of Visual Flight Regulations. He promised them they would touch down on the Victoria waterfront before seven o'clock.

\#

Littlemick woke up just after six. Some kind of dream pulled at him, but he burst through it into consciousness. He lay curled on the bed, naked and blinking in the early morning quiet, then pushed himself up and went into the bathroom.

He got under the shower and soaped himself. The head of his penis was sore, the sensitive nerves outraged from overuse. He cleaned it carefully, then let the hot water sluice over his belly and rinse away the lather.

Four suits hung in the bedroom closet, along with a flock of white shirts -- french cuffs, no buttons -- and several striped ties. He chose a charcoal gray with a six-button vest, and admired its fit in the closet's full-length mirror. It hung flat down his back, with not even the suggestion of a wrinkle of fabric between his hard shoulders.

When he was fully dressed, Littlemick opened the bedroom door and went through into the sitting room. Michael's woman was where he had left her, bent lengthwise over the desk.

Last night, she had assumed the position willingly -- at least at first. He remembered the sequence of events very clearly.

She'd come out of the bedroom wearing the commissionaire's uniform. He liked that. At his urging, she had lain face down on the polished mahogany, and reached her hands down to grasp the curved french provincial legs. He had moved quickly then, producing the duct tape from the shopping bag. First, he taped her wrists in place, then bound her ankles to the legs at the other end of the desk. A short length of tape closed her mouth.

He'd stood behind her and slowly raised the fabric of the uniform skirt like a theater curtain climbing up her thighs and over her bare buttocks. He'd put a finger inside her and found her dry, but that didn't signify. He unzipped and pushed himself into her. She jerked and made a sound that was muffled by the gag. He thrust harder, and that brought more noises from her. It was only seconds before he came, slamming himself into her so hard he drove the desk almost a foot across the carpet.

He pulled out and wiped himself clean on the skirt, then positioned the chair a few feet behind her and sat down. He listened to Michael's woman making angry noises. He watched her pulling against the bonds, but he had taped her thoroughly.

Eventually, she stopped struggling and making sounds. He sat in the silence for a few minutes, looking at her. Her delicate parts were red and swollen. He got up and moved into position again. When he touched her, she tried to shrink away.

He did it four more times during the night. Inbetween, he sat for long periods in the padded chair until the cold ache rose again in his groin. He slept a while before the last one. It hurt him to enter her. His penis felt as if it had been flayed and the woman moved only spasmodically.

He had scarcely a drop left in him, and his climax was like the thrust of a red hot needle along his urethra. When he pulled out of her swollen grip, it was like knives cutting at him. His legs trembled.

He had staggered to the bedroom and torn off the suit,

leaving it puddled on the floor. Shutting the door on the woman's noises, he had fallen onto the bed and slept solidly through the remainder of the night. He thought there might have been a dream about the sister-thing, but he couldn't recall it.

Now, as he came into the sitting room, the woman heard him. She began to squirm and make noises. He checked her bonds, found them still secure. She flung her head left and right in rage, but he paid no attention.

He stood behind her and watched. She was very red and puffy between her legs. A smear of semen had run down one thigh and dried into scaly flecks. He fondled himself through the cloth of his suit trousers, found only soreness -- no stirring of desire. He was finished with her.

He asked Michael what he thought should be done with her. There was very little of Michael left now; he had dwindled to a small voice far back in an out-of-the-way corner of Littlemick's mind -- although, when necessary, he could be taken out and worn like a mask.

Michael's voice said they should leave her tied up in the bedroom closet, with the *do not disturb* sign on the outer door. By the time anyone came to check, they'd be sipping champagne on the Singapore Airlines flight.

The image of the wine glass reminded Littlemick that he was very hungry. He felt the hunger as he felt all physical desires lately; the craving was maddening, almost irresistible.

He'd been too busy to have dinner the night before, but the hotel coffee shop would be opening soon. He would go and get something tasty -- anything he wanted -- and bring it back to the room. He'd eat it all up, then he'd take care of Michael's woman.

He put Michael back to sleep, then checked to make sure that the sister-thing was also sleeping. When he got settled in his new place, he would have the strength to deal with her. She would not be like Michael, retained in a diminished form, to be brought out whenever a face and voice were needed; the one who now called herself Dory would be devoured utterly. He would not leave even a whisper of her to annoy him.

As for Michael's woman, the bedroom closet would hold her. But there would be no need to tie her up. He hung the *do not disturb* sign on the door handle and went downstairs.

#

The six-seat DeHavilland Beaver rattled like a tin hut in a hurricane and bounced alarmingly in the turbulence that occupied the narrow zone between the low cloud cover and the gray waters of Georgia Strait. To Harry, it seemed as if the plane's nose usually pointed more west than south, but the pilot assured them they were on course for Victoria.

Mack sat in the co-pilot's seat, wearing the spare set of headphones so that she and her boyfriend wannabe -- his name was Terry, she had said -- could converse over the roar of the single engine. Harry peered out the window as they ran out of water and flew over a dark mass of land. The plane banked a little to the left, and the detective could see a thin blade of wet road cutting through the second-growth forest that blankets most of eastern Vancouver Island.

He's following the Island Highway. Harry thought. Aloud, he said, "Can this thing go any faster?"

Neither Mack nor Terry heard him through their earphones. They were too busy talking into their little chin mikes.

The little plane flew south, bumbling over the farms of the Cowichan Valley, then gradually climbing as the highway made its way over the rise called the Malahat, then snaked down the other side.

The clouds broke here, as they often do, leaving Victoria in the clear. Harry looked ahead and saw the sun glaring silver off the tongue of the sea which thrusts up from the Strait of Juan de Fuca into the tip of the island, creating the natural harbor which had first induced the Hudson's Bay Company to build the fort that would grow into the province's capital.

Harry had read up on the history of British Columbia when he moved to the coast. He had been a voracious reader then. Now, he tried to think about the old dates and facts to keep his mind away from what he might find when they touched down in the harbor. But it wasn't working. The way Dory had sounded on the cell phone kept creeping into his mind.

The Beaver banked again, and they fell abruptly, sickeningly, through a pocket of air. They were low over Victoria's northern suburbs now, looping around to the west so they could come in from the south. The pilot was talking to the harbor air control, getting clearance to put down in the space between the marinas and taxi across the water to the seaplane dock.

They hit the water, bounced once, then came down for real. The pilot cut back on the throttle and angled them toward the little floating jetty. A man wearing grimy coveralls and a peaked cap that advertised a brand of motor oil came onto the dock and hitched a rope to the plane's wing.

The moment the door opened, Harry was out of the plane. He stepped over the float to the wooden planks before the propeller stopped turning and headed for the stone steps that led up to Government Street. He could see the mansard roof of the Empress above the granite lip of the promenade wall. It was big enough to be a castle in the early morning light.

He wasn't thinking at all now. His mind was narrowed down to its purest concentration, to an undiluted need to *act*. The prospect of Dory in danger drew him like a greyhound after the mechanical lure.

Mack thanked the pilot and came after him, running up the stone steps onto Government, empty now in the early morning, looking somehow naked without its usual covering of tourists and souvenir hawkers and street kids banging on home-made drums.

She sped across the pavement, shouting, "Whoa! Wait a minute, Harry! Hold up!" but he did not slow the metronomic pace that was carrying him toward the Empress.

She caught up with him halfway down the hotel's broad front walk, grabbed his arm and half pulled him around. The look on his face sent a rush of mingled fear and pity through her.

"Harry, wait up! Please!" she said. "We can't go busting in like a two-horse cavalry. We have no jurisdiction here. We at least need the guy from the Victoria PD to come in with us."

She would have felt better if he'd shouted at her, but his voice was low. There was pain in it. "I'm not here to be a cop," he said. "This is just about me and her. She's there. She's in trouble. How can I not go in?"

"Christ, Harry," she said, "we don't know what we're going into." She told him she had used the plane's radio-telephone to call Victoria PD and ask them to contact the detective handling the commissionaire assault. "He's coming down to meet us. Let's wait for him."

"I told you, I can't," he said, and moved to take his arm out of her grasp. "I have no choice."

But she didn't let go. "Okay, you're going in, I'm going in. But first we get something straight."

"Later," he said.

"No, Harry -- now. You need to rescue the princess from the goblin castle, I understand that. And I'm here, I'm the faithful sidekick. But you're not the only one with needs, partner. I need something. Not the white knight, I'm no princess. I need the rest of you, Harry."

"You don't know if there is any rest of me," he said. "I don't know if there's anything there."

"Oh, there's plenty, Harry, and I want it. I want it all."

She put her arms around him, pulled him into her. He opened his mouth to say something, but just then the hotel fire alarm went off and drowned him out.

#

Monica heard the elevator chime ring. She waited, counting to sixty three times, to be sure he was gone. Then she gathered herself for the effort.

He had hurt her. She felt a burning soreness in the ring of muscle that closed her vagina. But worse than that were the cramps in the backs of her thighs, knots that she couldn't straighten while she was bound to this desk.

Now that she was alone, she didn't bother pulling at the layers of tape that held her to the polished wood. She'd tried that enough times in the night to know that she could not get loose that way. She'd had plenty of time to think through her situation as the night slowly wound its way to morning. She now knew that there was more to Michael than she had thought.

At first, when he had shoved himself painfully into her, she had wanted to think it was only play-acting. He was fantasizing, pretending to be the three-piece rapist from the tabloid pages. But then, as he came at her over and over, always in silence, paying no attention when she moaned in pain and tried to wriggle free, the chill realization crept up from the bottom of her mind that this was no fantasy he was working out on her unwilling body. *He's the one*, she thought as the pain ripped through her.

She remembered the newspaper stories, remembered reading

about what he had done to those women. *That's where the money came from*, she thought. *From women like me, tied up, feeling pain and fear, and wondering what he was going to do next. And I'm part of all that. I* helped!

The papers had said there was a knife. That would have been the old Nazi dagger he'd had her thrust into the wood of the office door. The cops had that one, but did Michael have another weapon now, somewhere in the suite?   When he'd finished with her, would he pack his bags, cut her throat, and walk out the door?

She hadn't dared to try anything while he was in the bedroom, even when she heard him snoring. If she made a noise, he might come out with a knife in his hand and end it all. She'd felt terror when she heard him get up and stumble around in the darkness; the fear had not been relieved when she heard Dory's voice. *He's cracking up!* she thought. *I don't know who's going to come out of there next.*

Then he emerged in the morning, cold faced and dressed like a banker. She'd steeled herself not to make too much of a fuss if he raped her again, just grit her teeth against the pain,   get through it and hope he'd go downstairs for breakfast -- she was sure he wouldn't be ordering from room service.

When he went out without a word, her hopes rose. Then they'd fallen as it occurred to her that he might be playing a sadistic game -- waiting outside the door to rush back inside and ruin her plan. So she'd counted the three minutes from the elevator chime, then counted another sixty seconds before she put the plan into effect.

She couldn't pull herself free of the tape, but she was not immobile. The bonds held her only at the wrists and ankles, and her limbs were not stretched to their ultimate length. Her arms had some play in her elbows and shoulder joints; her legs could flex a few degrees at hip and knee.

She'd experimented a little during the night. Now she did it for real. She slid her torso as far as it would go to the left, lifting as much of her right side as she could from the desk's surface, then she threw her body as far to the right as it would go.

She was strapped lengthwise to the piece of french provincial furniture, her head hanging over its right-hand edge, her legs over the left. The sudden jerk to her right lifted the slender back legs of the desk slightly off the carpet and caused the single shallow drawer under the top to slide out a couple of inches.

But then the desk's back legs thumped back onto the carpet. She took a deep breath, gathered herself, and tried again. This time, she remembered to fling her head to her right, along with the rest of her body.

The back legs came up a little higher -- she felt the tilt increase this time -- and the drawer inched out a bit farther. But the desk's back legs dropped back onto the floor.

Monica hauled herself as much onto her left side as she could, straining to gain height above the polished wood so she could increase to the maximum the force of momentum her body would hurl against the desk's inertia.

She tried to force her aching, cramped limbs to stretch a little more, just another quarter inch of total height. She told herself that each attempt increased the odds of success: the desk drawer extended out like a lever, the thick tourist guidebook it contained would add its ounces to the total effort. *It has to work*, she thought.

Poised to fling herself once more, she heard the elevator chime. For the first time, tears flooded her eyes. *Son of a bitch! He's coming back!* For a moment, it was too much; for a moment, she was just a tired, battered woman, helpless and in pain, seeing her one chance unfairly ripped from her grasp.

She heard a lock turn and a door open. But the sounds were distant, somewhere down the corridor, in another suite.

The moment of despair passed, and rage drowned the spot where the hopelessness had drably flowered. Monica threw her weight to her right, the desk's back legs came off the floor, high, then higher yet. The drawer rasped farther out, and she willed it to help her.

The desk leaned, teetering on its front legs. Monica pulled to her right, stretched the joints in her left shoulder and hip to their utmost, craned her neck to increase the downside weight.

The desk drawer slid another fraction of an inch outward, and then -- slowly, so slowly -- the desk toppled forward onto its front, pinning the woman's right arm and leg under it.

Monica didn't care about the pain from the pressure of the desktop's thin, hard edge against her upper arm. Nor that the drawer had slid free and ended up underneath the inward curve of her waist.

She was triumphant now. Able to move a little, she scooted sideways, pushing the desk ahead of her, still spooned against its polished surface. When she had put some room between her and the drawer, she rocked until she could roll onto her back.

Now the desk rested upon her. She was thankful the hotel used fancy furniture. She didn't know the name of the style, only that it was lightweight, with thin curved legs. The whole thing weighed no more than a coffee table.

This was the ultimate test of her plan, worked out during the long, pain-ridden hours of the night, while the monster snored and grunted to itself in the next room. Bound facedown to the desk, her full weight resting on it, there had been no way to break free. Once she got onto her back, there were only a few lengths of wood between her and escape.

She began to stretch. This was how she had envisioned it. Lying on her back, she would push her legs down toward the floor. At the same time, she would draw her arms back and above her head. The desk's spindly legs would break or be torn from its corners. And then she would be free.

She stretched. She strained with all the strength her cramp-knotted muscles could muster. She was rewarded by a slight creak from one of the desk's joints. She drew up all her reserves, grunted like a woman in childbirth, clamped her jaws tight till they ached, and pulled at the mahogany with her bound wrists and ankles.

But nothing happened. The thinness of the dark wood was deceptive. It was strong, and the glued dowel pegs that held its legs in place might as well have been bolts of steel. She could not pull the desk apart.

No tears came this time. She lay on her back in the ridiculous blue uniform, legs and arms in the air, a piece of furniture stuck to her. She stared at the ornate plasterwork on the ceiling, until it seemed that she was again strapped face down onto the desk, hovering in space over a white floor that was figured in flowers and arabesques. She was spent, inert, beyond saving now.

Then, from out of her belly, out of the burning ache in her groin, came a burst of roiling rage that overtopped anything she had ever felt. She looked at her hands, suspended two feet apart above her head, and she willed them to *come together*.

A sound grew in her throat, the thick, growling breath of an animal pushed to its last extremity. Her thin biceps stood out like marrows. Her forearms corded and shook from the pressure. Her diaphragm clenched and, behind the tape gag, the growl became a snarling roar.

And the legs of the desk snapped like dry kindling. Her arms suddenly came free, each now wearing a wide bracelet of tape that snugged a short length of broken desk leg to a wrist. The splintered end of one of them had ripped the skin of her inner arm. She paid no attention, but tore the sticky fabric away until her hands were clear.

She sat up, with difficulty, having to lever up the top of the desk that still pressed against her front. She scrunched around the obstacle to rip the tape from her ankles, working fast, her ears tuned to the sound of the elevator chime.

The last piece came away and she threw the desk off her. She sat on the carpet and rubbed the backs of her thighs, digging her fingers into the tortured flesh, then reaching down to pull her toes toward her, stretching the long muscles.

Then she rolled over and rose from her hands and knees to her feet. *First things first*, she told herself and tottered into the bedroom. The notebook computer was on the night table.

Okay, she thought, *let's get the hell out of here*. She yanked off the sweat-drenched commissionaire's tunic and let the baggy skirt fall to the floor. She badly wanted a bath, but there was no time. She pulled on panties, jeans and a sweater, found her purse and sat on the bed to stuff her feet into runners.

She never heard the elevator. She was pushing her heel down into the second shoe when she caught the sound of the outer door opening. She came up off the bed fast, but there was nowhere to go. He was between her and the only exit.

He stood in the outer doorway, a plastic-wrapped plate of pastries in one hand, and a paper cup of coffee in the other. She saw the surprise in his face give way to ungovernable rage.

She dove for the bedroom door, slammed and locked it, then ran to the window. It opened for her, but outside was a sheer drop of fifty feet to the roof of the entrance pavilion. She looked around, and saw the phone.

There was no dial tone. Instead, she heard a recorded voice listing various amenities the hotel had to offer. She swore. He had thought of it before she had, had used the phone in the sitting room to dial up an internal number, tying up the line and preventing her from calling for help.

She heard the bedroom door handle rattle, then came a thump as he threw himself against it. She knew the wood was solid, but enough effort would eventually tear the lock out of the jamb.

She went back to the window, looked up and down the dawn-lit street. Just one early walker would do, someone she could scream to, someone who could get help, dial 911. But, at this hour, the harborfront promenade that would be filled most of the day with gawkers and hawkers was deserted.

A seaplane was taxiing to the dock down below the promenade. She saw a man pulling on its wing. Then two passengers got off, a man and a woman chasing him. Monica yelled to them, but the roar of the plane's engine ate her voice. Then they dropped out of sight below the sea wall.

Two more thumps hit the door. A hairline crack appeared in the jamb. She needed time to think, to *plan* something, but he wasn't giving her any. She scooped up the notebook and her purse and fled into the bathroom, slamming the door after her.

Chapter 14

Warren had been a bellhop most of his sixty-three years, and he had seen it all. But when he heard the heavy *thumps* coming from the honeymooners' suite, he knew he had to investigate.

He put the meal cart that carried somebody else's continental breakfast against the wall of the corridor and went to the newlyweds' door. He listened, heard more muffled noise, and rapped sharply on the gilt trimmed wood.

There was sudden silence from within. Warren knocked again, said, "This is the floorman. You folks need any help?"

Again, there was no answer. Warren produced his pass key, put it in the lock, turned it and opened the door an inch. He knocked again, said, "Floorman," and slowly opened the door, giving whoever was on the other side time to compose himself.

It was the man, Warren saw. The room was a mess -- *Christ, they've busted the desk!* -- and the man looked more than a little frazzled.

The bellhop was torn. Like most long-service employees, he thought of the Empress as his home. The desk was an antique, probably shipped around the horn from Europe before there was a Panama Canal. Seeing it broken was like losing one of his own possessions.

On the other hand, it was obvious this was a relationship that needed all the help it could get. He elected to ignore the outrage -- the hotel's restoration staff could probably repair the damage.

"Now, now," he said, coming right into the room. "Having trouble with the door, sir?   Sometimes these old locks will stick. You do know that your room key can open any of the locks in the suite?"

The man said nothing. He had already struck Warren as being what Warren called a curious specimen. He was breathing hard, like a man pretty wrought up about something, but his face was as deadpan as a wax dummy.

"Had an accident, I see," the bellhop said. "Not to worry. Housekeeping can send somebody up."

"Later," the man said. The voice seemed odd to Warren. But he saw that the man's face was looking almost normal now. And he was taking out a wallet and offering a twenty dollar bill.

Warren made the money disappear with practiced speed. "Don't you worry," he said again. "Sometimes these things take a little time and gentle persuasion. If I can be of any assistance, just buzz the front desk and ask for Warren."

The man said, "Thank you," and formed a vapid smile. Warren let himself out.

#

The phone in the bathroom was playing the same stupid recording. Monica jammed the hand set back into the receiver. She put her ear to the door and listened. She thought she had heard another voice.

She opened the bathroom door to hear better, only a crack. She put one eye to the opening and peered through, just in time to see the door to the sitting room open and the monster coming through it, the key in his hand.

He looked at her, and for the first time she saw him smile. It was not a good thing to see. She slammed the bathroom door and locked it, thinking even as she turned the little deadbolt, *He has a key*.

There was a complimentary toothbrush in a basket on the sink. She snatched it out, slid it under the door and kicked it until it jammed. Immediately, she heard the key turn in the lock. The door came in a fraction of an inch, all of his weight on the other side.

The toothbrush stopped him. But he forced it again, and the plastic shaft skidded a little on the tiled bathroom floor. The door opened an inch more.

Monica looked around her. There had to be something she could use. "You're not getting me, you dickless son of a bitch!" she said.

There was a sound that might have been a laugh, and he hit the door again, driving it open another inch.

"Bastard!" she screamed, and cast her eyes around the little room. There was a razor, but it was a disposable plastic thing that couldn't do more than scratch him. Nothing heavy enough to hit with -- even the ashtray the hotel provided was a delicate piece of work that matched the furniture.

But the ashtray gave her an idea. She slapped the drum of toilet tissue on its hanger on the wall, so that it unrolled and spilled onto the floor in a pile of soft paper. She scooped it up and wadded it into a loose ball.

The monster hit the door again, once, twice, the third time driving it back enough to get an arm in and reach for her. His nails clawed her wrist, but she stepped back out of reach.

The hotel ashtray was on top of the toilet tank. It held a small box of matches, thin wooden ones not much thicker than toothpicks. She tucked the wad of paper under her arm, got the box open, her hands shaking, took one out and scratched it against the striking strip on one side.

The match broke.

The monster pulled his arm back out of the door and slammed his shoulder against it again. Down on the floor, the toothbrush had done all it could. When he stood back, they both knew there was more than enough room for him to squeeze through the door.

But Monica hadn't waited. She dug out another match and struck it. This one lit. She put it to the wad of paper in her other hand and set it ablaze.

He saw what she had done, and smiled. He leaned forward and put his face into the wide space he had made between the door and the jamb and laughed at her. It was an ugly sound -- a dry *Heh-heh-heh-heh*, the kind of laugh a sadistically intelligent toad might give just before flicking out its tongue to seize an insect and crush its thin, brittle carapace to flinders.

Monica thrust the ball of burning paper toward him, but he scarcely bothered to move back from the small fire. His flat, stony eyes regarded her through the flicker of blue and orange flames. He smiled and gave his ugly laugh again, then pursed his lips and blew the little heat back toward her.

That was when she brought the aerosol can of hair spray from the back of the sink and shot it straight through the fire into his face. The highly flammable chemical hissed from the nozzle, ignited over the burning paper with a whuffling rush, and bathed his face in fire.

His skin peeled back. His eyebrows and eyelashes were singed away. The pain was sudden and horrific. Instinctively, he gasped, drawing superheated fumes into his windpipe, to sear and dry the moist flesh. He stumbled back, coughing, his hands thrown up in front of his face.

Monica stepped through the half-open bathroom doorway, the smoldering wad of paper still in her hand.

"Here," she said. "Have some more."

She held the fire close to his chest and gave him another long shot of burning hair spray that shriveled the flower in his lapel and set the suit jacket on fire. He fell backwards, but she followed him, dousing him with flame.

He gave a croaking scream now and rolled on the floor, trying to beat out the blaze she had ignited on his chest. But the chemical had soaked into the suit's fabric and would not go out. He got to his knees, tore the jacket off over his head and flung it from him. It landed against one of the gauzy, floor-length drapes that framed the bedroom window. The thin fabric caught immediately. Flames climbed the wall and licked at the wooden valance above.

Littlemick stood up, coughing, slapping at a small patch of blue flame on his vest. He looked for the woman, but she was gone.

\#

Warren was clattering back down the hall, the room service cart loaded with used dishes and cutlery, when the door to the honeymooners' suite flew open, and he saw the bride came running out, clutching something to her chest. A waft of acrid smoke trailed after her.

The bellhop had seen that before too, and knew what to do. There was a CO_2 extinguisher next to a fire alarm on the wall across from the elevator. He grabbed the one and pulled the other, then strode into the suite.

"No need for panic, sir!" he shouted over the *braaannnggg* of the fire bell, as he entered the bedroom and began spraying chilly clouds of carbon dioxide in the direction of the fire. "Please walk to the nearest fire exit!   Remember to take the stairs!   Don't use the elevators!"

The groom snarled at him, pushed the bellhop out of the way and ran from the room. *Errol Flynn did exactly the same thing back in '56*, Warren reminded himself, tilting the extinguisher to smother the flames sneaking along the top of the window.

\#

The hotel put its most experienced staff on the front desk

early in the morning, the time when tour groups arrive and depart and chaos is never more than a small mistake away. The polite young man Harry confronted was a seasoned professional, not one to be flustered by any combination of fire alarms, agitated patrons and a pair of police detectives shouting questions at him.

"No, sir, you may not go up there," he replied. "It appears to be on fire."

"Room 705!" Harry shouted over the din of the alarm bell, for the fourth time.

The imperturbable clerk sighed and spread his hands, palms down. Harry thought Pontius Pilate couldn't have done a better job of disavowing responsibility. "Please use the stairs to your left," he said, and indicated the main staircase.

Harry and Mack turned toward the stairs just as a young woman in jeans and a sweater came jittering down the bottom steps, a notebook computer clutched to her breasts. She legged it across the lobby and out the side door to the cab stand. In her wake, a trickle of guests, some of them in nightclothes, swelled into a thicker flow.

The clerk turned to a woman whose blue hair matched both her voluminous nightgown and the ribbon around the neck of the small, highly vocal dog she clasped to her capacious bosom. "How may I help you, madam?" he inquired.

Harry and Mack took the stairs two at a time, staying against the inner wall, pushing through the growing mass of hotel guests flowing down the stairway like a waterfall of limbs, torsos and bobbing heads.

"Harry," Mack shouted over the noise of feet and voices, "we should stay in the lobby. Catch her coming through!"

"I can't wait!" Harry said, pushing up and rounding a corner to the next flight. He could feel the pull, drawing him upwards, against the flow of panicky people coming down the stairs. He was being drawn toward an ending, a final culmination. It terrified and elated him.

Most of the fleeing guests were older: the Empress attracted more retired travelers than some of the newer, more commercially oriented hotels in the downtown. It was not that hard to move them out of the way.

The detectives squeezed between the bodies, Harry leading with one shoulder, his head ducked, firmly wedging aside the downward flow of aging flesh.

Then his passage was blocked by a younger form, a male body that reeked of smoke and singed hair. He looked up and recoiled. The face was burned, the eyebrows and the front of the hair gone, patches of dead white skin hanging loose, separated from the raw, red flesh beneath.

Harry instinctively stepped back. It was as if he had come face-to-face with a creature from one of his darker dreams. His gaze met the other's gray eyes, saw that they were maddened by pain -- and by more than pain, Harry thought.

It crept into his awareness that there was something familiar -- horribly familiar -- about those eyes. Then the man snarled at him, a literally bestial noise from deep within his throat, and roughly pushed past.

Harry turned to look. He could not take his eyes away from the smoke-stained figure. The man went down a few steps, growling, shoving the slow-moving elderly out of his path. He went past Mack, and descended a couple of steps more.

Then his steps became unsteady. He began to move like an amateur's first attempt at animating a movie monster through stop-motion photography, his arms and legs jerking spasmodically, his neck twisting.

Now Harry was frozen. He knew that something was about to be made plain, that some horrid completion would now be laid before him. He watched the burned man's head rotate toward him, saw the jaw muscles writhing as if he struggled for control of his own speaking apparatus.

As the head turned, Harry saw it in profile: the long, straight nose, the line of the jaw. The detective made a incoherent sound. His mouth opened and could not close around a word.

The burned head continued to turn, fighting against its own body's resistance, until the man was looking back over his shoulder at Harry. Now, the seared features seemed to writhe and distort themselves, as if beneath the skin were extra sets of muscles that could create expressions foreign to normal human experience.

It was a war waged across a human face. Then the tumult of conflicting aspects abruptly resolved itself into a unity. It snapped into place from within, like a computer-morphed trick image from a hair commercial.

Seeing that face appear, although by now he knew it would come, was the worst of it for Harry. His knees softened. A thick, cold shiver twitched the muscles of his back and pulled his shoulders tight. His neck locked and his teeth ground together like pebbles rolling along the bottom of an icy stream. A trembling began in his lower belly and spread to his chest and arms.

He sat down on the stairs. The knees of the still descending flood of hotel guests battered his shoulders and the back of his head. He felt none of it.

He stared. Even beneath the burns, the bald brow, there was no mistaking who was looking back at him through those pale, lashless eyes.

"Harry," Dory called to him, across the tide of still moving bodies. "Help me."

Harry swallowed, fighting down hot bile that suddenly billowed up from his stomach. He wanted to shut out the sight before him, but his eyelids remained treacherously open. Now everything else in the stairwell -- the jostling people, the hammering fire alarm, panicky voices, the whiff of smoke, Mack's upturned face just below him -- it all faded to the dimmest gray. The only light was in the center of his vision, and in the light was a truth he could not bear to confront.

"Harry," the voice -- *Dory's voice* -- said again. "Please."

Mack heard the voice. She looked from her partner to the burned face. "Oh, my god," she whispered.

"Harry," the Dory-voice said, one last time. But Harry was beyond helping anyone. He could only stare.

Mack acted. "Hold it!" she said. She struggled toward the man with the woman's voice.

And at that, the face changed again. Dory sank helpless beneath its surface, and in the place where she had been there rose up once more the snarling mask of the monster. He turned to run down the stairs.

"Police!" Mack yelled, yanking her service automatic from beneath her coat. "Stop right there!"

The burned man turned back. There were people between him and the detective with the gun -- a small elderly couple and a fat woman in a voluminous robe of rose colored silk. The man snarled, raised both hands and put them against the large woman's expansive bosom. He pushed her back up the stairs, so that she stumbled and crashed into the diminutive older man and his wife, who both fell back against Mack.

Now the man swam down through the crowd in the stairwell, shoving aside anyone in his way. As gently as she could, Mack helped the elderly couple regain their feet. The fat woman had slid off them, gotten up and continued down the stairs without a backward look. She moved surprisingly fast.

"Harry!" Mack called. "Come on!"   She followed in the big woman's path, around the corner of the stairwell and down the next flight.

Harry heard his partner's voice receding, shouting, "Police! Clear the way!"   He found that if he concentrated on Mack, on her need for help, he could move. There was something ironic about that, he was sure, something a little comic. He pushed down an urge to smile.

He reached for the railing and pulled himself to his feet. He took a step downward, his legs moving of their own volition, then another step. It was like stepping into empty air and falling free. The flow of the crowd carried him along. He was not really in charge of anything that was happening to him now.

#

Littlemick was raging. He smashed Dory back into a narrow crevice on the farthest edge of his domain. He didn't care about the cops behind him. He had to get Michael's woman. Most of all he had to get the notebook off her. Everything -- the money, the private estate in southeast Asia, the fulfillment of his dream -- everything was in that computer. Years of his life, in her hands. He would kill her. No one would stop him.

He burst through the doors of the stairwell, into the lobby. The bell was still ringing, and outside he heard sirens growing louder. A flock of hotel guests milled in his way. He shoved them aside. *Where was she?*   He couldn't see her anywhere.

He asked Michael: *Where would she go?   What would she do?*   The answer came back: *Taxi.*

He knew the side entrance where the taxis would be waiting. He began to push toward it. Most of the crowd was shuffling toward to the front door, which was set back from Government Street by steps and a long walkway. He cut across the flow to the smaller entrance, shouldering the people aside.

He was almost in the clear. He could see the arched doorway where she would have gone. He would find a cab, have Michael talk to the driver, spin some tale about being separated during the panic, find out who had picked her up and where they had gone.

He would find her.

He broke free of the crowd. He could see a yellow cab through the doorway, its engine idling. He sped across the lobby toward it.

Suddenly, the noise of the siren reached a crescendo and died away. The cab lurched forward, out of its pick-up zone, and in its place appeared the side of a fire truck. The hotel doorway immediately filled with fast moving men in yellow helmets and heavy canvas coats. Littlemick tried to dodge around them, but there was nothing to do but wait until they cleared the way.

He flattened himself against the big display window that formed the corridor wall. His feet moved of their own accord, eager to be back to the chase. The seconds crawled by until the firemen were past him, the doorway clear.

He took a first step toward the exit, but before he could take a second, a smashing blow to the left hinge of his jaw staggered him. He fell sideways. He turned at the same time to see who had hit him. A pudgy fist came again to split his upper lip and flatten the end of his nose.

The fat woman from the stairwell had dogged him step for step across the lobby. Her name was Alice, and nobody had pushed her down since the fourth grade. She had responded then to the insult by doing exactly what she was doing now.

But as Alice cocked her fist to deliver another right cross, the burned man spun and drove his fist hard into her midriff. The punch whooshed the air out of her lungs, and she had to bend over and put her hands on her knees.

Littlemick ground his teeth. He wanted to do more damage to the woman who'd had the nerve to touch him, wanted to see her blood. But there was no time. *Michael's woman. The notebook. The plan!*

"Hold it!"

The policewoman had come through the crowd after him. She now stood ten feet away, the squared muzzle of her automatic pistol pointed at him. Her hands scarcely wavered in their grip on the weapon.

"Put your hands on top of your head, turn around and face the wall," she said.

He glared at her, his eyes as cold as granite pebbles at the bottom of a stream. His bleeding upper lip curled back to reveal his teeth.

"Do it!"

Littlemick looked past her. The other cop was coming now, the one Dory had called to, his face haunted, the skin as gray as ancient putty. He wove through the crowd toward them, slow and hesitant as an old man.

"Come on, now," said the female cop. "Let's be reasonable."

Those were always the words Littlemick could not bear to hear, the words of betrayal, the words of contemptible weakness. They acted like a trigger to fire his deepest rage.

Now all thought of Monica and the notebook fled his mind. The fury in him boiled high and spilled over. He gave in to the surging frenzy of purest hate. His mouth opened to its widest, the lips skinned back from the teeth. A howl distended his throat as it poured from his belly. His feet danced and his hands hooked into claws.

The fat woman had her hands pressed to her middle, sucking air, trying to straighten up. Littlemick reached and sank the fingers of one hand into the dyed, frizzy hair. He swung her up and around in front of him.

At the same time, he flung back his other hand and smashed the display case behind him. The shattered glass cut his knuckles to the bone, but he paid no attention. Without looking, he reached among the Victorian toiletries, groped until his hand closed around the cutthroat razor.

When he pulled it out and flicked it open, blood sprayed from his gashed hand. He held the blue steel edge to the woman's throat and backed toward the side entrance, dragging her with him.

"Let her go!" Mack yelled. She followed him toward the doorway, the gun steady in her hand.

Harry stepped forward from the crowd. He came up beside his partner. He had not drawn his gun. He blinked slowly.

Littlemick stopped and smiled his ugly smile at the two

police officers. He used the razor to lift the fat woman's chin. Her eyes bulged. She swallowed and stared at Mack.

Harry searched the face of the man with the razor, saw only the hideous, cold rage. There was no hint of the woman he had talked with, touched, been touched by. Yet he knew she was in there, somewhere behind the mask of hate.

He took a step forward. "Dory?" he said.

Littlemick made a phlegmy noise in his throat.

"Dory?" Harry repeated. "I know you're there."

The burned man's face *rippled* from within. Harry saw again the clash of personalities, the struggle to control the shared features. For a moment, Dory looked through the gray eyes. The bleeding mouth opened to speak.

Littlemick fought back, lashing out at her with vicious power. But the sister-thing was surprisingly strong. She had never exerted herself so powerfully against his consciousness before, had always gone back in the box when he had no use for her. Her resistance caught him off balance.

The hand that held the razor tight against the fat woman's throat dropped an inch or two. That was all Alice needed.

She had caught her breath. Now, her right hand came up, and its palm pushed against her captor's wrist. Her left arm snapped forward, then drove her elbow back, hard and fast, into his lower ribs. She spun her body with the blow, putting all her considerable weight behind it, and broke free.

The woman's elbow caught Littlemick in the floating ribs. Pain stabbed through his left side, and a flash of fresh rage flooded through him. He crushed the sister-thing, flattened her and ground her down inside him. Her strength was nothing before his fury.

It took only a second, but the second was enough for Harry. He saw the monster retake control, knew that Mack would shoot.

But Dory was in there, needing him, waiting for him to help.

"Mack, no!" he shouted, and threw himself at the burned man. He got a two-handed grip on the wrist of the hand that held the razor. His momentum carried them both to the floor. Harry struggled to pin the man down, but the body was all wire and muscle.

Littlemick hit Harry hard with his free hand, three fast chopping blows to the face. He enjoyed that. He'd wanted to smash that face every time he'd peeked out through the sister-thing's eyes and seen its moondog simper. It just begged to be broken.

Harry held on. "Mack!" he cried. "Help me!"

But Mack had made up her mind: as long as the man was armed, she would take the first clear shot she was offered. The only thing stopping her now was that her partner covered the burned man. She moved around the struggling pair, looking for an opening. "Harry, get clear!" she said. "I'm ready!"

Harry was holding on against the blows. "Dory!" he called, then again. But the man squirmed beneath him and drove his knee up into the detective's groin, twice.

The first impact brought an astonishing pain. The second eclipsed the first. Harry's vision closed in, became a channel of light surrounded by flickering red shot through with yellow veins. He tasted bitter acid at back of his throat.

Littlemick rejoiced to feel the policeman's grip slacken. He tore his hand free from Harry's grip and poised the razor to slash him deeply. His other hand seized Harry's hair, yanked back his hair and bared his throat for a killing stroke.

"Bye bye," breathed the monster into the detective's ear. He had the voice of a little child.

Littlemick sliced down with the razor. Harry reached weakly to block the stroke, but he knew even as he did so that the man was too strong.

Time slowed. He saw the flash of the steel toward him, saw where the hairs on the back of the man's hand had been singed away. The blade came inexorably down. *Nihil obstat*, he thought. Nothing could stop it.

There was a convulsion in the hard body beneath him. The features contorted, and in a moment he knew it was Dory's face was looking at him. The grip on his hair loosened and the razor stopped an inch from his flesh.

"I'm sorry, Harry," she said. She had fought her way back across the expanding range of Littlemick's being, across a vast, dark continent of violence and hate and rage. She had been able to seize control just long enough to stop the monster from killing the only man who had ever cared about her.

Then Littlemick struck back with a storm of shrieking spite, his immense malice rearing over her small flickering light like a black and glistening tidal wave of filth. She saw him descend, and knew that she would not rise again.

She knew she had only seconds of existence left. She drew up her knees and used Littlemick's machine-built muscles to throw Harry clear of their shared body. She saw him fly from her, as her vision withdrew and faded to black.

The effort had taken every flickering speck of energy that clung to her shrunken being. She had almost nothing left when Littlemick's backlash roared over her. This time he would carry her far down, into the deepest, iciest realms within him, and there he would grind her to nothingness.

Littlemick reveled in his power. He smashed the sister-thing, smothered her, swallowed her, drove her helpless toward final oblivion. It was the work of only seconds.

Mack crouched over the spasming shared body, her automatic pointed at the chest. She saw the struggle that would carry Dory away, saw the dwindling moments of the woman who so had obsessed her partner resisting the onrush if the other.

Mack heard Harry say a single word. His voice was thick and indistinct. It might have been the woman's name.

The policewoman saw Dory's eyes flicker toward her partner. Then they came back to Mack. The steady gray gaze held her a moment, moved to the muzzle of the gun, then came back in an unspoken plea. The lips silently formed words that Mack could read: *Do it. Now.*

Harry had struggled to his hands and knees. Mack saw Dory's resistance fading. The last vestige of her was being obliterated from the burned face. She saw the monster flow into the place where the woman had been, saw the eyes become stones again.

She waited until she saw his grip tighten on the razor, until he was gathering himself to leap up.

Then she shot him through the heart.

Harry was behind Mack. He had risen to his knees, one hand extended to his partner. When the sound of the shot slammed off the walls of the hotel lobby, he lowered the hand and sank down until he was sitting on his calves.

Mack put her gun away, and squatted down in front of him. She took her partner's hands in hers and said, "Harry, it had to be."

He raised his eyes to hers. "I know," he said.

"It'll pass, Harry. You'll be all right."

"No."

"You have to," she said.

"No."

"Yes. You owe it to her. To Dory."

He stared at her.

"She loved you," Mack said. "She protected you, gave everything she had to save you. You can't turn your back on that. At the end, she didn't have much, but what little life was left to her she willingly gave up. For you. You can't let that mean nothing."

"Jesus, Mack."

"You can't look away from it, Harry. It was all she had, and she gave it up cause she loved you."

She helped him to his feet. His balls ached, and the bad taste was thick in the back of his throat. Harry looked down at the dead face. There was nothing there now.

"You got to take it on, Harry," Mack said.

"I don't want to hear it."

"Doesn't matter. When you're worth everything to somebody, you've got to be worth something to yourself. Now you owe it to her to make some good come out of this."

"Let's go home," he said.

#

They went back to Vancouver the slow way. Mack didn't want to deal with the amorous pilot. By the time they'd gone through the Victoria PD's mill, it was early afternoon.

They caught the ferry out of Schwartz Bay. The morning's overcast had evaporated, and Georgia Strait was showing them the spectacular composition of green sea, white capped mountains and blue sky that was usually reserved for tourism brochures. They went up on deck as the big stretched boat entered Active Pass.

Harry said, "You know, there had to be an accomplice. Somebody who stuck that knife in the office door."

Mack watched a gull maintain station with the moving boat, seeming to hang in the air off the starboard bow.

"Oh yeah," she said. "Had to be. But, far as we know, any accomplice was only in on the money end. Which the companies are too embarrassed to talk about. So nobody's going to want us asking awkward questions. Especially not Inspector Mason's old buddy from school."

Harry looked at her. "It's not right."
"No, it isn't right. It's just how it is."

Epilogue

The original owners of the two names embossed at the top of the sheet of creamy paper had been dead for years, but the law firm they had founded was one of Vancouver's best. The letter invited Katherine Tower to visit their offices at a certain time, if it was convenient, to "learn of matters which may well be of benefit to you." She called but the lawyer who had signed the letter, a senior partner named Yvonne Fletcher, would give no more information, except that the benefit was what she called substantial.

The address was on the upper floors of Bentall Four, and when Katherine stepped off the express elevator an efficient-looking woman took her immediately to a small conference room done in oak and leather. Arranged around the table were three familiar faces: Ellen Wiens, Maria Chen, and Carla Gonsalvez.

It had been more than a month since the events that had brought them all together. When Katherine entered the room, no one spoke. It was obvious that the atmosphere was strained. She took a seat equidistant from the others.

The silence lengthened, until Katherine couldn't take it any more. She leaned forward, making the leather of the chair squeak under her, put her elbows on the table and said, "What the hell, we don't need to take it out on each other."

"I'm going to lose my job, Katherine," Ellen said. "Maitland's not saying anything directly, but it's there."

"They're not too happy with me, either," said Maria. "Suddenly, a couple of my best accounts are on other people's desks."

Carla said nothing. They knew she was sending out resumes.

"I'm not doing too good myself, ladies," Katherine said. "It doesn't matter that he's dead. I close my eyes, I see him coming through the door at me."

"I can't believe the whole Dory thing," Ellen said.

The door opened to admit a strong featured woman in a well tailored suit. She laid a briefcase of finely tooled leather on the table, and undid its straps.

"Ladies," she said. "I am Yvonne Fletcher. I want to thank you for coming."

"What's it all about?" said Katherine.

"We are acting according to our client's instructions."

"Who's the client?" Ellen asked.

"I am not at liberty to say," the lawyer said.

"As you may know," Katherine said, "all of us here have had our fill of mystery lately, Ms. Fletcher. My personal tolerance level for parlor games has worn pretty goddamn thin."   She stood up.

"I'm instructed to give you this," Fletcher said. From the briefcase she extracted a plain sealed envelope, and handed it to Katherine. She distributed one to each of the women.

Ellen shrugged, and opened hers. "Good God," she said. "It's a cashier's cheque for three million dollars."

"What?" Carla said, and ripped the end of her envelope. The others followed suit. Each envelope contained a cheque for the same amount, drawn on a trust in the Grand Caymans.

"What are we supposed to do with this?" Katherine said.

The lawyer shrugged. "That's up to you. My client says, and I quote, 'you can turn it over to your employers, or you can keep it. You've earned it.'   She wants you to know that she was partly responsible for what happened to you. I quote again, 'I didn't know, but maybe I didn't want to know. In the end, he did it to me, too.'"

When the lawyer had finished speaking, there was a silence in the room.

Maria broke it. "But it's stolen money," she said.

"I didn't hear that," said Yvonne Fletcher. She bid them good day, and left the room.

Nobody said anything for the better part of a minute. Then Carla spoke.

"Fuck it," she said. "She's right. I earned this. We all did."

Ellen and Maria nodded.

Katherine looked at the row of zeros on the cheque, then at the three women. She put her elbows on the table. "What do you say, we put together a company," she said. "We hire some talent -- then we kick some old-boy ass."

Yvonne Fletcher heard the laughter all the way down the hall.

www.ingramcontent.com/pod-product-compliance
Lightning Source LLC
Chambersburg PA
CBHW031950170626
46807CB00006B/2433